BESOTTED

THE FAIREST MAIDENS

THREE

Books by Jody Hedlund

Knights of Brethren Series
Enamored
Entwined
Ensnared
Enriched
Enflamed
Entrusted

The Fairest Maidens Series
Beholden
Beguiled
Besotted

The Lost Princesses Series
Always: Prequel Novella
Evermore
Foremost
Hereafter

Noble Knights Series
The Vow: Prequel Novella
An Uncertain Choice
A Daring Sacrifice
For Love & Honor
A Loyal Heart
A Worthy Rebel

Waters of Time Series
Come Back to Me
Never Leave Me
Stay With Me

The Colorado Cowboys
A Cowboy for Keeps
The Heart of a Cowboy

To Tame a Cowboy
Falling for the Cowgirl
The Last Chance Cowboy

The Bride Ships Series
A Reluctant Bride
The Runaway Bride
A Bride of Convenience
Almost a Bride

The Orphan Train Series
An Awakened Heart: A Novella
With You Always
Together Forever
Searching for You

The Beacons of Hope Series
Out of the Storm: A Novella
Love Unexpected
Hearts Made Whole
Undaunted Hope
Forever Safe
Never Forget

The Hearts of Faith Collection
The Preacher's Bride
The Doctor's Lady
Rebellious Heart

The Michigan Brides Collection
Unending Devotion
A Noble Groom
Captured by Love

Historical
Luther and Katharina
Newton & Polly

BESOTTED

THE FAIREST MAIDENS
THREE

JODY HEDLUND

NORTHERN LIGHTS PRESS

Besotted

Northern Lights Press

© 2020 Copyright

Jody Hedlund

Jody Hedlund Print Edition

ISBN 978-1-7337534-7-0

www.jodyhedlund.com

Scripture quotations are taken from the King James Version of the Bible.

Cover Design by Roseanna White Designs
Interior Map Design by Jenna Hedlund

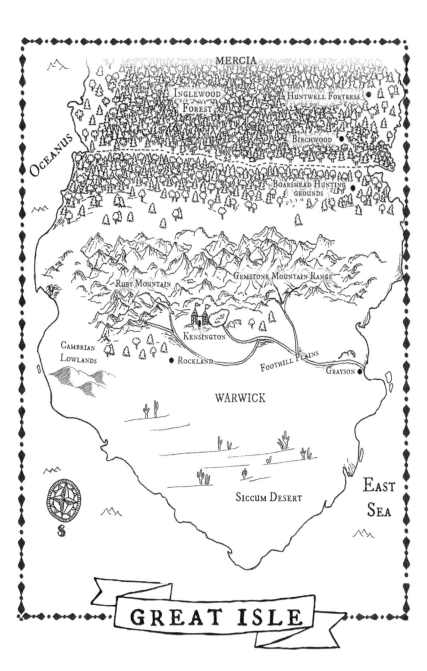

Chapter 1

Kresten

Hunger raged through my stomach like a boar on an attack. I plucked a handful of red currants and stuffed them into my mouth, but the tart berries couldn't begin to sate my appetite.

"We need to hunt today." I reached for another plump bunch, and the ripe berries slid off their stems into my palm.

Jorg stood beside me, feasting ravenously on the wild currants. "We should have hunted yesterday instead of frolicking with Walter's daughters." He spoke through a mouthful, even as he shoveled in more berries. His ragged garments hung loosely on his tall, lean frame, elbows and shoulder blades protruding sharply. His overgrown dark beard couldn't hide his sunken cheeks.

Guilt chopped into me like a back-cut threatening to fell me.

We'd grown thinner over the past four months of travailing in the wilderness, bearing witness to the hardships we'd endured since I'd started my Testing. But Jorg fared worse than me to be certain.

"You're right," I said. "As usual."

"Of course I'm right."

"But we had a jolly good time, did we not?"

"Yes, that we did."

I dumped more berries into my mouth, as did he, and we lapsed into silence. The trilling of hawfinches filled the early morning air along with the distant squawk of blackbirds. Though I preferred the commotion and busyness of court, I'd adjusted to life in the lonely forest, and the quietude and slower pace wasn't as stifling as it once had been.

A ray of sunlight slanted through the leafy ceiling and touched upon a dew-drenched spiderweb, glistening like a diamond crown. Thick moss cloaked the stately trees like kingly robes. And ground elder covered the forest floor like a royal carpet rolled out for a prince.

Except here I wasn't a prince. I was a lowly wood-cutter without crown, robe, or carpet. I didn't have a home to call my own. I hadn't had a roof over my head or a bed to sleep on since early May when I'd arrived in Mercia and the vast, overgrown Inglewood Forest.

Only two months until I finished my Testing and could return to Scania. Fifty-eight days to be exact. But who was counting?

I snorted, earning a raised brow from Jorg.

I shook my head and remained silent. My scribe had already heard enough of my complaining about how much I disliked being in the forest and living as a pauper. No sense in saying more.

I was under no illusion that I had any prospect of winning the Testing and becoming the next king of Scania. I'd never had a chance, not when lined up next to

Vilmar and Mikkel, who could both do no wrong in my father's eyes. Instead, to him, I was a disappointment, falling short of being the man he wanted me to be.

The truth was, I hadn't wanted to join the Testing, hadn't seen the purpose in subjecting myself to harsh deprivations when the kingship was out of my grasp. Nonetheless, I'd endured the past months for the sake of tradition and honor. I couldn't spurn the Testing, not when every Scanian prince underwent the challenges and had done so for centuries.

My stomach gurgled from the sour berries—and with a craving for meat. If I'd been home in the great hall in Trommen Castle, our summer residence, I would have been sitting down at the morning hour to hot, salty porridge and sizzling bacon slabs.

The growling in my stomach rumbled louder. "Never mind porridge and bacon to break my fast. Give me a feast of roasted venison, stuffed duck, and a loin of veal."

"Is that all?" Jorg asked wryly.

"Not in the least. I'd also like a bowl of plum custard as well as a hundred cherry tarts."

"Perhaps we should do some fishing first this morn before the woodcutting?"

"Yes, maybe you're right." I tossed a last handful of currants into my mouth, then reached for my sack containing all the possessions I'd carried with me during my homelessness. The contents didn't amount to much— a change of garments, blanket, flint, fishing net, a couple of traps, and the special scarf my mother had given me. I might not be my father's favorite child. But at least my mother cared.

"You may have to forfeit everything else for the Testing," she'd said to me on my last night in Bergen when she handed me the scarf. "But your family will be with you always, no matter how far apart we may be."

I wanted to believe her—had tried to believe her—but I'd never felt as though Mikkel or Vilmar had much interest in me, except when they needed something from me.

"Where shall we fish?" Slinging my sack over my shoulder, I startled at a red squirrel darting out from underneath a cluster of tall ferns and scurrying up a fine mature oak free of scars and rot, one that in a few years would be ready for cutting.

Though we'd witnessed no signs of any basilisks in the area, we could not help but be wary of every movement of every creature nonetheless.

Jorg draped his sack over his shoulder and followed me. "We had good fortune the last time we fished along the ravine. Do you want to return there?"

It was a distance of several leagues from our woodcutting domain, the section of the forest Walter Matthews had assigned to us when we applied for our woodcutter's licenses. We would waste precious work time traveling to and from the river. But I didn't know how we would last the day without more sustenance than the berries and roots we scavenged.

"Yes, the fish there are plentiful, and we shall catch enough to last us a few days." I changed my course to the northwest, having grown accustomed to the forest paths nearly invisible to the untrained eye. I'd also learned to be ever alert for the basilisks, watching for the telltale signs of their presence, namely the patches of barren, blackened, and scorched land surrounding their burrows.

Growing up, I'd heard tales of the deadly king serpent with a finlike crest upon its head, glistening scales covering its body, and a sharp, pointed tail. But I hadn't believed the miniature dragon-like creature existed any more than I believed in the large fire-breathing dragons of legends.

However, Jorg and I had lived in the woodland only a day before we nearly stumbled upon one. Thankfully, we'd been traveling with another young woodcutter who noticed the barren area and warned us to cover our mouths and noses so we didn't breathe in the basilisk's poisonous vapors.

We glimpsed the basilisk at the base of a hollowed-out stump, standing on its two spindly legs, hissing at us and spewing its venom into the air. Not only did the vapors have the power to wither and scorch vegetation, but they had the power to dull the mind and cause prey to fall unconscious, allowing the basilisk to creep up and strike with a poisonous bite.

Our companion also instructed us not to look the basilisk in the eyes lest we become victims of its lethal gaze. We heeded him and attempted to put a safe distance between ourselves and the serpent.

Now, after many weeks, we'd grown adept at staving off basilisks and learning where those in the vicinity made their homes. However, traveling any distance was never without risk, including for hunting or fishing.

Jorg was indeed correct that we should have hunted yesterday on our day of rest. Instead, we'd lingered in the hamlet of Birchwood after delivering our quota to Walter and receiving our compensation.

As warden of the eastern region of the forest, Walter divided up the deliveries of deadwood and white fuel amongst the peasants and tradesmen. He was also tasked with ensuring only licensed woodcutters labored under his supervision, swiftly punishing poachers.

From the start, Walter had taken a liking to me. And when he invited us to stay after our deliveries, I always had a hard time saying no, especially because his daughters provided us a meal and were amusing company. I expected Walter hoped we might take an interest in his pretty girls, as they were of marriageable age. But little did he know marriage was the last thing on our minds.

Even so, we usually lingered in Birchwood well into the evening. And by the time we left, we'd lost valuable hours to secure game that could last us through the week. Part of me argued that we deserved one day of pleasure after being exposed to such toil and peril all week long.

Furthermore, Jorg never complained. He seemed to have a merry time right along with me, so much so I sometimes forgot he was my scribe sent along by the Lagting to record my daily activities and give them a firsthand account of everything I said and did during my Testing.

Jorg was but a few years older than my twenty-one years. We'd become fast friends, and I no longer thought about the fact I was royalty and he wasn't. It was easy to forget since we were both living in such wretched poverty together. In addition, Jorg spoke the language of the Great Isle flawlessly because he'd lived in Warwick for most of his childhood, until his father, one of Queen Margery's courtiers, had sought sanctuary in Scania.

Jorg didn't reminisce about his childhood other than to say his father hadn't been able to stomach the queen's cruelty, nor had he been able to support her with a good conscience. As a result, he'd made a bold move in escaping from the country with his family. At the time,

Jorg had been a squire, working toward becoming an elite knight. Although Scania didn't have the same elite regiments that existed on the Great Isle, Jorg's father had found a Scanian knight willing to finish preparing him for knighthood.

Now, as we traversed through the forest, Jorg took the lead, his training lending him a keen eye that would alert us to danger. Our empty stomachs prodded us onward. When we reached the woodland near the ravine, we had to wind our way through particularly heavy shrubs. The rushing of rapids beckoned to us. As we broke into the river clearing, morning sunshine poured over my head, warming me and making me pause to take in the grandeur of the rocky cliffs and magnificent river.

For the beginning of September, the water level was diminished from what it had been in early summer. Because of its remote location, few people fished this far inland. Thus we always had success netting carp and trout, and we'd also found crayfish, which were small but edible.

I dug my fishing gear from my bag, eager to sate my appetite. Then I tossed the sack into a tall cluster of woodrushes only to have squeals erupt—the angry squeals of a boar that didn't appreciate being disturbed.

I threw down my gear, and with a burst of energy borne from fear, I sprinted along the riverbed, keeping to the cleared area for ease of escaping. I leapt over brush and rocks and splashed in the shallow water.

Even so, the boar's enraged squeals resounded much too close to my heels.

"Run faster!" Jorg shouted from where he stood upstream.

I was tempted to respond sarcastically and thank him

for his astute advice. But I was too focused on staying one step ahead of the boar. I unsheathed my sword and held it in one hand, while pulling my axe out of my belt with the other. I took a backhand swing at the creature and managed to make it stumble over loose rocks in the river, slowing it a little.

I used the moment to push myself harder, scanning the steep cliffs for a place I might escape. Covered by thick vines and brush, the rocky surface was twice as high as the thick walls of a castle, impenetrable and unable to be scaled—at least not by natural means alone.

As the squeal sounded nearer again, my gasping breath and lagging speed warned me I couldn't keep going indefinitely. I was too tired from the short night and weak from hunger and needed to find a hiding place, somewhere I could rest until the boar lost interest or my scent—whichever came first.

The thick brush against the cliff would conceal me better than the more open riverbank on the opposite side. As I rounded a bend, I made a quick turn and hacked at the ivy and hawthorn, clearing an opening. I pushed through until I felt the uneven granite of the cliff. Even then, I chopped branches out of the way and worked my way farther down the river.

At the snorting and squealing a mere dozen paces away, I held myself motionless, praying the creature would give up the chase and move on. The irony of my situation wasn't lost on me. Under normal circumstances, I should be the one cornering the boar—along with the others of a hunting party. But then, in coming to Inglewood Forest for my Testing, everything familiar and comfortable had been turned upside down.

My only hope was that Jorg was aiding me by pursuing

the boar with the intent of killing it for a feast of our own. If I could distract it, he might be able to get close enough to slay it before it slashed him.

With a fresh spurt of energy, I sliced my axe into the thick vegetation, piling it up and making a barricade. I worked swiftly and expertly, the mound growing. As the boar caught a fresh whiff of me and barreled toward me, I dove over the heap.

I tucked myself as I landed, expecting to roll into the base of the cliff. Instead, I found myself tumbling down into a cavern. As I cascaded to a stop, I scrambled to my knees, on the alert for a basilisk. Scant light made it past the layer of shrubs covering the opening, but it was enough for me to see the cave was low, hardly big enough for a man to sit without bumping his head.

Strangely, the cavern seemed to extend backward into the cliff. Keeping my weapons at the ready, I crouched low and crept through the passageway. I was surprised when it widened, allowing me to partially rise and leading me uphill. Natural light filtered through the tunnel, so much so that I suspected I was approaching another opening.

I scrambled up the last of the incline to find a layer of thick vines shielding the exit, preventing me from viewing what lay beyond. Cautiously, I used the tip of my knife to peel back the curtain of vegetation until I was able to peer through.

More of the same overgrown woodland lay beyond. Naught was unusual or different about the landscape than the rest of Inglewood Forest. Nevertheless, as I crept from the cave, my senses were on high alert.

Could I really even call it a cave? It felt more like a long-forgotten, secret passageway through the ravine.

And if it was a secret passageway, did something in this area need to be kept secret?

As I straightened and took in my surroundings, the thrill of adventure lured me as it always did. A small jaunt through this new part of the forest wouldn't hurt anyone, would it? I needn't worry about Jorg. He'd pick up on my trail and catch up to me in no time.

I found a slight deer path that seemed to have some use and followed it. Perhaps I'd find castle ruins. Or what if a dragon, like in stories of old, lived in the area? Maybe I'd find an ancient treasure.

More likely there was nothing. Even so, anticipation led me farther from the ravine than I knew I should go. Though I kept a lookout for the dead, barren areas that signaled a basilisk, the forest was as lush and fertile as I imagined the Garden of Eden had been.

Occasional sunlight pierced the covering of oak, birch, and hazel. A slight breeze rattled the branches, and while the leaves hadn't yet begun to shed the green from summer and don the color of autumn, the cooler nights of late meant the change would begin erelong.

While I found no hint of basilisks, I also found no hint of anything secret. My hunt was futile, and the growling of my stomach reminded me I needed to return to fishing. As I spun on my heels and began to retrace my steps, a faint voice wafted on the wind—or at least what sounded like a voice.

I halted but heard only the brushing of leaves overhead. Intrigued once more, I reversed my path, heading deeper into the forest and keeping my tread light so that when the voice rose on the wind again, I knew I hadn't imagined things.

I craned my ear. Was someone singing?

Another breeze rippled through the trees, bringing the sound with more clarity. A woman was most definitely singing.

I picked up my pace, my anticipation mounting. Tracking the direction of the voice, I veered off the deer path onto another trail of some kind. Since arriving in Inglewood Forest, Jorg had decided I was his pupil and he needed to pass all his knowledge to me. Of course, I'd already had rigorous training from some of the best knights in Scania as part of my education as a prince.

But I could admit, Jorg's skills had saved our lives on more than one occasion, and I'd benefitted under his tutelage. Even now, I took in every bent blade, crushed leaf, and broken twig, seeing far more in the forest than I would have a year ago.

The singing grew more distinct until I was almost upon the person. Through the shrubbery ahead, I caught a glimpse of blue before it was gone. I inched forward, making sure to stay hidden behind tree trunks and stumps until I reached the edge, where the forest opened into a small glade filled with long grass and wildflowers.

A woman was dancing.

I peered through thick branches, guessing this was the woman I'd heard singing. But now she was twirling and humming a familiar tune. In a simple blue gown, her skirt rustled and swished with each turn, showing bare feet underneath. Her unbound hair flowed in long blond waves that reached to her waist. As she spun, her hair floated around her, sunlight turning it to gold. A crown of dainty, light-blue flowers graced her head, the same flowers that dotted the clearing.

When she paused and brushed her hair out of her face, I sucked in a breath at her beauty, the arresting violet-blue eyes, elegant nose, rosy cheeks, and full lips.

At my intake, she paused, her hum fading and smile disappearing. She scanned the woods, and I ducked, hoping the foliage concealed me.

A moment later, as she resumed humming, I raised my head and peeked at her again. She'd returned to dancing except slower, her arms out as though she had an imaginary partner.

I could only watch speechless at her grace and poise, stunned all over again by her exquisite beauty, unlike any other woman I'd met—and I'd met many in my life whom I considered beautiful.

Who was she? And why was she here in the middle of the forest by herself?

In addition to the woodcutters, who were allowed a certain quota of trees and windfall, Inglewood Forest was also home to a fair number of charcoal burners. Such men and their families had a more isolated existence, and they oft went months before they ventured to Birchwood and other hamlets that bordered the forest. Jorg and I had met most of the charcoal burners within our woodcutting vicinity, but perhaps we'd yet to encounter those in this hidden area.

The young woman danced a few more steps, then stopped and shook her head. She bit her bottom lip and attempted the move again. The courtly dance was one my mother had taught us, one she'd learned while growing up on the Great Isle. In my mind, I played out the next few steps, and I was tempted to call out to her to use her right foot forward instead of the left.

Of course a poor peasant girl like her wouldn't know the dance and would need instruction. But why bother telling her when I could show her?

Cautiously, so I didn't startle her unnecessarily, I stood and parted the brush. The branches crackled and drew her attention. As I stepped through into the clearing, she halted and gasped, her eyes widening. She stood frozen in place, her body taut.

"Looks like you could use a partner in your dance." I gentled my tone and offered my most winsome smile.

Bunching her skirt, her gaze darted toward the opposite edge of the clearing to a basket and her discarded shoes. From the fear rippling over her beautiful features, she was like a doe about to bolt. And once she did, I might not ever see her again.

"Wait. I know the dance and can teach it to you."

She held herself rigid, her shoulders straight, her head high. I could almost hear her inner debate about whether to trust me or whether to race away as fast as her feet could carry her.

"I assure you, I'm quite good at it." I stepped with my right foot forward and flawlessly performed the dance step she'd been trying to learn.

She watched, unable to hide her curiosity.

I twirled the next several complicated moves. When finished, I bowed with a flourish. "Kresten, at your humble service, my lady."

Chapter 2

Aurora

I couldn't keep from staring at the young man. He wore the common, threadbare garments of a woodcutter—a simple long tunic belted at the waist above loosely fitting hose. But his bearing and mannerisms were like none of the woodcutters I'd ever seen.

Granted, I'd only met a few woodcutters in passing during my sheltered life. Even so, none had looked like this one—muscular, handsome, and yes, even dashing. He was the kind of man who existed in fairy tales but not in real life.

His hair, a soft woodland brown, was overlong and in need of a trim. And his scruffy face required a shave. Even so, the shagginess couldn't hide the rugged lines of his jaw and strong contours of his cheeks. His smile added to his charm, revealing clean and even teeth. Most of all, his eyes beckoned me. The pale blue resembled the same shade as the cornflowers I'd threaded together and placed on my head.

"Shall I show you the dance again?"

"No." I couldn't stay. And he needed to leave. Right away. My mind echoed with Chester's command urging me to run, hide, and stay secluded until the stranger was gone from the area. If Chester had accompanied me, he would have dragged me off. In fact, he would have heard this man coming and whisked me away to safety long before I was exposed.

As it was, Chester was gone for the week to the market. And though he'd bidden me to stay close to the cottage during his absence, I'd ventured from home each morn with my blackberry picking anyway. Aunt Elspeth and Aunt Idony hadn't minded. Agreeable and good-natured, they never hovered over me, probably because Chester had enough caution and concern for all of us combined.

Nevertheless, my aunts would have wanted me to dash away the moment this man appeared as well. They wouldn't approve of me striking up a conversation, much less taking dancing lessons from a stranger, no matter how harmless he might appear, especially since I'd wandered much farther from home than I normally did.

"Please?" The young man lowered himself to one knee and held out his hands to plead with me, his expression earnest. "I beg of you, my lady. Give me but a moment of your time, and you shall make me the happiest man to ever walk the face of the earth." The soft smile playing across his lips made him even more handsome. And irresistible.

It wouldn't hurt to have him teach me the next steps in the dance, would it? What could come of spending just a few minutes with him?

"*No!*" Chester's command barked in my head.

"Never talk to anyone. Don't trust anyone. Stay far away from everyone." Sir William had always said the same thing before he died, so his litany rose up and joined with Chester's.

I understood why the father-son pair had always been so protective. They counted it their sole duty in life to watch over me. In fact, Sir William had given up comfort and prestige to move to the cottage and be my guardian, bringing his motherless son with him. Even if Chester was but a few months older than me, he'd taken over as guardian after his father's passing, unwilling to think of doing anything else but protecting me.

"A lady of your loveliness must have an equally lovely name," Kresten commented from where he still knelt.

I glanced beyond him to the forest, searching for anyone else who might be lurking. What if he was one of Queen Margery's spies? Chester claimed she had more soldiers looking for me than ever before, since I was nearing my twentieth birthday, the age when I could rule Mercia in my own right.

With only two months to go, I couldn't jeopardize my security. Not after my aunts and Sir William and Chester had worked so diligently to keep me hidden from the queen.

"I'm alone." He followed my gaze. "I vow it."

"You are certain?"

"Yes." His expression turned solemn, his eyes even bluer.

My stomach did a strange flip, especially at the intensity of his full attention upon me. "Why are you here?"

"I was planning to do some fishing in yonder river when I accidentally came upon a boar. He wasn't too happy about being disturbed and gave me a fair chase."

"But how did you come to be here?" I motioned to the clearing.

"In my haste to outrun the beast, I stumbled upon a cavern that led me into this part of the forest."

Those who happened into the area almost always came from the far western edge, which was inhospitable and difficult to traverse with its many crags and cliffs. But few ever discovered the whereabouts of the ravine entrance. Already in a remote spot of the forest, the ravine provided an extra barrier that had made the charcoal burner's cottage an ideal place to hide a queen all these many years.

"I heard your singing and came to investigate."

"Where are you from?"

"I'm a woodcutter several leagues away from here." He hesitated just enough to let me know he wasn't disclosing the full truth.

A shiver prickled the skin at the back of my neck. Had Queen Margery sent him? And if so, how could I possibly outrun him and make my escape? Now that he'd discovered the ravine entrance, next time he'd return with a whole regiment of soldiers.

"I can tell you don't believe me." He rose to his feet and took his axe from his belt. "So to prove to you I'm a woodcutter, point out the twig you'd like me to sever, and I'll do it from here. No matter how high or far away."

I ought to make my getaway while I still could, but his offer intrigued me. "Truly any twig?"

"Truly any."

I studied the surrounding trees and located a misshapen limb high up in a nearby oak. I pointed at it. "What about that one?"

He covered his eyes to shield them from the morning sun as he followed my direction. "The twisted one with the nodules?"

"Yes. Precisely."

He lifted the hem of his tunic, yanked the fabric, and then ripped it with a loud rending.

I jumped back, wariness returning with full force.

He finished slicing off the strip. Then he dangled it out to me. "Blindfold me."

I hid my hands behind my back.

He extended the strip even farther. "Use this linen to cover my eyes, and I'll sever the branch without looking."

I glanced again at the limb I'd singled out and then back at him. Such a cut would be difficult with two good eyes. It would be impossible without sight. "You must be jesting."

"I'm entirely serious." His hand didn't waver as he held out the linen.

This man seemed to have a knack for piquing my interest. I tentatively took the cloth from him. "Very well. Since you apparently enjoy making a fool of yourself, I shall indulge your endeavor."

His grin made an appearance, one that lit up his eyes and gave him a boyish aura. "You're too kind, my lady." He used the proper address flippantly. At least, I thought he did. He didn't recognize me as one nobly born, did he?

He knelt again and bowed his head, waiting for me to blindfold him. Dare I engage with him further, or should I use the opportunity to flee?

At the humble bend of his head and the view of his handsome profile, I approached him, unwilling to part ways yet, though I knew I should. I draped the cloth around his eyes, winding it until I was able to tie it behind his head. I tried to be careful not to make contact with him, but my fingers brushed his hair nonetheless, and I was surprised at the softness of the strands.

Once finished, I clasped my trembling fingers. I didn't think I was afraid of him. I was more overwhelmed by the realization I was interacting with a man, something I'd dreamed about but hadn't expected to do until I returned to Delsworth.

"Ready, my lady?" he asked gently, as though he sensed my trepidation and feared he might frighten me away.

Was I ready? I swallowed hard and pushed away my misgivings for a final time. "Very well. If you insist."

"I insist." He climbed to his feet.

I took a step back, intending to give him plenty of room to accomplish the throw.

But he fumbled at the air as though searching for me. "At the least, you'll need to point me in the right direction."

Would I be required to touch him again? I cautiously reached for him, then drew back at the last second.

He held out his hand, palm up. "Come on with you. Just a nudge."

I stared at his thick calluses, the sign he was indeed a woodcutter, wielding his axe day after day. Maybe I was worrying for naught.

Before I could talk myself out of it, I wrapped my hand over his. As my skin made contact with his, I sucked in a rapid breath. And when he encircled his fingers lightly around mine, I was rendered immobile. I stood watching him, taking in his face again. Even with his blindfold, he was striking, so much so that my heart raced forward at an unsteady pace.

"My lady?" he asked after a moment, a smile tugging at his lips.

Did he sense how his presence affected me? Giving myself a shake, I pivoted him until he was facing the tree. Then I jerked my hand free and tangled it within my skirt. Even then, the warmth of his touch remained.

He seemed much too calm. He lifted his chin and attempted to gain his bearings but did so gracefully, as if he made an everyday occurrence of meeting young women in the forest and proving his worth.

Since he wore the blindfold, I studied him unabashedly, glad for the few moments to admire him without his knowledge. He likely had many women who fancied him, perhaps even had a girl somewhere interested in marrying him.

"I'm not sure I can concentrate with you staring at me so intently."

I dropped my gaze, a flush stealing through me. "You can see through the blindfold?"

"No. I vow I cannot."

"Then what makes you believe I am staring?"

"I can feel your interest."

"'Tis rather arrogant of you to think I am interested in you. What if you are only imagining it?"

"Am I?" He shifted just slightly so he was pointing directly at the tree.

I'd always counted myself truthful but couldn't admit how fascinated I was by him. So I remained silent, likely giving him the answer he sought.

He thumped his axe against his palm several times before he lifted the blade and poised it above his shoulder. "Have no doubt, my lady. I am interested in you. Very much so." As the last word left his mouth, he swung his axe behind him and then brought it swiftly forward, releasing it and letting it fly end over end.

It landed with a *thwack*, embedding into the trunk right at the spot where the limb was attached, hacking it off in one quick blow. I wasn't surprised at his ability or accuracy, not after seeing his calluses. But I was surprised at the swift swelling of my admiration.

As the branch crackled through the others and fell to the ground, Kresten tugged off the blindfold and watched the limb make the last of its descent. When it landed, he jogged over, retrieved it along with his axe, and returned to me, dropping to his knees and holding the branch out as if it were a laurel I'd won.

"My lady, your wish is my command."

"Is it?" I took the limb.

He bowed his head. "Whatever you wish, I shall be your servant and do it."

"Then you will go on your way, never come back, and tell no one of my presence here." That was what I wanted, wasn't it?

He remained motionless for a heartbeat, and I half-hoped he'd protest. "Very well, my lady." He looked up, meeting my gaze, his blue eyes so bottomless I wished I could retract my words.

"I shall do as you bid," he said. "But first, will you allow me one dance?"

One dance? My heart thudded with the sudden desire to have a real dance with a real man instead of the imaginary partners I'd always used. But as before, I could hear Chester cautioning me, telling me to be on my way.

My whole life I'd been careful, living within the boundaries Sir William and Chester placed upon me. Straying a little farther from home once in a while for my berry picking was as bold as I'd ever gotten.

Did I dare do something as adventurous as accepting a dance in the woods with this handsome stranger?

He stretched his hand out. "One dance, and I promise I shall never return here or reveal your whereabouts if that is what you truly wish."

I wanted this. Wanted to learn the dance. Wanted to be with him. Wanted freedom, even if only for a few minutes. Without giving myself the chance to think further, I thrust my hand into his.

At his smile, I couldn't stop from smiling in return. A thrill wound through me, drowning out the warning that I was making a mistake.

He led me to the center of the clearing and bowed, still smiling his pleasure at my acceptance of his offer. I curtsied, not caring that my smile radiated my pleasure.

Keeping hold of one of my hands, he situated the other on his shoulder. Then he rested his hand upon my hip. The contact seared through my skirt so that for a moment, I forgot to breathe. And even though he maintained a proper arm's length distance from me, I was keenly aware of his presence so near.

"Shall we both hum the music?"

I wasn't sure I could concentrate on anything but his touch and was afraid I'd make a fool of myself by mumbling or tripping over my feet. But I nodded. And as he hummed, I somehow managed to join in.

When we reached the part of the dance I didn't yet know, he paused and patiently talked me through the steps. We practiced it several times before I caught on. Even then I fumbled through the final quarter of the dance.

Upon reaching the end, I couldn't say no when he suggested we do it once more. And when we finished a second time, I was the one to propose doing it over. By the time we completed our fifth attempt, I could perform the steps almost as flawlessly as Kresten and laughed at myself when I tripped and nearly fell.

He steadied me. "You're a quick learner and will be an expert in no time."

"And you are a very good teacher. Much better than my aunts."

"Your aunts?"

The moment he repeated me, I realized I'd said too much, and I tugged away from him. "I must be on my way." I couldn't allow him to touch me again, or I would be helpless but to continue dancing. If it were possible, I would dance with him all day long.

He angled his head, almost as if he were reading my thoughts. "If you'd like, we could meet and dance again on the morrow."

I could think of nothing I wanted to do more. In fact, waiting until the morrow would seem like an eternity. Even so, I hesitated.

"I shall teach you another dance."

"I cannot."

I expected him to try to convince me otherwise. Instead, he backed up, letting his gaze sweep over me. "You're the most beautiful woman I've ever met."

My heartbeat stilled at his high praise, only to start tapping again at double speed with the pleasure of knowing he found me beautiful. "I still cannot meet again." I spoke the words Chester would want me to.

Kresten nodded. "Very well. I did promise that if you danced with me, I would do as you wished and go away and never come back."

"And tell no one of my presence."

"I would never do that, for I would keep you to myself."

"You would?"

"Very much so."

I forced myself to retreat one step, then two. He remained in his spot, unmoving, without pursuing me. When I bumped into my basket and shoes, I realized he truly intended to keep his promise and let me go. If I departed now, I'd never see him again. And that thought filled me with a strange emptiness.

I grabbed my belongings and hurried to the path that would lead me home. I couldn't resist a glance over my shoulder. Kresten stood where I'd left him, solemnly watching my departure.

What harm could come of meeting him one more time? After all, I hadn't even told him my name. "I might return to this clearing on the morrow to pick more berries."

His smile broke free like a burst of sunbeams. "And I might just happen to be fishing near here again."

I tucked my chin and hurried onward. But I couldn't contain a smile of my own.

Chapter
3

Aurora

"There you are, my sweeting." Aunt Elspeth didn't pause in her weaving as I entered the cottage. While her feet were pressing both pedals of the loom, her fingers flew between alternating threads, slipping the shuttle with its bobbin in and out.

Her plump frame spilled over a three-legged stool. Even with the cushion she'd fashioned for the stout little chair, I couldn't imagine sitting on it for hours a day as Aunt Elspeth did. I had a hard enough time staying still for just an hour or two focusing on my myriad of lessons.

I crossed to her and looped the wild cyclamen garland over her head so that it hung like a necklace. The silvery-pink flowers grew in profusion in the shade on the forest floor and were amongst Aunt Elspeth's favorites.

"Oh my!" She stopped her weaving and lifted the floral necklace to her nose, breathing in the delicate scent. "Just what I was hoping you'd bring me."

I smiled at her typical reaction to the flowers I gave her almost daily in one form or another. The jar filled with pale-peach begonias graced a nearby windowsill. An arrangement of snowdrops sat in a pot at the base of the loom. And a display of gladioli decorated the fireplace mantel.

"You're such a dear heart." Aunt Elspeth patted my cheek, her eyes shining with love.

"No, you are the dear heart." I bent and kissed the top of her head covered by a simple scarf. Although I tried, I couldn't express to my caretakers just how much I loved and appreciated them for the many ways they nurtured me.

As Aunt Elspeth returned her attention to the loom, I carried my basket to the table, woefully low on berries. After my hours away, how would I explain picking so few? "I am heartily sorry to be gone so long."

"Oh, you have naught to worry about." Aunt Elspeth's rounded cheeks were rosy and her smile was as ready as always. "You may as well get all the berries you can before they're gone."

With a sinking heart, I skimmed a hand across the scant layer hardly covering the bottom. My conscience nudged me to tell this sweet woman the truth about my encounter with the young woodcutter. But at the same time, there was something special about the meeting I wanted to privately cherish for a while longer.

Besides, if I told Aunt Elspeth or Aunt Idony I'd met a man in the woods, they probably wouldn't allow me to go out by myself again. In fact, they might even require me to stay home.

"I became distracted today," I said hesitantly, "and I neglected to pick as many berries as I should have."

"You'll get more on the morrow."

"Yes. I shall try."

"Will the promise of a blackberry pie help motivate you?"

"It surely will."

Aunt Elspeth loved to bake more than anything else. When she wasn't behind her loom, she dwelt at the hearth, creating delicious tarts, jams, breads, or other goodies. She made more than we needed. Even Chester, with his mammoth appetite, couldn't eat it all.

"I may even bake blackberry tarts if you find enough."

I doubted I'd find enough to make a pie, much less tarts—not if I revisited the same clearing and met Kresten again. For half the way home, I convinced myself I would return to dance. But for the other half, I decided I needed to be content with one meeting.

Even now, the battle waged within me. My heart pattered with the strange need to see him once more. But my head reminded me of what was most important—staying secluded for the final two months of my exile. After so many years of success at evading Queen Margery, I couldn't fail now, not when I was so close to the end.

I'd never understood her desire to slay me and take Mercia's throne. Why did she believe she had more claim to the queenship than I did? During history lessons, Aunt Idony had tried to explain the predicament, detailing how my grandfather, King Alfred the Peacemaker, had divided Bryttania upon his death between his twin daughters. My mother, Leandra, had inherited Mercia, and Margery was given Warwick to the south.

From what I could tell, Warwick, with its rich gemstone mine, had been the better inheritance compared to Mercia, which had iron mines and smelters. I'd become even more convinced of that when I'd learned of the wealth Queen Margery had extracted from the mine. Only within recent years had the reports become negative, indicating the mine pits were no longer as productive.

Leandra had also been tasked with guarding three keys to an ancient treasure fabled to be buried somewhere in Mercia. Margery, on the other hand, had inherited the white stone, believed to be the most important ingredient in the alchemy process.

In my view, Margery ought to have been satisfied. But Aunt Idony had explained that Margery believed she deserved everything according to the laws of primogeniture that governed Bryttania. Such laws stated that the oldest son became the next ruler upon the death of the king. If no sons were available, then the power would pass to the firstborn daughter. Since Margery had come into the world several minutes before Leandra, Margery claimed King Alfred shouldn't have divided the country.

Aunt Idony explained that King Alfred was known for his wisdom and for being a peacemaker. As such, people had trusted and accepted his decision to split Bryttania, particularly those who knew Margery and feared her leadership. They believed the king hadn't wanted the older twin to rule at all. But unable to prohibit her, he'd done the next best thing by claiming the twins had equal rights. In dividing the nation, he'd insured its survival. Or at least, he'd hoped Mercia could stand strong against Warwick . . .

My mother had ruled Mercia well. She'd earned a reputation as a fair and kind queen. Since her death, my father had served as regent, ruling just as fairly and kindly. Now Mercia's future depended upon me.

My aunts had spent years training and preparing me in everything I needed to know to become the next queen. And while I was eager for the challenge, doubts oft crept in to taunt me about whether I would be worthy enough, whether I could be the queen the people needed, whether I'd have enough fortitude, purpose, and courage to lead. After all, how could a young woman who'd been raised in the woods away from everyone have what was necessary to guide a nation?

Though I might doubt myself and Margery might call into question my right to be queen, Father and Aunt Idony had assured me Mercia's people would accept me as their ruler. And the only way Margery could take away my crown was by force, which according to Chester wasn't likely, since she didn't have a large enough army to attack.

Two months . . . I needed only to survive two more months of isolation and I would deliver Mercia from the threat of Margery's rule—a threat that had been hanging over the country for almost two decades. I couldn't put my future or Mercia's well-being into jeopardy for any reason. Especially not because of a silly desire to dance again with a handsome woodcutter.

The silence in the cottage brought my thoughts back to the present. Aunt Elspeth's hands and feet had grown idle, and a deep groove formed between her brows. "Something ails you, my sweeting."

As before, I knew I ought to tell her about my encounter with Kresten. It had been so unusual, so unlike anything I'd ever experienced that I would do well to seek her counsel on the matter.

But I had merely to think of Kresten's engaging smile, his beseeching eyes, and his tenderness in teaching me to dance, and I squelched the impulse to speak of him. I couldn't lest she forbid me from seeing him.

"What is it?"

"I am wondering about men." Even as I spoke the words, I could feel a flush stain my cheeks.

Aunt Elspeth's mouth rounded into an 'o,' and she blinked several times as though she hoped she would wake up from a dream to find my question had disappeared.

'Twas indeed a bold question, and I ducked my head as my own embarrassment swelled.

"Well now." Aunt Elspeth's voice squeaked unnaturally high. "I don't know much about that topic . . . I'm not exactly equipped to speak on the matter . . ."

"What matter is that?" Aunt Idony breezed into the cottage. Her wind-tossed, wiry gray hair frizzed out in all directions, and she brought with her the scents of soil, sunshine, and the dozens of herbs she grew in the garden behind the cottage.

Aunt Idony approached the table with her usual brisk manner and deposited bunches of basil, rosemary, and mint. Over the past several weeks, she'd been in the process of harvesting and drying the herbs she used in her medicines. Some she tied together and strung from the ceiling. Others she clipped and dried more rapidly over the heat of the fire.

She started to separate the plants, but at our continued silence, she paused and glanced between us. "What matter are you speaking of?"

I plucked at a lone leaf in the berry basket, unable to utter the query again.

Aunt Elspeth cleared her throat. "Our sweeting is wondering about—about—well, she'd like to know about . . ."

"Spit it out," Aunt Idony snapped.

"Oh dear." Aunt Elspeth fanned her face with her hand, her ample bosom with the wild cyclamen garland heaving up and down. "Oh dear."

"Surely, it cannot be as bad as that."

"She wants to know about . . ." Aunt Elspeth's whisper dropped low. "Men."

I couldn't meet either of their gazes and instead rolled the berries around the basket, pretending to pick out more leaves.

It was Aunt Idony's turn to clear her throat. She did so twice, the second time louder. Even then her voice cracked as she spoke. "What would you like to know, Aurora?"

I shrugged even though it was unladylike.

The two older women remained silent, likely exchanging glances as they did whenever I behaved in a way they found amusing or interesting. Or in this case, embarrassing.

I couldn't forget that, before they'd brought me to the cottage as a wee babe, they'd both lived as nuns, sheltered and secluded. They hadn't been around men any more than I had.

"Let's see." Aunt Idony lifted the basil and placed it on the opposite side of the rosemary only to shift it right back. "Men. They are big, talk too loudly, and eat too much. I think that sums it up."

"I don't think that's what our dear child wants to know," Aunt Elspeth hissed to Aunt Idony as if I couldn't hear.

I'd grown up with Chester, who'd turned into a fine man. But he was just a friend. I'd never forgotten to breathe around him or felt like my skin was on fire at the merest contact or had tingles rush over me at a smile.

But I had with Kresten. Was such a reaction to a man normal? In the fairy tales I'd read, some couples married for love, but others wedded for convenience or for other arrangements. What would it be like for me?

Aunt Idony coughed, trying to clear her throat. "What else can I tell you about men?"

"Will I marry a man I love?" I blurted. "Or must I marry for other reasons?"

"Oh dear," Aunt Elspeth murmured, fanning her face again.

Aunt Idony lowered herself to the bench and beckoned me to do the same. Once I was seated, she folded her hands on the table. From the frown puckering her forehead, she seemed deep in thought, trying to formulate the best answer, and I appreciated that about Aunt Idony. She took her duties to teach me seriously. She kept the cottage stocked with many books, including a secret cabinet where she stored the oldest and most valuable of the history books of the

Great Isle. Along with history, she made sure I was versed in science, geography, languages, mathematics, and all the other subjects a future queen would need to know for ruling a country.

Alas, we'd never talked about love or marriage. Naturally, I expected to get married in the distant future. I had to in order to produce an heir. And, of course, I'd begun daydreaming about what it would be like to mingle with people my age, including the men at court. I was excited to get dressed up for the royal ball that would introduce me to my kingdom. 'Twas precisely for that reason I'd wanted to perfect my dancing.

"Your Majesty." Aunt Idony reverted to my royal title as she had more and more lately. "From what I understand from the most recent correspondences, your father and his advisors have begun making arrangements for your betrothal to a man who will bring about an advantageous political and financial alliance for Mercia."

"Then I shall have no say in the matter?"

"Knowing your father is so kind and wise, he has taken your needs into consideration."

She was right. My father was wonderful. Two or three times a year, I traveled by night to the far-eastern regions of Inglewood Forest. There, I entered a secret maze of tunnels that eventually took me into the dungeons of Huntwell Fortress. I was hidden in a crate and carried to my father's chambers. He would dismiss his servants, and I would come out and spend the day with him, talking and soaking in every second of his company.

The time always went too fast. And Father

lamented that it did as well. Though we longed for more occasions together, Father and Sir William had agreed it was too perilous to consider meeting elsewhere or for any greater lengths. Already we risked one of Huntwell's servants discovering my presence, spreading the word, and giving Queen Margery clues to my location.

In recent years, the clandestine meetings had grown fewer. And once Sir William died, Father sent word to Chester that I wasn't to come at all, that I was to remain at the cottage until I could return to Delsworth.

I'd missed seeing Father during the past months, but even if I'd had the opportunity to be with him, I doubted I would have asked him about my future spouse, not when we always had so much catching up to do about everything else.

No, 'twas better to direct my inquiries to Aunt Idony, even if doing so made us both squirm. "What you are telling me is that not only will I have no choice, but 'twill not matter at all if I am attracted to the man or he to me?"

Aunt Idony unfolded and then refolded her hands, still coated in dirt from her work in the garden. "I cannot claim to be an expert in these matters, but I have heard many royal marriages turn out to be amiable."

"Friendly?"

"Friendship is a solid foundation for any marriage."

"But I am friends with Chester and have no wish to marry him."

"Of course not. You must marry royalty."

Royalty. That meant I would never be able to marry

a pauper like Kresten who had no name, no wealth, and no alliance to offer. Not that I wanted to marry him. "So I must resign myself to a loveless marriage with a man who may or may not be attractive to me?"

"As I said, I'm not the expert, but I do believe if you put forth effort, you might learn to love the man you marry."

I understood everything the dear woman was telling me—that I would need an advantageous match, one that would be for the greater good of Mercia. As queen, my duty and loyalty to the country superseded my personal desires. Attraction, love, and any other feelings paled in comparison to Mercia's strength and well-being.

Even though I agreed, I couldn't keep disappointment at bay. After the whirlwind of emotions I'd experienced while dancing with Kresten, I hoped to have more of the same in my future. But I had no guarantees.

I sat up taller and straightened my shoulders. I was the queen of Mercia and must do what was expected of me. But that didn't mean I couldn't meet with the handsome woodcutter again, did it? If I might not ever get to feel the deliciousness of attraction with my future husband, at least I could experience it one more time with Kresten.

Chapter 4

Kresten

She wasn't coming. I sat back on my heels in my hiding place, worked the kink out of my neck, and tried to shrug off the dismay.

A dozen paces away, Jorg mouthed, *Let's go.*

I held up a finger, indicating one more moment, and peered again through the thick foliage into the glade where I'd danced with her yesterday. She'd said she *might* return to pick berries, not that she definitely would. And apparently she'd decided not to.

I should have guessed so. She'd likely had too much time to think over the matter and come to the conclusion that a rendezvous in the middle of a deserted forest with a stranger wasn't such a good idea. I didn't blame her.

On the other hand, I had hoped she'd sensed I meant her no harm and that she could trust me. Obviously, I'd failed in that regard.

A pebble hit me in the back, and I glanced over to find Jorg nodding in the direction of the ravine, his brows furrowed with irritation. Already we'd expended valuable labor time by hiking to the river, locating the secret tunnel, and traveling to the clearing. And now we'd been waiting for over an hour for her to appear.

'Twas past time to leave.

But for some inexplicable reason, I couldn't force myself to go. In fact, I had half a mind to locate her trail from yesterday and track it to her home. The only thing holding me back was the vow I'd made to go away and never come back if that was what she wished.

Certainly, that wasn't what she wished. Was it?

Again dismay settled over me, chasing away the hope that had grown since yesterday's meeting. After I'd left and made my way back to the ravine and the river, Jorg had taken one look at me and almost punched me. Even with his superior tracking skills, he hadn't been able to locate the hidden opening and had searched for me all the while I'd been gone.

Though I hadn't planned on telling him about the young woman, I'd needed to placate him in some way.

"She is the most beautiful woman I've ever seen," I'd said after describing how I'd outmaneuvered the boar, landed in the cavern, then explored the woodland beyond, only to hear her singing.

"You think every woman is beautiful." Jorg's scowl could have scared away a basilisk.

"Not like this one." I hadn't been able to stop smiling or reliving every moment of my time with the young woman. "She was truly God's most exquisite creation. And I must see her again."

"We're already behind on our labor schedule today, and we can ill afford it again."

I gave Jorg a playful push. "Loosen your belt and live a little."

He seemed to wage an inner war for control before he breathed deeply, relaxed his shoulders, and forced a smile. "You're right. I'm sorry for getting upset."

I paused long enough to study him and for an instant saw the situation as he had. He'd been given a great honor to accompany one of the three Scanian princes to the Great Isle for the Testing. But it also came with great responsibility. No doubt Jorg wanted to please the king and the Lagting with how he handled his duties. In addition, his reputation as a great knight was at stake.

With so much pressure, Jorg was bound to be worried about me now and again, especially since one of his duties was keeping me alive for the duration of my Testing.

I clamped him on the shoulder. "I was insensitive. Please forgive me for causing you undue anxiety."

My rare apology left Jorg speechless. I shoved him and laughed, hoping to resume our usual banter. However, the rest of the day, we'd both been strangely quiet. I'd been preoccupied with thoughts of the beautiful young woman—even in my slumber—so much so that by this morning, I'd been almost desperate with the need to see her again.

Though I wanted to keep the ravine opening a secret, Jorg had been adamant about accompanying me. I'd acquiesced so long as he promised not to speak or show himself to the young woman. She'd already been nervous enough with just me, and I had the feeling she wouldn't stay if she saw anyone else.

As always, we'd used caution during our trek, especially through the unknown section of the forest, attempting to stay clear of the scorched ground that indicated the presence of basilisks. As with yesterday, I hadn't seen any signs of the creatures. Jorg had remarked upon their absence as well, growing more careful the farther we ventured into the new territory, as if he expected the basilisks to play a trick on us.

I gave the clearing a final sweep and then stood. I needn't have worried. She wasn't coming, and now I needed to honor her request to depart and never come back. But first . . .

I shouldered through the thick growth and made my way into the sunny field where we'd danced. I knelt at the first cluster of flowers and picked them. At the very least, I'd carry a handful of the dainty blue flowers with me to remember her and the way she'd looked with a crown of them in her hair.

At the crack of a twig on the opposite side of the clearing, I glanced up. She stood there, the sun spilling over her golden hair that fell again today in long, loose waves to her waist. Her blue eyes were dark and uncertain, and she twisted the handle of her basket, poised as though to flee at the first word I spoke.

I wanted to race to her. But I made myself proceed casually. I couldn't say the wrong thing and send her scurrying away. "For you." I held out the flowers.

She tipped her basket to reveal flowers of all shapes and sizes.

Obviously, she didn't need any more. Still, I wanted her to have them. "For you, so that you might make another crown."

She took a timid step toward me. "Do you think I need a crown?"

"You are unrivaled in beauty and have no need of it. But you deserve one nevertheless."

Pink infused her cheeks, and she dropped her gaze only to look up a moment later, shyly, her eyes full of interest.

"You can teach me how to make the crown." Doing so would afford me more time with her in addition to the dancing lesson. "Unless you think such a feat is beyond the realm of my ability."

Her lips started to curve upward. "'Tis simple enough."

"Then I shall be your willing pupil."

"Very well. Although, I must say I am rather surprised to find you are interested in weaving flowers. I had not thought a man would give himself over to such a task."

I'd give myself over to any chore, no matter how menial, to spend more time with her, but I bit back my pathetic remark. "To be sure, the task may be too delicate for the sensibilities of others of my gender. But you'll find I'm not so prejudiced."

Her smile widened.

I lowered myself to the grass and patted the spot next to me. She hesitated but a moment, before she made her way over and sat, careful all the while not to get too close. She fanned her skirt out around her, one that was patched and frayed along the hem.

Once she was situated, I placed the bundle of flowers I'd picked onto her lap, and at her instructions gathered additional flowers, leaving the full stem attached and as long as possible.

For several minutes we collected flowers and bantered, until she halted and tilted her head, watching me. "I was beginning to think you would not come this morn."

So she'd been waiting in the woods for my appearance? Pleasure wafted through me. "I wouldn't have been able to stay away today. Not even if an entire army tried to stop me." Apparently, I was doomed to making pathetic remarks to this woman. How had I become besotted so quickly?

"I tried to talk myself out of coming," she admitted softly, as she twisted several flowers. "But the convincing did not work."

"I'm heartily glad you failed at it." More than glad, but I managed to keep the pitiable comment to myself this time.

"You must plait the stems." She wove the stems in and out. "Like this."

I watched her, marveling at the slenderness of her fingers, at her grace and her capableness.

"Now you try it." She picked up three flowers and extended them to me.

"I may need to watch you longer." I'd watch her all day if I could. But I figured saying so would only make her self-conscious.

She thrust the flowers at me. "The best way to learn is by doing."

"Very well." I took the flowers. I'd braided my own hair oft enough in the style of a Scanian nobleman, with a simple single strand off to one side. Since coming to Mercia, I'd done away with the practice, hoping to blend in with the other woodcutters and disguise my true identity. And now as I twisted the stems, I did so with practiced ease.

She leaned in to watch, her shoulder brushing mine and her breath near enough that I caught the sweet scent of mint.

"'Twould appear you are quite good at plaiting and need no practice."

I held up my simple braid. "Then you deem it worthy of the crown?"

"Indeed. Perhaps you have entered the wrong trade as

a woodcutter and should consider flower weaving instead." She tucked her chin, as though embarrassed by her jest.

I tapped her shoulder with mine, hoping to encourage her to continue with the banter, or at the very least, not to be uncomfortable with it. "With such high praise and incredible wisdom, how can I do otherwise?"

She laughed, and the sound settled around me as warm as the sunshine.

"In fact," I continued, taking courage from her openness, "once I have made a fortune as a flower weaver, I shall be indebted to you and give you a portion of the wealth."

"That would be most kind of you. Although, I shall consider your debt paid if you give me another dancing lesson."

"Just one?"

"Perhaps two?" Her expression held anticipation. Was she as excited to be with me as I was with her?

"I'll let you be the judge and shall offer my expertise on the dance floor until you deem my debt paid in full."

"Very well." She placed the braided flowers in front of me and gathered three more. "Enlighten me, how did a simple woodcutter such as yourself learn to dance so eloquently?"

I was at a loss for how to answer her without an outright lie. I couldn't tell her I was Prince Kresten, the third-born son of King Christian of Scania. I'd scare her away.

Moreover, I'd accomplished four months of my Testing without revealing my royalty. I could go the final two months, couldn't I?

"Forgive me," she started. "I did not mean to pry—"

"No, you have no need to apologize. I was simply thinking of my previous life." My mind raced with how to go about sharing some of who I was. "I have spent time at the royal court in a foreign country."

"You did?" Her expression contained no disbelief, only awe.

For a peasant girl such as herself, perhaps the very concept of court life was too much to imagine. Now that I'd been away from the glamour and comforts, I could see more clearly the opulence and privileges I'd taken for granted.

"My father . . ." I fumbled to explain myself. "My father spent some time there, and I accompanied him." It was the truth, even if not the whole truth.

"Can you tell me what the court was like?" she asked almost breathlessly, as if she'd like nothing better than to visit a royal household for herself.

I breathed out my relief that she didn't ask why my father had been in the royal court. I didn't want to deceive her any more than I already had.

For a short while as I braided and as she showed me how to weave the strands together into a circlet, I answered her questions about court life, about the feasting and dancing and parties. I tried not to give too many details lest she comprehend how knowledgeable I truly was. But then, a poor woman like her wouldn't know any difference, and I certainly had nothing to worry about.

When we completed two matching wreaths of flowers, I raised my crown above her head. "May I?"

She gave a quick nod, then nibbled at her lip. I liked her sweet innocence. It was a refreshing change from other women I'd known.

I lowered the flowers until the crown rested on her head. Wisps of her hair fluttered around her face in the morning breeze. And before I could stop myself, I brushed a strand back and tucked it into the crown, relishing the soft silkiness.

She drew in a wobbly breath but didn't back away.

"There. Perfect," I whispered, my breathing unsteady too. My hands twitched with the need to touch her hair again, but I lowered them to my lap. "Your turn."

She lifted her flower wreath, her hands shaking slightly. As she pressed it into position, she brushed at one of my strands. And when she tucked it into the crown, her bright and curious eyes met mine.

I held myself still, and as she reached for another piece of hair and combed it back, I uttered not one word of protest. Wonder filled her expression, and I guessed she'd never touched a man's hair before.

I would have allowed her to continue, except her wreath of flowers tipped forward and almost fell off her head. She reacted before I did, situating it back into place.

I offered her my hand. "Now that we are crowned as king and queen, shall we dance?"

Her eyes widened with wariness. "King and queen?"

"Yes. We can pretend, can we not?"

She studied my hand and then placed hers into mine. "I suppose we can."

I closed my fingers over hers. "Will you not tell me your name? I should like to know it."

She started to withdraw.

"Please don't go." I clung to her. "'Tis of no consequence. Your company is all I need."

She focused on our clasped hands, hesitation warring across her features.

"To be sure." I squeezed gently. "Disregard that I even brought it up—"

"Rory."

"Rory?"

"Yes."

"'Tis the name for a young child."

"I shall turn twenty years soon. Would you have me change my name?"

I chuckled. "No, I shall call you whatever you wish."

She didn't meet my gaze. Perhaps she was using a nickname and hiding her given name. Though a part of me wanted to know everything about her, I shrugged off the desire. After all, I'd withheld information from her and couldn't expect more of her than I did of myself.

As we stood and she placed her hand on my shoulder, I was consumed with thoughts of her and her nearness. I had difficulty concentrating on the dance but forced myself to hum and twirl her.

She kept pace and didn't stumble once, and by the time the dance ended, she beamed with pleasure.

"Well done, Your Majesty." I released her and bowed.

Her face turned pale, and she took a rapid step away. "Your Majesty?"

"Yes, you are the queen, are you not?"

She glanced at her basket of flowers as though she wanted to bolt. What had I said to disturb her?

I tapped my crown of flowers. "And I am the king, remember?"

"Oh, yes." The stiffness in her shoulders eased. "I forgot . . . Your Majesty."

I held out my hand, desperate to keep her from running off. "Shall I teach you another dance?"

I was relieved when she returned and placed her hand

back in mine. And soon I swept her up in another dance, this one more complicated. We practiced the steps several times, the sun growing warm and bright with the passing of morn.

As though recognizing the same, she broke away, heading for her basket. "I must go. My aunts will be wondering where I am."

I began following her but then stopped. I had to let her go, even though I wanted to spend the rest of the day with her. "Will you meet me here again on the morrow?"

She picked up her basket and darted to the woods with such haste I feared she wouldn't answer me. But as she pushed aside brush, she cast a look over her shoulder. "Yes."

Then she was gone.

I watched her trail long after she disappeared. Finally, at the crackling of branches behind me, I crossed to Jorg where he still hid in the brush. His gaze was full of censure, likely because I'd taken so long. He opened his mouth to speak, but I shook my head, cutting him off.

Without a word, we started on our way, hurrying through the woodland. Not until we exited the secret passageway into the opposite side of the ravine did we slow down. Jorg led the way, his sharp eyes always scanning the landscape and his senses ever alert for danger.

"You're angry with me," I called from behind, breaking our silence.

He didn't answer, the sure sign I'd peeved him.

"Don't worry. We shall get the work done. I'll labor hard enough for two men the rest of the day. If I don't, I'll give you my coin next payday."

"That's not the issue."

"Then what is?"

"The girl."

I stopped, a wayward hawthorn branch slapping me in the chest.

Jorg continued for several more paces before he realized I was no longer on his heels. He halted and slowly pivoted.

Overhead, the thick leaves of yew, oak, and pine blocked the sunlight from reaching us, leaving Jorg's face in shadow. But the tautness of his body was easy enough to see.

"What about the girl?" I asked.

"Leave her be."

I bristled at his command. At times Jorg forgot I was the prince and he, my servant. Like now. Nevertheless, I blew out a breath and forced myself to remain congenial. "I like her, and I plan to see her again. What's wrong with that?"

"A girl like her doesn't deserve for you to toy with her."

"I'm not toying—"

"Spare me. I was there. I saw and heard everything."

"I treated her with the utmost respect. How can you say otherwise?"

Jorg shook his head, his body radiating frustration. "It's not about respect, Kresten. It's about the fact that you are a prince and she is a pauper. You will reside in a different country, and she lives here. You are worldly wise, and she is as innocent as a dove. Need I go on?"

"What harm is there in spending a few hours with her? I do so with Walter's daughters, and you feel no need to chastise me for it."

"That's different. They're simple and uncomplicated

and amusing. But this woman . . . she's not like them. You've never met anyone like her before."

He was right. Rory was unlike any other woman I'd met—peasant or noblewoman.

"I saw the way she looks at you, the same way all women look at you. And it isn't fair to allow her to think there could ever be anything between you."

"I'm not leading her on."

"Then what are you doing?"

"Enjoying a friendship."

Jorg released a humorless laugh. "If you witnessed what I did, you'd realize a great deal more than friendship was happening."

If I was completely truthful with myself, I would have to agree with him. The feelings I had around Rory were intense and the pull to her strong. Even now, my pulse pounded with the need to spend time with her again, to watch sunlight glisten in her hair, to witness her eyes light up with joy, and to bring roses to her cheeks.

"Maybe it doesn't have to be mere friendship," I said more somberly.

"And what hope do you have of anything more than that?"

I honestly didn't know. Likely none. Rory and I hailed from two different worlds. Worlds that could never mesh. Even if by some chance, a peasant woman could wed a prince—which was impossible—my father and the Lagting had already entered into negotiations with kings of other nations with regards to spousal matches.

From what I'd heard during my last days in Scania, three royal women from various countries had already been selected. Mikkel and Vilmar would wed the princesses of most importance. I would get the leftover, the one who didn't have quite as many advantages to offer Scania.

I'd have no choice in the matter and had always accepted that fact. I understood I must do my duty, and what did one strange woman matter over another? Except now, something inside shifted. Why must I marry a woman by default? Why could I not have some say? Perhaps I might suggest someone like Rory.

She was beautiful enough to be a princess, as well as poised, gentle of spirit, and a quick learner. Surely she could adjust to life at court.

I shook my head. I'd known Rory a total of two days. Why was I even thinking of marriage? "For the love of the saints, Jorg. Let's not make this more complicated than it needs to be. I want to spend time with a comely girl. You've never had a problem with me doing that before. Don't read more into this than exists."

"Be careful, then. I can tell she's special."

Rory *was* special. I sensed it too. Maybe it was because she wasn't fawning over me like the women at court. Maybe because she held an air of innocence that was so fresh. Or maybe because she was so alive and vibrant. Whatever the case, I wanted—no needed—to see her again.

"I'm going back on the morrow." I started forward, leaving Jorg little choice but to do the same, but not without an exasperated sigh. "I promise I shall be careful with her."

He tossed up his hands as though in defeat.

Misgivings rose to make me second-guess my decision, but I hastened to stuff them away. I would be careful. I vowed that I would.

Chapter 5

Aurora

I threw away caution and continued meeting with Kresten. One morn we picked blackberries. Another, we searched for wild elderberries. The next, I led him to a plum tree, and we filled my basket with ripe fruit, making sure I had enough for Aunt Elspeth so she could make all the baked goodies she desired. Every day, I insisted on giving Kresten a portion of the harvest, sensing his hunger—or at least witnessing his proclivity to eat more than he placed in the basket.

And always, he made every task enjoyable, and I loved how full of life he was. He taught me more about woodcutting, showed me how to throw an axe, and even performed more of his daring blindfolded chops. Sometimes we sat in the grass and just talked, and at other times we hiked. Once he even hung a rope in a tall oak, formed a swing, and pushed me on it for a short while before he attempted to repeat childhood tricks he'd once been able to do while swinging— flipping and twirling and other perilous feats.

For the most part, I'd been content with my simple life in Inglewood Forest. But hearing him speak of the outside world made me realize how much I still had to do and see and learn. His tales of his adventures sparked a longing inside me to experience more of the world the way he had.

On the day before Chester was due to return home, I tried not to dwell on the fact that this would be my last time with Kresten. I didn't want to spoil the day with gloomy thoughts, so I simply savored the hours we had together. As we finished the morn by picking crab apples, I went slower than usual, not ready for the time to come to an end.

"Watch this." He plucked a particularly high cluster. He waited for me to focus on him, and then he twisted his arm behind his back and tossed an apple toward the basket. It landed squarely on top of the others.

"'Tis only a matter of good fortune," I teased. "Not skill."

"I beg to differ." With bright eyes and a wide grin, he performed his trick again. Strands of his light-brown hair had come loose, and he raked them back, as charming and handsome as he'd been every other morn.

"'Twould seem you are a woodcutter of many talents. After all, not many men can claim to weave flower crowns and pick crab apples the way you do."

He chuckled. "I should say not."

I loved how easily we could banter. I'd never done so with Chester. He'd always been so serious and purposeful about everything he did. By contrast, Kresten's playful nature was unexpected and refreshing.

And I would sorely miss it... miss him... even though I'd known him less than a week.

Quietly, I plucked a final cluster and placed the fruit in my basket. 'Twas past time for me to return to the cottage. That meant it was also time to say farewell to Kresten.

All last night I'd tossed and turned in my bed, trying to figure out a way to continue seeing him without Chester or my aunts knowing about it. But I always arrived at the same conclusion—I couldn't sneak off and deceive them any longer.

I also couldn't tell them about Kresten. Not even if I tried to reassure them he was nothing more than a friend. Because that wouldn't be the truth either. Although I'd never interacted with a man the way I had with Kresten, I knew well enough that my attraction toward him wasn't mere friendship.

As I'd arisen in the morn, I'd decided there was only one thing I could do—put an end to our relationship. We needed to go our separate ways and not see each other again, and I couldn't allow him to persuade me otherwise.

"Is everything alright?" Kresten dropped a last handful of crab apples into the basket.

I could no longer hide my melancholy. "I must be on my way."

He nodded, his expression growing somber as though he, too, dreaded the end of our time together. "I'll walk you to the clearing."

We ambled through the woods, talking of small things. And when we reached the clearing a short while later, I forced myself to keep going.

KRESTEN

"I'll see you tomorrow?" I asked, holding myself back from chasing her.

I'd sensed her growing more comfortable in my presence with each passing day. She'd talked more about her aunts who'd raised her, giving me vivid descriptions of both of them, their quirks and personalities and interests. My stomach gurgled every time she described the food Aunt Elspeth made. And I liked the no-nonsense attitude of Aunt Idony, who had an herbal remedy for every ailment under the sun. Clearly, Rory doted on the two women and loved them dearly.

She'd also talked of her friend Chester, who had been a companion while growing up and had taken over the charcoal kilns after his father died. She'd explained that Chester's father had made great efforts over the years to capture weasels and then release them into the forestland surrounding the ravine. He'd strategically situated them along a wide perimeter, nurturing, feeding, and protecting the population so they'd increase in number. And Chester now oversaw that task in addition to wood burning.

As a result, the area was free of basilisks, for apparently the weasel was the only animal that could slay the deadly creatures. With the weasels living in the woods and forming a protective barrier, Rory and her aunts had never worried about the serpents. And as we'd traipsed about picking fruit or resting in the glade, she'd assured me we had naught to worry about either.

I found myself sharing more with her as well. Though I refrained from revealing my royalty, I talked of my past adventures—the cliff-diving into deep gorges, scaling steep mountains, and hunting for dangerous wild animals. She listened with rapt attention as though living out the escapades in my retelling.

Always in the back of my mind, Jorg's warning nagged me: *"A girl like her doesn't deserve for you to toy with her."* The warning was valid. I'd had a history of breaking the hearts of many a young woman, and I wasn't proud of it.

However, with Rory I was determined to be different, because I realized even more just how different *she* was from anyone else. She was humble and yet confident, shy and yet bold, lighthearted and yet serious, amiable and yet reserved. The dichotomy of her character resembled the rings of a tree, each one built upon the previous, lending her a depth that never failed to fascinate me.

"I shall not be back to see you anymore." She halted at the edge of the clearing.

In the middle of eating another of the small crab apples, I paused. "No. We must meet again—"

"Chester will return from the market today." She hefted her full basket higher on her arm, refusing to meet my gaze. "Once he returns, he will not allow me to wander off by myself."

"Bring him along."

"You do not know Chester. He would never approve of my meeting you here, even if he came to chaperone."

"Once he meets me, surely he'll see I'm a decent fellow."

"He is very strict about where I go."

"Perhaps I can come to your home instead—"

"No!" Her beautiful eyes widened with panic. "No, you cannot."

"Then somewhere else? He can choose."

"Please try to understand." Her voice softened. "As much as I have enjoyed these past mornings together, I must not see you again."

The bite of apple in my mouth turned bitter, and I tossed the remainder to the ground. She was putting an end to our being together.

"Why?" The question fell out before I could stop it.

The September morning was fair, and her cheeks were flushed from the cool air, making her eyes all the brighter and her beauty all the more radiant. With each passing day, I thought I would grow accustomed to how stunning she was and become less enamored with her. But I was only more besotted. All I could do was watch her, my longing for her likely starkly displayed upon my countenance.

"'Tis for the best, Kresten. We must go our separate ways now before doing so becomes more difficult."

She was all but admitting she had feelings for me too. I ought to be glad of it, but I couldn't abide the thought of going even a day without her. How would I go forever?

"I shall be miserable if you deny me the chance to see you again."

She tugged at one of the crab apples in her basket, plucking off its leaves. "You will eventually forget about me."

"Never."

"You must."

"I won't be able to, so please don't ask it of me." My chest began to ache in an unfamiliar way. I pressed my hand to it. Was this what it felt like to have one's heart broken?

"Forgive me, Kresten." Her eyes turned luminous with unshed tears. "I knew I should not allow false hope to spring up between us, but I ignored the warnings in my heart."

"What if it doesn't have to be false hope?"

"We can never have more." She spun and slipped into the brush.

"Wait!" I stalked across the clearing. I couldn't let her get away. Not without making her understand that we could have more. Because we could, couldn't we?

Jorg's words rushed back into my conscience: *"It isn't fair to allow her to think there could ever be anything between you."*

As she disappeared into the foliage, my steps faltered. *"We can never have more."* Her declaration echoed Jorg's. And deep inside I knew them both to be true.

For as much as I loathed having to stand there and let her leave for good, I had to respect her wishes, even if I might not understand her need to sever our ties. And I finally had to accept the truth of our situation—I would hurt us both if I allowed our feelings to develop further only to leave at the end of my Testing. This parting was difficult enough, and putting it off would cause even greater heartache.

'Tis for the best. I watched the forest grow still where she'd been moments earlier. The throbbing in my chest pulsed into my limbs, rendering me immobile. The throbbing also made me realize something I'd never understood before—just how selfish I was.

If she hadn't walked away today, I would have done this to her in less than two months. I would have walked away, leaving her confused and nursing a broken heart. And the very thought that I could have been so calloused filled me with a sense of shame. How many women had I hurt? How many young ladies had experienced despair on account of my insensitivity?

'Twas no wonder Jorg had been quieter than usual the past few days. Although he hadn't spoken words of condemnation as he had after the first meeting with Rory, I'd sensed his judgment anyway. I'd attempted to ignore it with extra jesting and frivolity. But I understood now that he'd seen the selfishness I hadn't wanted to acknowledge.

I stalked back to the wooded area where he was waiting for me. He'd already dropped from his perch in one of the gnarled yews, where he climbed most mornings to stay hidden from Rory and yet still act as my guard. Now he regarded me with wariness. No doubt he assumed I would attempt to follow her and drag him along in the process.

I brushed past him. "You were right. I'm a selfish idiot." Without waiting for him to agree, I forced myself into a jog, heading in the direction of the ravine.

As he fell into step behind me, my shoulders tensed in readiness for his "I told you so." If he so much as hinted at pity, I wouldn't be able to stop myself from slugging him. I didn't easily engage in brawls, but at the pain radiating from my heart, my fists balled with the need to hit someone or something.

By the time we reached our territory, midday had passed and so had a large portion of our workday. My gallivanting with Rory had already cost us a great deal of our workweek, even though we labored at our woodcutting far into the evening to make up for starting late each day.

Wordlessly, we picked up where we'd left off, collecting deadwood, brush, and twigs that littered the ground, which we then formulated into bundles of approximately six feet long by three feet wide and high.

We had yet to start on our white fuel quota, which consisted of the laborious process of stripping hardwoods of bark. Once we finished that task, Walter required us to coppice a certain number of trees per week, as the process of pruning the trees helped with new growth and prolonged the forest's productivity.

While I'd gained strength in my muscles and had increased my endurance since the first awful week as a woodcutter, the work was still difficult and tiring. And each night I went to bed hungry and exhausted.

Certainly I'd learned to appreciate the lowly paupers who spent a lifetime at the job. And certainly I'd grown in my ability to empathize with those who owned nothing except what they carried and had no home save the forest floor.

I'd also started to learn the lesson of my Testing, spelled out by the engraving on my sword: *Deny thyself.* Over the months of analyzing the charge I'd been given, I'd learned the words came from the Lord himself in Scripture, from the Gospel of Matthew: *"If any man will come after me, let him deny himself . . . for whosoever will lose his life for my sake shall find it."*

I'd always valued my material possessions and comfort. I could admit I loved rich foods, fine garments, and servants at my side. And I could admit I'd put too much emphasis on my wealthy life. To be sure, my Testing was teaching me to have a better perspective, to deny myself pleasure and to live sacrificially. I would return home a better man for all my experiences.

Even so, my father and the Lagting had given me the easiest Testing. They'd sent Vilmar to be a slave in the dangerous gem mines of Warwick, and they'd relegated Mikkel to Norland's Isle of Outcasts, where he would have to survive amongst brutal bands of warring exiles.

Yes, I was poor and hungry. And yes, the basilisks and boars posed a threat. But mostly, my everyday existence had been uneventful, even boring. And now with the loss of Rory, my last days in the forest stretched bleakly ahead of me.

Though I hadn't wanted to acknowledge the truth, this Testing had proven it—my father viewed me as the weakest of his sons. He didn't think I could handle anything harder than woodcutting. And at times, I feared he was right.

Chapter 6

KRESTEN

THE WORKWEEK ENDED TOO RAPIDLY, AND WE DIDN'T REACH OUR quotas, which was no surprise. Regardless, on our day of rest, we started the trek to Birchwood with bundles of wood piled high upon our backs.

An hour into the trip, Jorg halted suddenly.

With my head bent under the loads upon my back, I nearly bumped into him. "For the love of the saints, Jorg—"

"Basilisk." His tone was low and urgent.

He didn't have to say anything more. The one word was all the warning I needed.

I followed his attention, peering through the foliage to a blackened patch of earth that appeared as though it had been destroyed by a wayward campfire spark or lightning strike. A reptile-like creature stood at the center of the area on its thin legs, its head raised and its crest rounded and full.

No bigger than a hunting dog, the beast hissed, its long, forked tongue flicking out as though to warn us to stay away.

"Cover your mouth and nose." Jorg ripped off a strip of his tunic.

Already sensing the dulling of my mind from the poison in the air, I slipped out my knife and slashed mine too. We worked rapidly to cover our mouths and noses, and at the same time, backed up.

The basilisks weren't known for attacking outright. Instead, if the creatures felt threatened, their hissing expelled more venom. They waited for their victims to fall unconscious from their deadly vapors, then closed in and administered a lethal bite.

As we crept away, the basilisk darted toward a hole in a blackened stump. Only then did I see what it had been standing upon. A human body.

I held out a hand and stopped Jorg. "Wait. Someone's there."

A brawny man lay facedown in the leaves and windfall within the basilisk's burned-out territory. Though I couldn't see much of his body, I glimpsed an axe attached to his belt.

A fellow woodcutter?

"We need to get him." I began to loosen the straps on my shoulders. "He might still be alive."

"If he is, he won't be for long."

I lowered my bundles of wood to the ground. Then before I changed my mind, I darted forward.

"No!" Jorg's fingers grasped at my tunic, but I wrenched away.

With my axe and knife both at the ready and my eyes on the basilisk burrow, I did nothing to conceal my approach. Speed was more important in this instance than stealth, and as I reached the body, I dropped to one knee and rolled him over.

Immediately, I recoiled. 'Twas the young woodcutter who'd guided us when we first arrived at Inglewood Forest. His blue, bloated face was hardly recognizable. The bruising and swelling continued down his neck to his torso and limbs. His fingers were so distended they were double their normal size.

"He's dead." Jorg spoke from beside me. "Now let's go."

I sheathed my weapons. "We cannot leave him here for the basilisk to feast upon." Grabbing hold of the man's arms, I tried to lift him, but a wave of dizziness hit me, and I wavered on my feet.

Jorg's brow creased, his worried eyes trained upon the basilisk's lair. But as I dragged the woodcutter backward several paces, he took hold of one arm, and I kept a grasp on the other. Together we stumbled to put as much distance between ourselves and the basilisk as possible.

With every passing second, my mind turned fuzzier and my vision blurred. Fatigue overwhelmed me, making me want to lie down and go to sleep. When I fell to my knees a moment later, Jorg shook his head curtly and motioned for me to keep going.

Only when we reached a point far beyond where we'd dropped our wood did we release the woodcutter. Jorg and I collapsed to the ground, tore off the coverings over our mouths and noses, and gasped in the clean air.

When our minds cleared and we regained our strength, we hastened to retrieve our wood and finished the hike into Birchwood. After delivering our paltry cuttings to Walter, we went back for the woodcutter, then brought him to town so Walter could inform his family of his death.

This week, even with Walter's invitation to stay for a

meal, I had no desire to linger. After purchasing a few supplies, we returned to our territory and attempted to hunt but to no avail. As the afternoon waned, Jorg suggested we use the remainder of daylight hours to provision ourselves with fish for the week. At the prospect of facing hunger in the week ahead, I acquiesced.

Initially, I didn't want to go back to the ravine area. After two days since last seeing Rory, I was still too consumed with thoughts of her and had no wish to stir up my heartache by returning to the spot where I would only think of her more. But we needed to fish, and the river near the ravine never failed to give us what we needed without the threat of basilisks.

After lowering our net into the rapids and securing the lines, I scavenged along the shore in the tall grass for duck nests, hoping fortune would smile upon me and reward me with eggs to fry with the fish.

I found myself wandering downriver in the direction of the secret passageway, and the closer I drew, the more I wanted to throw caution away and hike back to the clearing. Rory wouldn't be there at so late an hour—she wouldn't be there at any hour. Yet, I longed to go anyway, simply to revel in the memories of our short week together.

"Aha!" At a glimpse of greenish-gray lumps in the shadows, I parted the weeds to find four eggs partially covered in dried grass.

"I've found gold!" I shouted over my shoulder toward Jorg on the opposite bank, grinning for the first time since leaving Rory.

"What?" he called above the rushing water of the rapids.

I picked up two eggs and lifted them for him to see.

He started to grin, but then his eyes widened. He had his axe out in an instant, but before he could throw it or I could make sense of what was happening, something sharp sliced into my thigh, plunging deeply like a knife.

At an enraged squeal, I realized a knife wasn't digging into my flesh. It was the razor-sharp tusk of a boar.

With a swiftness Jorg had drilled into me, I swung my axe, knowing I needed to cut off the tusk before the creature ripped off my leg. The difficult chop required every ounce of my concentration and fortitude. I brought the weapon in from the side, twisting just slightly, and in the process put pressure on my thigh.

Pain like fire raced up and down my leg. But I gritted my teeth and pounded the blade down on the tusk at the boar's skull. Though I aimed the strike as far from the entry point as possible, the blow set the boar free but left the tusk in my thigh, driving it deeper, tearing my flesh in the process.

Agony barreled through me, sending blackness over me like a veil. I released a cry and fought against the enfolding darkness, pivoting around in time to block another charge from the boar. Missing one tusk and bleeding from where my axe had grazed its forehead, the boar was more infuriated than before. It lowered its head and came at me again.

Weak and stunned, I couldn't move fast enough. The boar's remaining tusk sliced into my leg just above my knee. Though it stung and drew blood, it was just a flesh wound.

The boar thrashed with rage and plunged toward me again.

I swung my axe and aimed for its broadside, making contact but unable to knock it down. At each jarring step,

I feared it would be my last before I fell unconscious.

"Jump to the left!" Jorg's shout drew nearer, and from the corner of my eye, I could see him sprinting through the river toward me, his axe raised and ready to throw.

I tried to obey him but only managed an awkward tilt. It was enough for Jorg. An instant later, his axe whistled in the air past me. The blade embedded into the boar's head, dropping and silencing the creature instantly.

Was it the same boar that had chased me last week? I couldn't be sure, but part of me wondered if it lived near the secret passageway as a sort of guard, to keep intruders away.

Seconds later, Jorg was at my side. He sliced the boar's neck with his knife, ensuring it didn't try to attack again. Then he spun and caught me just as my knees buckled.

He draped my arm across his shoulder while he assessed my wound.

I closed my eyes and fought down the bile that had begun to rise. My pain was beyond endurance.

"If I pull out the tusk, it's possible you'll bleed to death." Jorg braced me higher, taking the weight off my injured leg.

"If you leave it in, it'll do more damage."

Jorg examined it more closely. "It's at an odd angle. If I remove it, I'll tear your flesh irreparably."

I tried to hang on to him but felt myself slipping.

"I need to find a skilled physician." Jorg's worry penetrated my haze. "Where is the closest one?"

"Delsworth?" I had no idea, but Birchwood and some of the other villages that bordered the forest wouldn't have a physician amongst them. Perhaps one of the outlying estates of a nobleman might have a skilled healer on hand. But that kind of trek would take us at least a day—probably more. Delsworth was even farther, and the journey there would be impossible in my condition.

As if coming to the same conclusion, Jorg released a cry that contained all his frustration. "Surely there is someone in this godforsaken forest who can help us."

"You'll have to do it, Jorg." Though I was grasping him as tightly as I could, my strength was fading.

Jorg was silent a moment. Then he sheathed his knife and axe before he straightened and bore more of my weight. "There is one place we might find aid. Let us pray there we will find friends and not foes."

Chapter 7

Aurora

"I shall go berry picking again on the morrow." **With** my spoon, I drew swirls in the gravy remaining on my trencher, pretty swirls in tune to the music playing in my head. Kresten was twirling me and smiling, the sunshine lightening his hair and turning it a warm wheat. His summer-sky eyes caressed my face, alight with pleasure and something else I couldn't name but that made my pulse quicken.

The clinking and clanking around the table faded to silence, and I glanced up to find everyone staring at me.

"We can use more fruit, can we not?" I asked.

"Well now." Sitting at one end of the table, Aunt Elspeth scanned the assortment of baked goods and other delicacies she'd been busy making. "I'm not sure . . ." She returned her attention to my face and then smiled and nodded. "Of course. Of course, we can use more—"

"Nonsense." At the opposite end, Aunt Idony

wiped her mouth with a napkin and pushed her empty trencher away. "We have too much already. In fact, if we eat any more, we're likely to turn into fruit cakes."

Chester guffawed and then resumed shoveling plum pudding into his mouth. With his broad shoulders and hefty girth, he filled the length of table across from me, especially with the way he slouched and spread his elbows wide as he supped. Black etched the grooves of his fingers from the charcoal burning. His dusty-blond hair fell over his freckled face, more contemplative than usual since his return the previous day.

Or perhaps I was the one who was more contemplative. "Very well. Then I shall collect more berries to preserve for winter."

With the lengthening shadows of autumn, the simple candelabra at the center of the table cast a cozy glow. The spicy scents of the drying herbs overhead and the soft crackle of the flames on the hearth— everything about the cottage should have contented me, but restlessness needled me instead.

I dragged my spoon through the sauce and completed the final twirl. This time when I looked up, Chester had paused in his eating, his spoon lodged in his mouth. His eyes narrowed upon me, the humor from seconds ago gone.

"Of course, my sweeting." Aunt Elspeth exchanged an anxious glance with Aunt Idony before she bestowed another one of her cheerful smiles upon me. "We can take the fruit with us when we leave, can we not, Idony?"

"Don't be ridiculous. Of course, we cannot take it. We shall need to pack sparsely in order to travel swiftly."

I let my spoon fall idle on my trencher. I'd forgotten. We wouldn't need to worry about storing up winter supplies this year. Or any other year. After All Saints' Day, I would be away from Inglewood Forest and ensconced in my royal residence, awaiting my coronation as queen of Mercia. There I would have all the provisions I could ever want.

A strange moroseness stole through me, the same that had followed me home the day I left Kresten behind in the woods after telling him I couldn't meet him again. I'd been unable to stop thinking of him or our time together. And I hadn't been able to stop wondering if I'd made a terrible mistake in severing our relationship.

Chester took his spoon from his mouth and sat up to his full, imposing stature. "I told you she's been odd since I got home."

Aunt Idony crossed her hands and examined me. "Her behavior and mood are slightly different, but with the impending changes, we can expect no less."

"Slightly?" Chester scoffed. "She's very different, and I want to know why."

"'*She*' is right here at the table with you, listening to your conversation about '*her*.'" I glowered at Chester, and he glowered back.

"Who would like a nice cup of mead?" Aunt Elspeth stood and hustled toward the hearth. "I've made it with the special blend of spices everyone likes so well."

"I would like to know what is going on with Rory." Chester's tone was as hard as his glare.

"And I would like a cup of mead." I refused to look away from him for fear he'd realize he was right. I was behaving oddly. 'Twas because of meeting Kresten. He'd awoken feelings I hadn't known existed—desire, attraction to a man, the need to experience love. And now that those longings were awakened, I couldn't make them go back to sleep.

"Why exactly do you want to go berry picking on the morrow?" Chester insisted.

Suddenly, I wished I hadn't brought it up. I didn't want Chester growing more suspicious and confining me inside the cottage for the next two months. Besides, even if I ventured to the clearing, Kresten wouldn't be there. Not after I'd told him we must go our separate ways and that nothing could ever happen between us. He'd proven himself to be the kind of man who would respect my decision.

Chester sat forward, his muscles stretching his tunic. "Why, Rory?"

I could feel Aunt Idony watching me, waiting for my answer and refraining from rebuking Chester as she did from time to time when he became over-bearing. Now was one of those times I sorely wished she'd put him in his place.

However, I sensed neither she nor Chester would be satisfied until I gave them some sort of answer. "I like the freedom of exploring."

"You should never have gone off by yourself." Chester slapped the table, causing the dishes to rattle. Aunt Elspeth, who was stirring the mead, hopped and pressed a hand to her chest.

"I stayed close enough—"

"We have two months, Rory." His voice escalated. "Just two months. Why couldn't you wait instead of putting yourself in peril?"

We'd already had this conversation several times since he'd come home and learned I'd gone berry picking by myself. I understood his perspective. His father had sacrificed much to serve me. And Chester was doing the same. Now that we were this close to surviving the years of being hunted by Queen Margery, he didn't want me to jeopardize what he and his father had labored so hard for.

I sighed and stared at the meal I'd barely touched. The swirly lines had turned into a maze amongst the congealed sauce. That's how my life had felt in recent weeks. Like a confusing maze. Things should have been simple. I was the royal heir to the kingdom of Mercia. I'd been raised and groomed to become queen. And now the time was near when I would take the crown and put into practice everything I'd learned.

Why then did I feel so unsettled, so restless?

If I was honest, the feelings had been pressing ever harder and closer for months.

Aunt Elspeth tiptoed back to the table. "Here you are, sweeting." She delivered the mead, her eyes wide upon Chester, as if she expected him to pound the table again at any moment.

I cradled the mug between both hands, letting the rising eddy of steam bathe my face.

Aunt Elspeth watched me tenderly, her big eyes teeming with expectation.

I breathed in the spiciness of nutmeg, cloves, and ginger, then took a sip and gave her the smile she was waiting for. "Thank you. You always know just what I need."

"Of course I do, dear heart. I know you better than anyone." She patted my arm, then began to clear away the remainder of our meal.

"Well?" Chester plucked a tart from a platter even as Aunt Elspeth whisked it away. He popped the entire delicacy into his mouth and chewed, never once taking his gaze from my face. "Why couldn't you wait?"

"I love all of you. I really do." I let my gaze touch each of the faces of the dear people who were like family to me. "But I am weary of being confined, and I long to see the world beyond the cottage." Once the words emerged, I knew them to be true. Maybe as a child and young girl I'd been content with this home and life. But of late—and especially after meeting Kresten—I found myself wanting to explore farther and travel to places I'd yet to discover.

"Ah, Rory lass." Chester reached across the table and held out his hand, palm up.

I set my mug down and placed my hand in his as I had many times in the past.

The anger in his features softened. "I know this isn't easy for you. But you'll soon be away from the cottage and be able to go wherever you want. Can you find it within yourself to make do until then?"

"I shall try."

"Good." He smiled and squeezed my hand before he released me and pushed back from the table, apparently satisfied I would remain safe.

"Wait." Aunt Idony hadn't moved, and she continued to study my face as though seeing deeper into my confession than even I had. "If Her Majesty would like to have an excursion now and then beyond the usual boundaries, then Chester, you must take her."

He shook his head, his face clouding again. "With the influx of new arrivals over recent months, we can never be certain when we might encounter someone. We cannot take any chances of her being seen."

Although I hadn't seen any newcomers to Inglewood Forest, Chester brought back tales every time he went beyond our boundaries. Earlier in the summer, he'd returned with news of discord in Warwick, that the slaves who worked in Queen Margery's gemstone mine had revolted. Most shocking of all was the news that one of the Scanian princes had been at the mines as part of some kind of kingly testing and had led the uprising. Afterward, the prince and the slaves had traveled to Inglewood Forest to hide and stave off the wrath of Queen Margery.

Upon Chester's return from this most recent trip, he'd delivered more shocking news. Queen Margery had accused her daughter Princess Pearl of treason with another one of the Scanian princes who was also on the Great Isle for kingly testing. The queen had captured the couple and sentenced the princess to death by beheading. Somehow Princess Pearl and the prince had escaped. Now they also sought refuge in Inglewood Forest.

"Her Majesty will benefit from getting out of the cottage now and again during these last long weeks of waiting." Aunt Idony's tone was kind but left no room for arguing. "You will accompany her."

Chester stiffened at the order, but he didn't offer any protest. Instead, he bowed his head toward Aunt Idony in deference.

I'd never liked when my aunts made concessions or doted on me because of my royalty. I always felt self-conscious and spoiled when they did so. Like now. "Please. 'Tis not necessary. I shall learn to be content for the remainder of our confinement."

Aunt Idony rose, her head brushing against the newest bundles of herbs she'd hung to dry. "No harm came from your wandering this past week, and I do not anticipate anyone will find us here in our isolated part of the forest. But if you do wish to explore again, you will take Chester, will you not?"

"I shall. I—"

At a sudden pounding against the door, Aunt Elspeth jumped with a yelp. Aunt Idony turned pale and clutched the table. And Chester was off his bench, weapons out of his belt and in each hand before anyone could take a breath. I, too, rose and stared at the door, praying it was only a rare woodcutter passing by.

A fist banged against the door again, louder and more urgently.

"Who is it?" Chester inched closer to the door.

"I am a lowly woodcutter in need of a healer for my injured friend."

Aunt Idony moved forward, but Chester held out a hand to halt her. "There is no healer here."

"Please. He was attacked by a boar and suffers greatly."

Aunt Idony moved toward the door again, but Chester shook his head fiercely and then faced the door. "Go away. We cannot help."

Silence filled the space. Chester was using discretion the way Sir William had taught him. However, if someone was truly in need, I couldn't abide the thought of sending him away.

"I shall see to him," Aunt Idony whispered, clearly feeling the same way I did.

Chester held up a finger, bidding us to give him another moment.

"Rory?" came my name from the lips of the man outside.

The blood drained from my body in the same instant that everyone looked at me, alarm on their faces. The voice wasn't familiar. I had no idea how this man knew my name. Was this some kind of trap set by Queen Margery to lure me out of the cabin?

"Rory!" he called again. "Please! Kresten needs help."

"Kresten?" The name slipped from my lips before I realized it.

"Yes, he's been attacked by a boar and badly wounded. Please. Help." The desperation in the man's tone told me this was no trap. Kresten was hurt.

How badly? My pulse spurted with a new fear. I'd never witnessed the damage of a boar attack, but I'd heard Chester's tales and knew of the maiming and damage a boar's tusks could wreak. If Kresten wasn't speaking and had lost consciousness, then the injuries must be substantial.

I started across the chamber only to have Chester block my way. "We need to help him," I hissed.

"How exactly do you know Kresten?" Chester's face had hardened to iron, and his eyes flashed with accusation along with disappointment. Both Aunt Idony and Aunt Elspeth watched me, awaiting my answer.

Part of me wanted to hang my head in shame for deceiving my friends, but at another urgent knock against the door, I straightened. Maybe I'd made a poor choice in wandering away from the cottage and meeting Kresten. But now that it was done, I couldn't stand back and allow him to needlessly suffer and die.

"Open the door." I met Chester's severe gaze with one of my own.

"No."

I'd never exerted my authority over Chester's before, hadn't wanted to lord myself over him. But at this moment, I could only think of Kresten outside, bleeding and possibly dying. I lifted my chin and spoke words I'd never thought I would to Chester. "I command you to do it."

Something in his eyes wavered.

I pushed around him and stalked to the door.

"No, Rory." He grabbed my arm.

Holding the handle, I paused and looked at his strong fingers gripping me. "Unhand me."

He didn't budge.

Aunt Idony approached and laid a hand upon Chester's arm. "You must do as she says."

"We don't know who is out there—"

"Chester."

He dropped his hold. I nearly trembled at the prospect of defying my protector, and yet I lifted the latch anyway. I was doing the right thing in aiding a hurt man and would not deny him the care he needed out of fear of the repercussions and danger it might bring me.

I swung the door open wide, letting the candlelight fall upon a tall young man with a lean face and dark bushy beard, a stranger who peered at me with frightened eyes. He was holding up another man who was leaning heavily upon him, his head down and overly long brown hair hanging in disarray. Blood saturated his hose. Even in the growing dusk, I could see a gash in his flesh where his hose had ripped away. I held my breath. Was this Kresten?

As though hearing my unasked question, the injured man lifted his head and peered at me through the strands of his hair. Though his face was pale and his muscles taut, the handsome features belonged to none other than Kresten.

He fought to curve his lips into a smile. "I know— you didn't want—to see me again—but I couldn't resist." Each breath was halting, and he dropped his head again, sagging against his friend.

My body tensed with a sudden urgency. Kresten was indeed badly hurt. "Bring him in." I stepped aside and waved the taller man into the cottage.

In the next instant, Aunt Idony was at Kresten's opposite side, slipping her arm around his waist and lending him her strength.

"Thank you," Kresten's companion said, his voice cracking with relief. Stumbling under the weight of Kresten and half-dragging him, he stepped inside, then slid a wary glance at Chester, whose sword was raised in one hand and his knife in the other.

I leveled a glower at Chester. "You may put your weapons away. The only peril at present is that this man may lose his life."

Chester didn't move and instead continued to glare at the newcomers.

"Take him into my chamber," I instructed Aunt Idony.

Aunt Elspeth had frozen in front of the table, a dirty trencher in each hand, her wide eyes upon the strangers.

"Aunt Elspeth, we shall have need of warm water."

She tore her attention away and focused on me, nodding vigorously. "Yes, of course, my sweeting."

I followed Kresten into my room off the main living area. In recent years, as I'd realized the privilege of having a chamber to myself, I'd asked to have the dormer room, especially because the climb up the ladder was becoming more difficult for Aunt Elspeth. But my aunts had insisted I remain in the spacious room that contained the cottage's only bed, and they continued to slumber on pallets in the drafty loft above.

Now, with Kresten so gravely wounded, I was more than willing to give up my chamber. As his companion and Aunt Idony lowered him to the bed, they placed him there carefully on his stomach. Only then did I see the wound in the back of his thigh, the mangled flesh with the boar's tusk embedded deeply.

I gasped and had to grasp the door frame to keep from collapsing.

Aunt Idony's gaze darted to me, teeming with concern. "Chester?"

At her shout, instantly Chester was at my side, bracing me up.

I pressed a hand over my mouth, afraid I would be sick.

"Get her out of here!" Aunt Idony called, even as she stripped Kresten's breeches.

I clutched at the door, unwilling to leave just yet. Kresten had to live.

Chester gently peeled me away. "Come on with you, lass."

A part of me wanted to protest. But Aunt Idony

would work better at her doctoring if she didn't have to worry about me every time she turned around. So I allowed Chester to lead me to the table, where he pulled out the bench and helped me to sit. He motioned urgently at Aunt Elspeth, and she bustled over with another mug of mead, her face wreathed with worry.

"I am fine." I took the cup from her. "Please have no care for my well-being. Pour your attention upon Kresten. I beg of you."

I didn't want him to die. I was suddenly desperate to save him, desperate to have the chance to talk with him again, and even desperate for another opportunity to dance.

Chapter
8

Aurora

I sat at the table and buried my head in my hands, too shaken to be of much aid to Aunt Elspeth as she scurried back and forth from the hearth to the bedchamber with the water, linens, and herbal remedies Aunt Idony requested of her.

Chester stood stiffly outside the chamber door, whittling a stick with his knife. He'd gone out several times to scout the premises and ensure no one else was lurking in the woodland around the cottage. From his periodic checking out the window into the darkness, he seemed to expect more intruders at any moment.

I understood his apprehension. If Kresten had told one friend about the passageway through the ravine, then he might have mentioned it to others. Perhaps it would be only a matter of time before word spread and Queen Margery's spies came to investigate.

I'd compromised my safety, and I regretted it. But I didn't regret meeting Kresten. In fact, the longer Aunt Idony worked on him, the more fervently I prayed for

God to spare his life and limb. I blanched whenever I pictured the tusk protruding from his leg, and I marveled that Kresten had maintained the wherewithal to walk to our cottage in such a condition. It proved an inner fortitude and depth I'd glimpsed during our days together.

When Aunt Idony exited the bedchamber, I sat up, unable to breathe. She held a bloody towel and was wiping more blood from her hands.

Aunt Elspeth had long since finished cleaning up our meal and returned to her loom. Now the soft clicking of the pedals ceased, and her hands grew idle. "How is the young man?" she whispered loudly—so loudly she may as well have used a normal tone. "Will he live?"

"Yes, thank our Father in heaven."

"And his leg?" Aunt Elspeth continued in her overly loud whisper. "Will he be able to keep it?"

"I believe so. But only time will tell."

At the good news, the tension in my body eased. Hot tears pricked the backs of my eyes, and I lowered my head so no one would see my display of emotion.

"Jorg will stay with him," Aunt Idony said, as if answering an unasked question she'd sensed from Chester.

Chester heaved a sigh, likely one he'd been holding since the first knock on the door.

Aunt Idony finished wiping her hands. "They mean us no harm, Chester."

I was relieved by her declaration, but before I could say so, Chester shook his head. "You cannot know that entirely."

"Jorg is a kind young man who cares very much for his friend."

Jorg? Kresten hadn't talked about any companions. But it should come as no surprise that he had friends, since he was so likeable.

"We cannot trust them," Chester insisted. "We can trust no one. That's what my father always taught me."

"We must be cautious, but not at the expense of basic kindness and decency to someone in need."

I sat up again. "Yes, you have spoken my sentiments exactly. I shall never overlook the needs of others in order to save myself. I would be true and noble no matter the cost."

Chester sheathed his knife and pushed away from the door frame, his expression stormy. As he stalked toward the table, I braced myself for the argument that had been brewing since the moment our visitors knocked upon the door.

He stopped and towered over me. "Those are not my sentiments, and they never will be. My only sentiment is that of keeping you alive and secure no matter the cost."

I understood what he wasn't saying—that as queen of Mercia, my safety was paramount. I respected his position, but I also disagreed. What kind of leader would I be if I put my well-being above my people's and was never willing to sacrifice for them?

Chester lowered himself to the bench beside me. "The real question is, how did you meet these two?" With a glance to the half-open door of the bedchamber, he lowered his voice. "And the next is— why didn't you tell me?"

Aunt Idony crossed over and stood near us, clearly wanting to know the answer to his questions as well.

"I think you know why I refrained from telling you," I whispered.

"No, I don't."

"To avoid a confrontation like this."

"If you're so concerned about being true and noble, then you would refrain from deceit."

He was right. I hadn't been true or noble. While I hadn't exactly lied, I also hadn't been forthright. Deceit was deceit no matter how one portrayed it.

"I met Kresten at the clearing closest to the ravine. The first day was an accident, but the times after that we planned to meet." Embarrassment rushed in. "I did not speak of the matter because I did not want anyone to stop me from seeing him."

Chester's brow furrowed. "You know you can't harbor fondness for him, do you not?"

"We already had this conversation while you were gone." Aunt Idony gave me a pointed look. Now she knew why I'd asked her about men. "And Rory is well aware of her obligations."

The obligation to wed an important man, form an advantageous alliance, and become a worthy queen like my mother. Though Queen Leandra hadn't ruled Mercia for many years, her marriage to my father, Prince Stephan from Norland, had secured Mercia's northern border and solidified trade agreements. Within just a few years of her reign, she'd turned Mercia into a strong and independent nation, and she'd proven herself a capable and focused leader.

As a young and inexperienced ruler, I'd have much to prove too. I needed to follow in my mother's footsteps. At least, I prayed I would be able to live up to her reputation and be just as strong and purposeful. I couldn't jeopardize being like her, especially not before I'd even had the chance to begin.

"Yes, I am aware of my duty. That is precisely why I told Kresten we could not see each other ever again."

"And look how well that worked," Chester retorted.

"He is a man of his word. He chose not to seek me out. And he would have kept his promise if not for his injury."

"I find that hard to believe."

I glanced toward the door and lowered my voice even further. "I did not reveal myself."

"He'll discover erelong you are no peasant girl. And that is why he must leave on the morrow."

Aunt Idony protested at the same moment I did. "With the medicines I administered to dull the pain of his wound, he'll slumber for many hours. And when he awakens, he'll be weak and immobile, likely for many days yet."

A tiny thrill wound through me just thinking about him staying for a while.

As if reading my reaction, Chester scowled. "No good can come of this man staying here. He must leave on the morrow."

Aunt Idony rested her blood-coated hands on her hips. Though I'd never met a real physician, I doubted anyone could compare to her skill. And with the extent of Kresten's injury, she wouldn't cast him out so soon, would she?

Thankfully, she gave a curt shake of her head. "The leg needs time to heal before he puts pressure on it. Besides, I must clean and medicate the wound to keep it from putrefying."

Chester pressed his lips together.

I spoke before he could utter additional protests.

"We shall care for Kresten as best we are able until Aunt Idony deems he is well enough to travel."

Chester's shoulders slumped slightly, enough for me to know he was discouraged more than angry.

I reached out a hand toward him, my palm up. "Please try to understand . . ."

He didn't place his hand in mine but pulled away and stood. "What I understand is that you like him and are looking for any excuse to spend more time with him."

I let my hand drop, a strange sadness filtering through me. Chester was my closest friend and companion. He always had been. And though we didn't see eye to eye on everything, we never remained angry with each other. Was this, then, to be a rift we could not repair?

He glanced between Aunt Idony and me. "If you plan to disregard my concerns, then I insist Rory stay away from him for the duration of his stay."

I stood quickly, nearly tipping my bench. "You cannot ask that. No harm can come of keeping company with him—"

"Already the harm may be immeasurable."

"You are overreacting."

"And you are naïve."

"Chester." Aunt Idony's tone rang with censure.

He snapped his mouth closed against something more he wanted to say.

I pulled myself up, hoping I appeared more confident than I felt. I would soon need to make decisions every day—decisions that would be unpopular, that might even anger people. I may as well practice on Chester. "I give you my word. I shall be careful."

"But you have never spent time with a man and have no idea the wiles—"

"She will be chaperoned." Aunt Idony cut in. "At all times."

I hadn't been chaperoned with him in the woods, and we'd gotten along splendidly. But I wouldn't bring that up now.

"I pray I am wrong," Chester said, "but I fear we are making a mistake and that this will only lead to misfortune."

"Kresten is a good man and will bring us no ill will. You will see." Once Chester got to know the wood-cutter as I did, he'd realize his fears were unfounded.

Chester glowered at the bedchamber. Then without another word, he crossed and exited the cottage, slamming the door behind him.

Chapter 9

KRESTEN

MY THIGH BURNED AS THOUGH SOMEONE HAD STUCK A GLOWING brand into my flesh and left it there. Every time I moved, the burning speared the rest of my leg, forcing me to resign myself to lying on my stomach and staying as motionless as possible.

For the first day of my confinement, such a position was bearable. I slept most of the time, the herbal remedies making me drowsy so I was hardly aware of anyone or my surroundings.

However, by the second morning, the pain was still excruciating, but I was more alert. I wanted to roll over and take in my lodgings as well as get a better look at the people coming and going from my chamber. Mostly, I wanted to see Rory and was disappointed when she didn't come in all day.

Aunt Idony tended to my injuries, leaving my legs uncovered and packing the thigh wound with poultices and salves. She was efficient and brusque and not overly friendly, but she had saved my life, and hopefully my leg, with her healing skills.

Aunt Elspeth was more talkative and doting. Every time she came into the room, she brought food—custards, breads, confections, and more—the kind of food I hadn't eaten since leaving Scania. Though my pain had taken away my appetite, I was glad Jorg could partake of the offerings.

Chester either stood or sat directly outside the chamber door, always whittling with a sharp knife. I expected him to interrogate me about how I knew Rory, but the only attention he afforded me was an icy glare.

When I awoke on the third morning, my mind was clearer than it had been the previous days, and though the wound still burned, I sensed I'd made it through the worst and would heal.

As Aunt Idony finished spreading the salve, the strong aroma of the herbs I couldn't begin to name stung my nose.

"Thank you," I said, my cheek resting against the hay-filled mattress within the box frame. Though it was a simple bed, I was grateful for it, especially after the past months of sleeping on the ground with naught but my cloak and a blanket for comfort.

Aunt Idony wiped her hands on a rag. "Try not to move again today."

"I'll try, but I admit I am growing restless."

"How much longer before he is able to get up?" Jorg asked from where he stood at the foot of the bed. He'd spent a large portion of the past two days sitting on a stool nearby, and he must be as restless as I was, if not more.

"The flesh shows no signs of putrefying." Aunt Idony gathered her medicinal supplies from the edge of the bed.

"If that continues, he may be able to walk in a fortnight."

"A fortnight?" Jorg and I both spoke at once.

"The tusk went deep. You're fortunate it missed your bone."

I was fortunate. But I couldn't wait for two weeks to resume my woodcutting. Nor could I trouble this poor family that long. From what I'd gleaned, I was sleeping in Rory's chamber and on her bed, and I had no wish to inconvenience her any more than I already had, especially since she seemed to be avoiding me.

Perhaps she'd truly meant she had no wish to see me again and even now was holding herself aloof. If she was so determined to keep away from me, then I couldn't impose any longer than I had to.

I glanced toward the closed door, wishing for just one glimpse of her. But so far, I'd been relegated to seeing Chester's burly frame whenever the door opened. "You have been beyond kind to me. But as I have no means to repay you for your care and hospitality, we will be on our way by the day's end."

Aunt Idony paused in rolling a bandage. "If you try to walk, you'll break open every stitch I so carefully made, cause irreparable damage, and possibly lose your leg."

"Then allow me to bed down elsewhere—perhaps on the floor in the other room—so I don't impose upon Rory any longer."

"She wants you to have her chamber. Besides, right now you need the privacy." Aunt Idony looked pointedly at my bare legs. I was stripped of all my garments except my long tunic. While it provided some modesty, I agreed with Aunt Idony. It wasn't enough.

At the sound of raised voices from the other side of the door—one of them distinctly Rory's—all other thoughts fled from my mind save of her.

"I have waited long enough," she said in a low, angry tone. "You cannot ban me from talking with him again today."

"I can and I will," came Chester's calm response.

"We agreed I could visit him with a chaperone."

"You and Aunt Idony agreed. Not me."

My heart gave an extra thud. So she had wanted to visit me. And Chester was denying her the opportunity?

Aunt Idony had heard the commotion and was staring at the door. She pursed her lips but didn't make a move to intervene.

"Step aside and allow me to enter." Rory had talked of Chester and their childhood together. No doubt she was accustomed to bossing him around, although she hadn't struck me as a strong-willed woman.

"Please, lass. He's indecent. It wouldn't be proper, even with a chaperone."

At the ensuing silence, I saw my chance of seeing her rapidly slipping away. I couldn't let that happen. Suddenly, I didn't know how I could go another day, not even another minute, without being with her.

I motioned to Jorg. "Cover me. Make haste."

Jorg hesitated, glancing at Aunt Idony as if needing permission from her.

She nodded, her face reflecting weariness and age. "You may cover the wound for a short while."

Jorg draped a blanket over me. After he finished and Aunt Idony opened the door to leave, Chester was the only one I could see. Rory was no longer there.

"I'm entirely modest and decent," I called, hoping she could hear me wherever she was. "And am in desperate need of visitors."

Chester peeked in, scowling at me, his hand moving to the knife sheathed at his belt. It was clear he didn't want me in the cottage now any more than he had the eve I'd arrived. Jorg stepped between us, his fingers tight against his knife handle as well.

Aunt Idony whispered to Chester. He stepped stiffly aside, and a moment later, Rory appeared in the doorway. The morning sunshine streaming through the bedchamber window seemed to alight on her, giving her an ethereal glow. She wore a plain peasant skirt and tunic, and her fair hair hung in a simple braid over her shoulder, with loose tendrils framing her face. Even so simply attired, she was more beautiful than a dozen noblewomen wearing their fanciest gowns and jewels.

My breath stuck in my chest, and my heart refused to beat. All I could do was stare.

She anxiously examined me, as though attempting to judge the extent of my injuries. And I was relieved for Aunt Idony's prudence in sheltering Rory from seeing the wound. If it looked anything like it felt, I had no doubt the sight of it would turn her stomach.

"How are you faring today?" She started across the room toward me.

"Better now that you're here." It was the kind of flattery I'd wielded many times with other women, but with Rory it was actually true.

I thought I heard Chester snort from the doorway.

"Tell me the truth. How is your wound?" She stopped at the edge of the bed and lowered herself to a crouch so she was more at my level.

"Truly. Your presence is the medicine I've needed."

Another snort, this one more distinct, came from Chester's direction.

Rory cast him a brittle look. "You may close the door."

"Absolutely not. The door stays open, and I stay right here."

"Kresten's companion will act as our chaperone."

"And I will too."

Rory and Chester locked glares. Perhaps Aunt Idony would need to intervene again.

Thankfully, Jorg broke the tension. "Here, you'll be more comfortable sitting." He placed his stool next to Rory and motioned to it.

"Thank you for your kindness." She took her place on it, arranging her frayed skirt over her feet, but not before I saw her toes. She was barefoot again. "And thank you for bringing Kresten here. Aunt Idony says in doing so, you saved his life."

Jorg bowed his head slightly. "I'm grateful your aunt is willing to assist him. She's very skilled."

"Yes, she is quite gifted in the healing arts."

Aunt Idony had implied that Rory's visit must be kept short, and I wanted to make the most of every second with her. So when Jorg opened his mouth to continue the conversation, I spoke first. "I regret that I'm displacing you from your chamber."

"Think nothing of it." She folded her hands in her lap and studied them. "I am bedding down with my aunts in the dormer room above."

"We shall not stay long—"

"But I heard Aunt Idony say you must rest for at least a fortnight, that you will tear your wound open if you attempt to walk before that."

"Then you will not object to my presence?"

Her gaze flew to mine, and I found myself captivated by her endless violet-blue eyes. Though I couldn't deny I wanted to spend the next two weeks with her as much as her family would allow, I also didn't want my presence to be a burden. Especially after the way we'd parted when she said we must go our separate ways and never see each other again.

She cast a glance toward the door, then lowered her voice. "I admit I am glad to see you once more."

"I admit to the same."

A flush rose into her cheeks the same way it had oft during our dance lessons. "Are you in much pain?"

"'Tis growing more tolerable by the day."

She looked first at Jorg and then Chester before biting her lower lip as though she wanted to say something but didn't want our audience to hear. As a prince, I was accustomed to having people around me at all times. Even when in my private chambers, I'd always had servants along with knights and their squires lingering nearby. I'd long since learned to carry on as if they weren't present. But of course, Rory wouldn't be used to being a public figure and having minimal privacy.

She leaned in slightly. "Perhaps I can find ways to amuse you and take your mind off the pain."

"Your presence alone is all I could need or wish for. But if the amusements afford me more time with you, then I shall not object."

Chester snorted even louder this time.

"Chester, please." Rory cast pleading eyes upon him. The technique worked better than anger, for his eyes softened with what I could only describe as affection. Did Chester have feelings for Rory? Though she'd referred to him as being like a brother, perhaps Chester saw her as much more than a sister. Maybe that's one reason why he disliked me so much.

"Do you like chess?" she asked.

"I do play, although I've been told I lack strategy."

"Then I shall teach you."

My thoughts returned to when I teased her about teaching me to braid flowers in exchange for dance lessons. "I suppose you do owe me—"

She cut me off with a rapid shake of her head and the darting of her gaze toward Chester. She didn't want him to know about our dancing?

As if hearing my unasked question, she shook her head again in warning. "What about reading? I can read to you, if you would be agreeable."

"I would be very agreeable." Was she able to read? I didn't know of many women who had any learning, much less a peasant woman. Perhaps Aunt Idony was educated and had passed her knowledge along to Rory.

Whatever the case, it was becoming clearer with each day that this was no ordinary peasant's home, at least not like any others we'd visited during our time in Inglewood Forest. The furnishings, the food, and even the atmosphere had the feel of nobility. Perhaps once they'd been wealthy but had fallen onto hard times.

I shifted so I could see her better and held back a wince at the pain that shot through my leg. "Perhaps I shall teach you Tafl."

"And what exactly is Tafl?" She studied my face, her attention drifting to my brow, nose, cheeks, chin, and then my mouth. The innocence in her expression told me she didn't realize she was observing me so openly.

I couldn't hold back a pleased smile. "Tafl is a game like chess, with a king and army and war strategy."

"Very well. But I must warn you, I am a competitive game player and rarely lose."

"And I must warn you, I'm not in the least competitive but somehow manage to almost always win."

The hint of a smile graced her lips. "Then we shall be evenly matched."

Evenly matched? We were far from evenly matched, but I couldn't tell her that. Not now. Not after the way we'd parted that day in the woods. If she hadn't thought we had any hope before, she'd think so even less if she knew I was a prince. She'd likely run from the chamber and never return.

"Time is up." Chester stepped into the room.

She lifted her chin almost defiantly. "A few more minutes."

"I'm passing along Aunt Idony's instruction." Chester's gaze connected with mine for an instant, but it was long enough to let me know he'd listened carefully to our every word and still didn't like me. Not one bit.

Rory didn't move from her spot but reached for my hand where it rested near the edge of the bed. "Please do not feel you are imposing. You are welcome to stay here as long as you need." Her squeeze was amiable, but it sent a shimmer of warmth up my arm regardless.

Chester stiffened as his gaze locked on our connected hands.

I brought Rory's hand to my lips and kissed her fingers. At the gentle contact, she drew in a breath but made no move to pull away. Chester, however, growled his protest, and his boots clunked on the floor as he approached.

Jorg intercepted him, pushing himself to his full height, and the two men stood face-to-face, their chests almost touching.

With a shy smile, Rory rose and extracted her hand

from mine. Then without a glance at Chester, she strode from the chamber.

Jorg didn't budge. And Chester finally took a step back. "You're not woodcutters, that much is obvious. The question is, who are you and what are you doing here in Inglewood Forest?"

I tried to mask my surprise at how astute this man was. "Think what you will. But we are woodcutters. Go ask Walter Matthews in Birchwood. He'll vouch for us."

Chester studied my face, as if attempting to see past my deceit. Finally, he spun and stalked away, banging the door closed behind him.

For as much as the man irritated me, I couldn't fault him for his suspicions. He was concerned for Rory and wanted to keep her safe from any potential harm. If I were in his position, I might have reacted the same way to having two outsiders in my home, especially if they interacted with the woman I cared about.

I closed my eyes, weariness washing over me. I didn't want to hurt her in any way. Yet if I allowed our attraction to progress unchecked during my recuperation, I'd certainly cause her heartache when I left.

Friendship. Yes, that was the solution. I'd make a point of treating her as naught more than a friend. I would squelch the desire that surfaced so easily every time I was with her, and I'd facilitate friendship instead.

Surely no harm could come from just being friends.

Chapter 10

Aurora

I loved spending time with Kresten. In fact, with every passing day, the more time I spent with him, the more I wanted, not less. When I was busy with chores, I could think of nothing but finishing so I could visit him. And when I was with him, I dreaded Chester's intrusive command telling me my time was up.

At first, Aunt Idony allowed me to sit with Kresten for the briefest of lengths and only a couple of times a day. But after she gave Kresten permission to sit up in bed, she also allowed me to stay longer.

Just as he'd been when we met in the forest, he was an interesting, entertaining, talkative, and fun-loving young man. And he brought life and energy to our cottage that we'd never had before.

Aunt Elspeth easily fell prey to his charm, giggling and talking like a young girl whenever she was around him. While Aunt Idony was more guarded, at the very least she accepted his presence. It helped that Jorg asked to aid with chores, assisting Aunt Idony with weeding the garden, pruning fruit trees, and chopping wood for fuel.

True to his word, Kresten taught me Tafl, a game he'd learned while living in Scania. I caught on with haste, and we spent hours a day challenging each other in both Tafl and chess. He also liked when I read aloud to him. At first, I was uncomfortable when he watched me read, but soon enough I grew accustomed to the attention and rather enjoyed it.

At the end of the second week, Aunt Idony decided his wound wasn't healing well enough for his leg to bear weight. And though both he and Jorg insisted that they needed to be on their way, Aunt Idony persuaded them to stay longer.

Kresten seemed to take the news in stride, while Jorg was more agitated. By the end of the third week at the cottage, Jorg decided to hike to Birchwood and inform their warden what had happened and why they were failing to deliver their regular quota.

With Jorg gone for the day, I suspected Kresten would be more restless than usual.

"How are you faring?" I peeked my head into the chamber during one of the occasions Chester had gone outside to attend to his charcoal kilns. Though he didn't devote as much time to charcoal burning as others of the trade, he'd kept up the appearance of being a charcoal burner, as had Sir William before him, so if anyone questioned our means of survival, they would assume we relied upon the charcoal as well as living off the forest instead of a secret royal provision.

Propped up in bed with cushions against the wall, Kresten lowered the book he'd been reading and grinned at me in welcome. The sight of him never failed to send a flutter through my stomach.

He cocked his head toward the game sitting on the bedside table where we'd left it the night before. "I am waiting to resume our Tafl game. The one I'm winning."

"The one you are winning only because I am letting you."

"We'll see about that." His grin broadened, making him all the more appealing, and I wanted more than anything to abandon my embroidery at the table and sit with Kresten. Chester had restricted my visits to the times when he was able to supervise. But surely by now, Chester had realized how unfounded his fears were. No harm had befallen us as a result of Kresten and Jorg's presence. No one even knew we had them as guests.

No ill would come of spending a few minutes with him now. I hesitated in the doorway, not wanting to break the rules of being in his chamber without a chaperone. Less than a dozen feet away, Aunt Elspeth paused her weaving, glanced to the cottage door, and then spoke in an overly loud whisper. "Well now. I'm not supposed to allow you to enter. But I am ready to give my hands a rest and won't mind a short break to sit with you."

"Are you sure? I do not want to take you away from your labor."

She pushed herself up from her stool, wincing as she straightened. "It's no trouble, my sweeting. My poor old back cannot go as long as it used to."

I dragged in a more comfortable chair for her along with a footstool. Once she was settled, I tucked a warm blanket around her to ward off the chill of the autumn day and then took my place on a stool at Kresten's bedside, drawing up the table and resuming our unfinished game.

We talked and bantered and played. And, as with every other day, I relished being with him, feeling alive in a way I never had before. While I awaited my turn, I studied Kresten's face, his brows puckered in concentration.

I couldn't imagine a kinder, sweeter, more enjoyable man. Not only did I love spending time with him, but the strong lines of his cheeks and jaw and chin never failed to draw my attention. He had a perfect nose, a handsome smile, and the most stunning blue eyes.

"It's your turn." His voice was laced with humor. "But take your time admiring me. I don't mind."

I dropped my gaze to the pieces on the board, a flush infusing my face. "And what makes you think I am admiring you?"

"Because I'm irresistible."

I didn't dare look up for fear he'd see the truth in my eyes—that I did find him irresistible.

"Admit it," he whispered with an intimacy that sent my pulse racing. "You think I'm gallant."

"Hush." Kresten had never been this bold with Chester standing at the door. I could only imagine what Aunt Elspeth was thinking of this turn in our conversation. Her eyes were likely wide, and she was probably fanning her face with the force of a gale wind.

"Aunt Elspeth's asleep," Kresten whispered as though reading my mind.

I peeked her direction, and sure enough, her head

was tilted back, her eyes closed, and her mouth wide open, emitting the heavy breathing of slumber.

"You must still behave." I tried to study the game.

"You should know by now that I rarely behave the way I ought to."

The low rumble in his voice made my insides flip upside down. "You must try."

"Or what?"

Again, my insides flipped, leaving a ripple of pleasure in their wake. "Or I shall need to discipline you most severely."

He was silent for a heartbeat, and then I felt the pressure of his fingers under my chin, tipping my head up. "Will you allow me to do this?"

"Do what?"

He skimmed his thumb down my cheek to my chin. "This?"

The soft caress sent a tremor through me, one that traveled to my very core. "No, you cannot."

"Then what about this?" He brushed the pad of his thumb across my lower lip.

My breath stuck in my lungs, and I could only shake my head and whisper, "No."

"Maybe this?" He grazed my upper lip.

"No." I could hardly get the word out.

During the process of our whispered conversation, he'd leaned closer to me, and somehow I'd leaned closer to him so that we were now poised above the game, our faces mere inches apart.

With his attention squarely upon my lips, the desire that flamed in his eyes was undeniable. I couldn't deny the desire welling up within me either. For what, I didn't know. All I knew was that I longed for more, that the longing had been building with each passing day of being together.

These past weeks of his recuperation, he'd been chaste and reserved. He'd used caution, treating me with sisterly regard. Even so, an undercurrent had existed between us, something sweet and secretly thrilling, something I'd tried to ignore. But now that we had a moment of privacy, we could no longer let it lay dormant.

"If you are so adamantly opposed," he whispered, but without moving back, "then I guess I shall stop."

"No." The one word was breathless with anticipation.

The blue of his eyes darkened. And he drew closer, so that the warmth of his breath hovered above my lips. Did he intend to kiss me? I'd never experienced anything like this and wasn't sure how to react. Did I want his kiss?

My body tensed with need. Yet, I hesitated. Though neither of my aunts had spoken of kissing or showing physical affection, I understood that a kiss wasn't something to give away lightly. It was a precious means of connecting with someone special. And I'd always imagined I'd share my first kiss with the man I planned to wed.

Alas, I couldn't marry Kresten. Simply couldn't. Or could I? Could he come with me and stand by my side during the uncertain days ahead? Or what if I stayed here and let my father continue to rule as regent in my stead?

"Rory?" His whisper brushed my lips.

At the opening of the door in the other room, I jumped back, nearly toppling from my stool. I hastened to steady myself and pretended to study the board, noting from the corner of my eye that Kresten was doing the same.

Aunt Elspeth sat forward with a start, mumbling something incoherent under her breath.

Chester's heavy footfalls thudded through the living area.

I situated myself even farther away from the board and braced myself for his censure.

An instant later, he appeared in the doorway. "What's going on here?"

I wanted to hang my head at the anger in his tone, but I forced myself to move one of my army pieces. "We are finishing our game."

"I told you no visits unless I was inside the cottage."

"Aunt Elspeth is chaperoning."

I was thankful the dear woman had awakened and was now sitting forward, her eyes wide open. "No need to worry, Chester sweeting. I've been watching them except for a few seconds when I gave my eyes a rest."

Even though my turn had come and gone, I kept my focus on the board, unable to look at Kresten lest in doing so I gave myself away. And unable to look at Chester for fear he'd see the truth of how much I liked Kresten.

"I don't know why you cannot listen to reason." Chester's statement was loaded with frustration.

"And I do not know why you cannot stop treating me like a helpless child." I situated an off-center piece in the middle of its square. "I am a grown woman and do not require you overseeing my every action."

Chester pressed his lips together, likely to keep from saying something about how I was the queen of

Mercia and in need of more protection than the average woman.

What if I just wanted to lead a normal life?

Such a thought was traitorous. Especially after how diligently Aunt Idony and Aunt Elspeth had labored to prepare me for the task of ruling and leading a royal life.

Aunt Elspeth rose clumsily from her chair and ambled to the door. "Don't worry, dear heart. Let the two enjoy the company while it lasts. For all too soon it will be over." She patted Chester's cheek before she continued into the other room.

A moment later, the whirring and clacking of the loom indicated that she was back at her weaving.

Chester beckoned me with his hand. "Come now."

"*All too soon it will be over.*" Protest welled up within. I didn't want it to be over, not when it had just begun.

"We must give the patient a break," Chester insisted.

I expected Kresten to make a witty comment about how he was fine and didn't want or need a break from me. But he focused on the board, his forehead lined and his brows knit. Was he thinking about Aunt Elspeth's words too?

Kresten moved one of his pieces. He set it down next to my king, then rested against the cushions. "Game over."

I watched him, waiting for him to look up, grin at me, suggest another game—anything. But he crossed his arms behind his head and closed his eyes.

The silence in the chamber grew stifling. And a strange hurt pricked inside.

"All too soon it will be over." When it was over, this was how it would feel, except worse. Maybe it was time to stop ignoring the fact that we had no future. Maybe it was time to stop pretending today was all that mattered. And maybe it was time to stop giving away my heart—although a part of me suspected it was too late.

I rose and exited the room. I didn't want to talk to Chester, but he followed me outside the cottage into the cool afternoon.

"Be more careful, Rory," he said quietly as the door closed behind him.

I lowered myself to the bench underneath the window and retrieved the wreath I'd been creating from the variety of flowers I'd dried over the summer.

"Please, Rory," Chester said again after a minute.

I inhaled a deep breath, taking in the aroma of wood smoke from the kilns mixed with the dampness of fallen leaves. The distant trill of a weasel echoed in the soft stillness of the air. Aunt Idony, on her knees in one of her herb beds, paused to study us before she resumed her pruning.

Chester folded his arms and propped a shoulder against the door frame. Apparently, he had no intention of leaving me in peace until I replied.

I let the wreath fall idle in my lap. "I had hoped by now you could accept Kresten and see that we have naught to fear from him."

"And I had hoped by now you'd recognize that something about him doesn't match up with who he claims to be." Chester had mentioned his suspicion on several other occasions. And I'd reassured him that while Kresten may have had an unusual upbringing, there was no denying his skill with an axe or the brawny muscles and thick calluses of a woodcutter.

Perhaps I, too, found it unusual for a pauper to be so well versed about so many subjects. But I didn't question him for fear he might be wondering the same of me. If I remained silent on the matter, I hoped he would too.

"You're allowing yourself to get too close to him."

I'd already admonished myself to cease from giving him my heart. And my pulse already pattered with a strange foreboding. Nevertheless, I couldn't make myself cut things off with him yet.

Maybe a stronger queen like my mother would have been able to do so. I needed only to envision her portrait hanging in my father's chamber at Huntwell Fortress to be reminded of my own shortcomings. She'd been regal, her eyes alight with purpose and her chin high with determination. She'd accomplished everything she set out to do. Aunt Idony and my father had always spoken highly of her, lauding her many feats.

How could I manage ruling a country when I could hardly manage my emotions? Surely once I arrived in Delsworth, everyone would be disappointed that I wasn't as strong and purposeful as my mother. They'd view me as plain, simple, and ignorant, unfit to rule. What if they decided they didn't like me or want me as queen?

Maybe I ought to consider staying at the cottage after all. For several seconds, my insecurities seemed to join forces with the desire to stay here with Kresten.

But as Chester released an exasperated breath, I released the idea, letting it float away on the breeze.

"You need not worry." I spoke the words expected of me. "As Aunt Elspeth said, the time with him will be over erelong. And then I shall never see him again."

If only I could convince my heart that's what I really wanted.

Chapter
11

KRESTEN

I SIGHED FOR THE HUNDREDTH TIME, EARNING ANOTHER RAISED brow from Jorg. Sitting on the stool by the window for light, he paused in writing in his journal where he kept record of our daily activities. "Do you need another book?"

The history book lay open on the blanket covering my outstretched legs. Though I'd found the history of Mercia fascinating and appreciated Saint Bede's tales of the early settlement of the Great Isle, today I took no pleasure in reading. Every time I tried, the words blended together, and all I saw was Rory's earnest face, the desire in her eyes, and the readiness in her open lips.

I could have kissed her. I would have kissed her, and she would have let me . . . if not for Chester's return.

Part of me longed to finish the moment, to press my lips to hers and savor the sweetness of a kiss. But another part of me was relieved Chester had arrived when he did, preventing me from carrying through with it.

We had to remain friends. And until yesterday, I'd

maintained the boundaries—or at least I thought I had. If Aunt Elspeth hadn't fallen asleep . . . But even as I blamed the older woman, I could only place the responsibility upon myself. First I made the mistake of flirting with Rory. Then I made the situation more intense by touching her. If I'd kept my focus on the game and behaved properly, things wouldn't have escalated.

And she wouldn't be avoiding me . . .

I peered beyond Chester to the living quarters but didn't see her anywhere. I hadn't glimpsed her since she'd walked out of the room yesterday after I so abruptly ended our game.

I reclined and tried to make myself comfortable. I was fooling myself into thinking we could only be friends and that nothing need change in our relationship. In truth, I'd been besotted with her before being wounded and ending up at her cottage. And now, after spending countless hours with her, I cared about her so deeply that it hurt.

Leaning my head back, I stared at the ceiling. I was falling in love with her, maybe already did love her. But such a love would bring grievous affliction—to me when I had to return to Scania without her, and to her when she learned I'd left her behind.

Jorg stood and set aside his journal and ink pot. "I can check if there's another book that might hold your interest better."

"No, this is fine." I picked the book back up and pretended to read.

Jorg watched me for a moment, then chortled. "Since when have you made a practice of reading books upside down?"

I focused on the pages only to realize I was indeed holding the book the wrong way. I snapped it closed and tossed it next to me.

At the doorway where he was whittling, Chester's lips cocked with the beginning of a grin.

Of course he was happy Rory and I were out of sorts. "You don't need to stand guard any longer. I've obviously provoked her, and she's not coming to visit me."

"True enough." With a cheerful salute, he left his post. A moment later, the door banged closed behind him, and the sound of whistling filled the air as he made his way across the yard toward the kilns.

Jorg watched out the window, following Chester's trail. As soon as the burly guardian was out of sight, Jorg stalked to the doorway, poked his head out and spoke to Aunt Elspeth, then shut the door.

"I told her you needed privacy, for . . . you know . . ." He nodded at the chamber pot as he grabbed his stool and positioned it near the head of the bed. As he sat and leaned forward, his severe expression confirmed what I'd guessed. He had news, and it wasn't good.

Ever since his return from Birchwood late last night, I'd sensed an undercurrent of tension in his demeanor. During the couple of instances when Chester had stepped away momentarily, Jorg had started to share something with me but had been interrupted by Aunt Elspeth and Idony, almost as if they were determined not to give us any time alone.

"I must speak with haste," Jorg whispered. His features, which had begun to fill out again after eating Aunt Elspeth's baked goods, were etched with urgency.

"What is it?" I pushed myself up, but the movement was too fast and jarred my wound.

"While in Birchwood, I learned both of your brothers are in Mercia."

I shrugged, attempting to make myself comfortable. "'Tis of no consequence to me."

"It is now."

I halted my restless positioning, a shimmer of trepidation shooting through me. "I suppose you will tell me why whether I want to hear it or not."

He nodded. "They have both married."

"Married?"

"Aye, married."

At one time I might have scoffed at my brothers for the news, but feeling as I did about Rory, my heart swelled with compassion for them. If they had experienced even half of the emotions I had, I understood well their motives for getting married. "Whom did they wed?"

Jorg shared all he'd learned, that Vilmar had led a slave revolt in Warwick's mine pits, married one of the slaves, and was now on the run from Queen Margery. Mikkel had wed the rebellious Princess Pearl, Queen Margery's oldest daughter, and was also on the run from the angry queen, having recently taken refuge in Inglewood Forest.

"You do know what this means, do you not?" Jorg asked as he finished relaying the news, glancing over his shoulder toward the door.

Unfortunately, yes. "It means they both will earn the disfavor of the king and the Lagting alike."

"Exactly."

Although the rules of the Testing didn't explicitly prohibit marriage, everyone knew that once we completed the Testing and the Lagting decided upon Father's successor, the arrangements for our brides would be finalized and we would soon be married. That meant we had no right to choose for ourselves or to wed without permission.

Why had my brothers defied tradition? Especially the two of them, who were so much more careful than I was about following the rules. I didn't understand it. Almost didn't believe it. Except the seriousness of Jorg's expression told me 'twas true.

"They also both left behind their Testing," Jorg whispered.

"They may yet return to their assignments."

"With but a month to go? I don't see how it's possible."

The rules of the Testing stated that if we left our location for any reason, we must go back and finish. Moreover, if we abandoned our duty entirely, we would forfeit any claim to the throne.

"Your brothers have eliminated themselves from the kingship. And now you must consider yourself the next king of Scania."

"Me? The next king?" I almost laughed, but Jorg wasn't smiling. This was no jest.

"You will be the only prince to complete the Testing and, in so doing, prove your worthiness to take the throne."

Was Jorg right? Would I have the chance to prove I was worthy? After living in my brothers' shadows for so long, would my father finally value me?

"I don't know, Jorg." Uncertainty rushed in to taunt me with all my weaknesses. I wasn't responsible or levelheaded like Mikkel. And people didn't trust and like me the same way they did Vilmar. I was too lighthearted to be taken seriously, and people at court only looked to me when they needed fun or adventure or parties.

"You have less than four weeks," Jorg whispered. "Finish strong and show the Lagting you are ready."

I'd never imagined becoming king was within my grasp. But if both Mikkel and Vilmar had taken themselves out of the running, then I was the only one left. If I completed my Testing, it was very possible the Lagting would honor me with the crown of succession.

"There is one more thing." Jorg shifted closer. "Your brothers want to arrange a meeting with you."

"What? Why?" Of course, my brothers knew I was here in the forest doing my Testing. But why would they seek me out?

"They've been asking around for you. Walter and several other laborers in Birchwood made a point of informing me."

"Then the townspeople know of my true identity?"

Jorg nodded. "Aye, word of it is spreading."

"What did you tell Walter and the others?"

"I let them know you were injured by a boar and unable to see your brothers."

"Let's arrange a meeting." I'd already taken some steps earlier that morning, and Aunt Idony had predicted I'd regain full use of my leg within the week.

Jorg's expression remained grave. "Until we know your brothers' intentions, I don't think we can risk an encounter."

"What kind of intentions might they have?"

"Since they have failed the Testing, what if they wish to eliminate you?"

I shook my head. "No. They wouldn't—"

"It's possible."

While I could admit I'd been jealous of the ease with which my brothers accomplished whatever they set out to do and for earning our father's affection, I didn't believe they were capable of treachery against me. Then again, I'd never believed either of them would disregard the Lagting and the Testing.

Whatever the case, I couldn't ignore them, not if they were in need. If they were running from danger, I could do nothing less than come to their aid the same way they would rush to mine. In doing so, however, I didn't want to involve Rory or her aunts.

Hitherto, I'd bided my time at the cottage. Though I hadn't liked burdening them, Aunt Idony had given me little choice but to remain. I'd determined to make the best of it, especially with Rory. But now that people knew who I was, I risked bringing attention to her, something that would happen if anyone suspected I'd spent time at her cottage. People would assume the worst, and any connection to me as a prince would surely ruin her reputation.

That meant I had to put aside my own desires and stop spending time with Rory.

Protest roiled through my stomach, but I scooted to the edge and swung my legs over. "Help me up."

"Aunt Idony said—"

"It doesn't matter. I need to start strengthening my leg. Now."

Jorg assisted me to my feet. At the full weight of my body upon my injured limb, pain jarred me so that I wanted to cry out.

"You're not ready yet."

I clenched my jaw. "I need to get ready."

Strengthening my leg would be the easy part. Saying farewell and leaving Rory behind would be the hard thing—perhaps the hardest I'd ever had to do. But it was for the best. Especially for her. I couldn't forget that.

Chapter 12

Aurora

I avoided Kresten for as long as I could by spending the majority of the day helping Aunt Idony harvest the root vegetables in the garden. Though we wouldn't have need of them during the winter, we would eat what we could over the next month and then have Chester distribute the rest to our nearest neighbors.

But even as I avoided the cottage and the temptation to visit Kresten, my thoughts returned to him again and again.

Thankfully, the October day was sunny and warm, a hint of cooler temperatures nipping my cheeks and nose. I sat back on my heels and admired the leaves, vibrant with the colors of autumn—fiery red, burnt orange, and flaming yellow.

Beside me, Aunt Idony did likewise, her hands dark with soil, her fingernails crusted, and her cheeks smudged. She made a sudden tsking noise, pushed herself to her feet, and slapped her hands together to dislodge dirt.

"I did not give you permission to walk so far a distance," she called.

I followed her gaze, and my heartbeat stalled at the sight of Kresten limping next to Jorg in the cleared area to the side of the gardens. I climbed to my feet as well. What was Kresten doing out of bed? He wasn't ready. His wound needed more time to heal.

Kresten leaned on Jorg. His handsome face was taut, the telltale sign of his pain. As he ignored Aunt Idony's chastisement and continued walking, a new realization seized me. He was leaving. Perhaps not at this moment, but the determination in his expression was signal enough to know he was preparing to go.

As if recognizing the same, Aunt Idony wound through the garden and circled the cottage, heading toward him, a frown creasing her brow. She would make him return to bed. Surely she would. And then everything would return to the way it had been. Tonight, he and I would start a new game, and I'd read to him again.

I'd been silly to let his slight from yesterday hurt me. He likely hadn't meant anything by it. Naturally, he'd been as confused as I by the intimate moment when we'd almost kissed. And now, I needed to show him all was well, that I wasn't holding anything against him, and that I wanted him to stay.

"You're going to hurt yourself," Aunt Idony remarked as she walked beside him.

I couldn't hear Kresten's muffled reply, but I guessed he told her he wasn't planning to stop, especially as he pressed forward along the edge of the clearing with Jorg's continued assistance. I waited for him to spot me and for his eyes to light up as they usually did. But if he realized I was there, he gave no indication.

Aunt Idony huffed and then strode to the cottage, disappeared inside, and returned a moment later holding a cane fashioned from the blackthorn that grew in profusion around the area. "I've been waiting to give this to you when I thought you were ready. But if you insist on doing this today, then take it." She pressed the cane into his hand.

He halted and stared at the smoothly carved stick, frustration waging a war on his face. After a moment, he lowered it and used it to take a step. He nodded at Aunt Idony. "Thank you."

She watched him hobble forward, putting more weight on the cane than Jorg. "Do not tax yourself."

Again he didn't respond, which only served to disperse the dismay within me. As I resumed my duties in the garden, I couldn't keep my attention from straying to him all too frequently. And I was ashamed to admit my prayers for his healing had ceased.

Later in the evening after supper, when Chester stepped outside to feed the livestock, I approached Kresten's chamber, hoping to make things right between us. As I peeked into the chamber, I was surprised to find the candle extinguished, and that all was silent and still. I could see his outline on the bed under the coverlet.

"Kresten?" I whispered.

Jorg stepped out of a shadowy corner. "He's already asleep. The walking today wore him out."

I watched Kresten, hoping for some sign of recognition, that perhaps I'd awoken him. But he faced the wall and didn't move.

With a nod, I exited, the weight inside growing heavier.

The next day, I had no opportunity to speak with Kresten, since he spent the majority of time outside strengthening his leg, disappearing into the woodland with Jorg for hours. When they returned, Kresten fell into bed exhausted, his face contorted with pain.

I waited anxiously for him to awaken, but he did so only to eat before slumbering once more.

By the following morn, I was desperate to speak with him. I could no longer deny my feelings for him went beyond simple infatuation. They went deep, and the prospect that he would soon walk out of my life wrenched my heart.

Resolved to meet with him, I waited until Chester was at the kilns and my aunts were busy in the cottage before I devised an excuse to go outside. Once there, I trailed after Jorg and Kresten into the woods.

I lagged behind, uncertain what I should say or do to gain his attention.

"Stop following us, Rory." His call startled me, and I hastened to hide behind the closest trunk.

Except for my shallow breathing and the rapid tapping of my heartbeat, the forest was silent.

"We know you're there," he said. "Now return to the cottage."

I pushed away from the tree and showed myself fully. The two continued walking, hadn't even glanced in my direction, as if I were nothing more than a pesky insect.

Did he have so little regard for our time together these past few weeks that he could so easily dispose of me? "No. I shall not return. Not until I have the chance to speak with you."

He didn't break his halting stride. "We would fare better if we didn't talk."

The rigidness of his back testified to the difficulty of each step. He was a strong and good man. Why, then, was he running away from me? Was he afraid of something? Of leaving? Of a possible future with me? "I did not take you for a coward."

He halted, forcing Jorg to pause.

I waited, letting my fears give birth to anger.

Slowly, Kresten pivoted until he was facing me, his brows furrowed into a scowl. "I am no coward."

I glared at him the same way I oft did with Chester. "Then why are you avoiding me?"

"I'm not. As you can see, I have been busy. 'Tis all."

"Then you are a liar and a coward."

A wayward strand of his hair had fallen over his forehead, and he reached up to drag his fingers through it while expelling a long breath. "Very well, you're right. I have been avoiding you."

The acknowledgment speared my chest with a shaft of pain. "Why?"

He jabbed his fingers into his loose hair again, holding them there before he looked at Jorg. "I need a few minutes of privacy with Rory."

Jorg hesitated.

"What harm can come of it when we're leaving on the morrow?"

On the morrow? My heart stuttered to a stop, and my anger blazed hotter, bringing a sting to the backs of my eyes. Had he planned to depart with this rift between us? Without making amends?

"Go ahead. Leave." I spun and stalked away. "You have made clear enough how you feel."

"No. Wait." His voice rang with frustration.

I didn't care. If he could abandon our relationship so easily, then perhaps I'd been wrong about him. Perhaps he didn't care about me half as much as I did him.

"Stop, Rory." Twigs and leaves crackled behind me.

I continued, tears welling and nearly spilling over.

"Please."

I slowed my steps and finally stopped. This was why I'd followed him, because I needed answers. And now that he was about to give them to me, I wasn't sure I could bear what he had to say. Instead, I wanted to bolt, like a doe escaping a hunter's sharp arrow.

His heavy, uneven steps drew nearer, until he halted behind me. His breathing was ragged, and I could feel the tension radiating from his body.

I held myself stiffly. Perhaps we would fare better saying no more and thus keep from hurting each other further.

"Rory," he whispered, his tone low and filled with such longing I couldn't keep from turning. His eyes were troubled even as his gaze tenderly lingered upon my face.

Two dozen paces away, Jorg waited, his feet braced, his expression full of censure.

Kresten frowned at his friend. "Give me a few minutes."

"You shouldn't—"

"I shall." Kresten straightened, revealing an authority in his bearing I hadn't realized he possessed. Strangely enough, Jorg bowed slightly, then backed away.

When the other young man disappeared behind brush, Kresten reached for my hand, catching it in his before I could prevent it. He brought it to his lips and placed a tender kiss upon it. "I'm sorry. I beg your forgiveness though I don't deserve it."

I wanted to stay angry with him, but the moment his lips touched my skin, I could do nothing less than forgive him. "Very well. I forgive you."

"I have behaved as a coward."

"I should not have said so. 'Twas petty of me."

"No, you were right. I was hoping that by putting distance between us, our parting would be easier."

His statement reminded me of the one I'd made when we'd gone our separate ways the first time. "I understand."

"But I suspect the parting will be difficult no matter what."

"True." In a short time, we'd become closer than I'd ever believed possible.

"I hold myself responsible. You cautioned against allowing false hope to spring up between us, but I didn't heed your warning."

"I neglected to heed my warning as well." If hope had already taken root between us, then what were we to do about it? Did we have to go our separate ways?

"I need to leave," he said, reading the question that likely showed in my eyes. "As soon as possible."

"But you are not ready. Even Aunt Idony says so."

"If I put off departing for a few days, even a week, I shall need to go eventually. So why wait? 'Twill slay me one way or another."

He was right. A few more days wouldn't be enough. A week wouldn't be enough. Even a month or two wouldn't satisfy. Perhaps only forever would suffice.

Forever. The word burned a trail through me. Being with Kresten was impossible, and yet I could think of nothing I wanted more than to spend forever with him.

"Perhaps you can come back?" The question slipped out before I had time to ponder the ramifications. Even if he did return to the cottage, my time was running out.

"Do you want me to return?" He searched my face, his expression serious, the strong lines fiercely beautiful.

I couldn't imagine my life without him in it. But how could I reconcile my need to be queen with my need for him?

"Do you?" His voice turned low and insistent.

"Yes."

The rigidness in his shoulders fell away. "I don't know how long I must be away. A month, maybe a while more. Will you wait for me?"

A month? That was about when I needed to begin the journey to Delsworth. I could wait that long, couldn't I? If he wasn't back when I needed to leave, I'd find a way to convince my aunts and Chester to extend our time until Kresten arrived. Then I'd invite him to go with me.

I nodded, swallowing the last of my resistance. "I shall try."

He bent his head and pressed another kiss to my knuckles. Dappled sunlight touched upon his hair, turning the brown to honey. Before I could stop myself, I skimmed my hand over the strands, relishing the softness.

His grip around my fingers tensed, and I hurried to dislodge from him, not wishing to overstep myself. Before my hand fell away, he snagged it and placed it on his cheek. The scruffiness was coarser than the hair I'd just grazed, but no less pleasurable. I drew a line down his jaw to his chin as he'd done to mine the other night. His blue eyes filled with a heat that told me just how much he liked my touch.

I rounded his chin and continued up the other side of his jaw.

He took an unsteady step closer and lifted his hands to my cheeks, cupping them. As his attention dropped to my lips, my breath caught. He'd almost kissed me that night. I was sure that's what he'd intended. And if I didn't stop him at this moment, I guessed he planned to kiss me now.

I let my fingers brush against his lips, feeling the warm dampness of his breath.

He kissed my fingertips. "I've fallen in love with you."

The words whispered through me down to my soul, stirring me so I knew with certainty I loved him too.

He dipped in, and his lips covered mine so softly and sweetly I thought I might swoon. I must have swayed, for he situated one of his hands at the small of my back.

I hadn't been sure I wanted to kiss him previously, but I had no doubt this time. He'd declared his love along with his intention to return to me. Though the odds conspired against us, I would devise a way we could be together. Surely I could. After all, I was the queen.

His hand against my back tensed and drew me closer. At the same time, his mouth moved more firmly against mine, testing and tasting and teasing my lips, until I could do nothing less than respond in kind. My hands still on his cheeks, I rose on my toes to meet him more thoroughly, pressing into him and expressing my utter fascination and adoration of him.

Tender and slow, the kiss lingered, until with each passing moment, I was conscious of a growing need for more. He must have felt the same, for his responses became deeper and more impassioned until, with a gasp, he broke away.

He didn't release me entirely, and our labored breathing filled the space between us, making me wish to kiss him again and again and again, though we needed to stop now since we had no right to share these intimacies until we were wed.

"I love you." He leaned his forehead against mine.

My heart thrummed a melody, one that brought with it a sweet joy I'd never before known.

"You don't have to love me yet in return," he whispered. "I know it's soon. But—"

"I love you also." My cheeks filled with more heat.

Tension eased from his hold. I rested my head against his chest, savoring the long, solid length of him, feeling safe and protected. And at home. For the first time in my life, I truly felt I was home.

At the loud clearing of a throat, I stepped away as Kresten released me. Jorg stood a few feet away, and he cocked his head toward the clearing up ahead. "Chester is returning from the kilns."

I spun, but before I could dash away, Kresten caught me. "Wait." He laced his fingers through mine. "Let's tell him together—"

"No. He will not understand. None of them will understand."

"I shall explain my intention to return for you."

"Chester will be furious." To say the least.

"He's not your father and cannot dictate what we do."

My father. He wouldn't approve of what I was doing either. Even now, I could picture the disappointment in his eyes. I shook my head, trying to dislodge the image. I would figure something out. I had a month in which to do so.

"Please." I squeezed his fingers. "Let me speak with Chester—and my aunts—in my own time and my own way."

"Very well." Even with his acquiescence, his eyes remained troubled.

I broke away and started back toward the cottage, touching my swollen lips and pressing a hand to my hot face. I needed to go back into the house and pretend nothing had changed—even though my whole world had just turned upside down.

Chapter 13

KRESTEN

I WATCHED HER GO, TEMPTED TO CHASE AFTER HER, CATCH HER hand, and approach Chester together. I wasn't afraid of him, and I wouldn't hide my feelings for Rory. He likely already knew them anyway.

At the same time, I wanted to respect her wishes to tell Chester about us when the moment was right. Perhaps she was worried he might try to harm me and wanted to spare me a fight. Perhaps waiting until I left was for the best.

I leaned heavily on the cane to take the pressure off my thigh. The pain had begun to dull but still burned nonetheless.

"Your father and the Lagting will never approve of a peasant woman becoming the next queen of Scania." Jorg's quiet statement jarred me back to the reality of my predicament.

"That's assuming I shall become the next king."

"You are the only choice the Lagting has now."

I didn't want the crown simply because my brothers

weren't eligible anymore. It was no honor to become king of Scania by default. And yet, how could I spurn my duty to my country?

"I love her, Jorg."

"I know." His shoulders slumped, as if he'd somehow failed me.

"This isn't your fault. You warned me and did all you could to discourage the relationship."

"That I did."

I'd tried over the past two days to stay true to my resolve to sever the ties. I'd avoided her outside and turned my back on her whenever she came to check on me in my room. I'd hoped to anger her and make her dislike me enough that she would forget about me. I'd even tried to resist her when she followed us into the woods. I'd willed myself to keep walking.

But my love was too strong.

Was this what had happened with my brothers? Had they fallen in love and been willing to risk everything— even the kingship—for the women they loved?

I braced myself with the cane. "I'll finish my Testing. The month may drag by, but it will pass erelong. Then once my Testing is completed, I'm coming back here for her. I'll beseech her to go with me to Scania."

"And what if she hears the rumors about your identity while you're gone?"

"She won't. Not here." Unless Chester went out on another trip to town and learned the information. "Even if she does, what difference will it make? It won't change our love."

"She doesn't strike me as the kind of woman who will stand for deception."

Was I deceiving her? Or merely withholding the whole

truth? Was there a difference? "Then you think I should tell her who I am before I leave?"

"What would you have her do if the situation were reversed?"

I'd want to know the truth. But in her case, I had the feeling the revelation of my royalty wouldn't impress her, might even scare her away. On the other hand, if I told her before I left, she'd have the chance to adjust to my being a prince and grow accustomed to the idea of moving and living a life far different than what she'd ever known.

"Very well." I hobbled forward on the cane. "I shall tell her. On the morrow, before we leave."

"One more tart, dear heart. Surely you can eat one more." Aunt Elspeth picked up another tart from the table and pushed it into my already full hands before she dabbed tears from the corners of her eyes.

"Thank you." I bent and kissed the top of her head. "You have been just like a mother to me."

"And you're a dear, dear boy." She turned her head and blew into a handkerchief, sounding like a honking goose.

Aunt Idony held out a small bundle. "Salves, ointment, rags, and the like. Keep putting them on the wound."

I nodded. "You saved my leg and my life, and I shall never forget it."

With my hands already full of baked goods, Jorg took charge of Aunt Idony's gift, tucking it into his sack.

Morning light slanted in through the cracks in the

shutters, giving me a final view of the cozy cottage that would always hold a fond place in my heart. I'd waited for either of the older women to invite us to return, but neither mentioned it.

I chanced a glance toward Rory who was standing by the door and fiddling with a loose string on her cloak. She plucked at it and didn't look my way. In fact, since returning last eve, she'd been rather quiet and hadn't made any effort to seek me out. Perhaps I'd only dreamed of the kisses and words of affection we'd shared in the woods.

Or maybe after having time to consider our declarations of love, she'd changed her mind about us and didn't want to wait for my return after all.

I'd hoped for a chance to speak with her one last time privately, but I'd lingered overly long already, and Jorg was growing irritable to be on our way. With a long hike ahead of us to Birchwood—made longer because of my injury—I couldn't fault him.

"Thank you for everything," I said. "I don't know what I would have done without your help."

Aunt Elspeth nodded, wiped additional tears, and then blew into her handkerchief again.

I tried once more to catch Rory's attention, but she refused to look at me. I was half tempted to blurt out my feelings right there in front of Aunt Idony and Aunt Elspeth. With Chester out at his kilns, at least I didn't have to worry about inciting him.

I pressed my lips together to keep from saying anything. I'd promised Rory I'd let her tell her family, and I had to follow through.

I hefted my bag over my shoulder. The moment I did so, Jorg opened the door and stepped outside.

I gave each of the aunts a last smile, then headed for the door. As I passed by Rory, I paused. "Farewell, Rory. I shall miss you."

Finally, she glanced up. The blue of her eyes was bright and full of hope—dare I even say love?

My pulse gave an extra beat. And I waited, unable to make myself walk through the door. She turned to her aunts. "May I walk Jorg and Kresten to the wood's edge?"

Aunt Idony hesitated, but Aunt Elspeth waved her hands as if to shoo us from the cottage. "Of course, sweeting. Of course. That's very kind of you to offer."

Rory wrapped her cloak more securely and slipped outside before Aunt Idony could object. I followed her, breathing deeply, the air heavy with the scent of the charcoal burning in the kilns.

Jorg started across the clearing, giving us the semblance of privacy, except a glance over my shoulder showed both Aunt Idony and Aunt Elspeth standing in the open doorway watching us. I waved at them, and Aunt Elspeth waved back with a tear-filled smile.

Rory ambled quietly, almost shyly, beside me. I slowed my steps to match hers, which wasn't hard with my limp.

"I shall pray for your safe return," she whispered once we were out of earshot of her aunts.

"And I shall pray the next month passes swiftly." My whisper came out more impassioned than I'd intended, earning a small smile.

"If you are ever close by, please come to visit. Even if only for a short while."

"I shall, but I noticed your aunts didn't extend such an invitation, and I have the feeling Chester hopes he'll never see me again."

We reached the edge of the forest all too quickly,

even with our slowest pace. Jorg had already started in the direction of the ravine, but I stopped, unable to make my feet move another inch forward.

Rory darted a look over her shoulder toward the cottage, and I did likewise, surprised to find that the aunts had gone back inside and closed the door behind them. She hugged her arms above her cloak, the chill of the night still lingering, especially in the long shadows of the woodland where we stood.

"Will you try to come before All Saints' Day?"

The holy day fell on the first of November. My Testing ended the day before on All Hallows' Eve. "Yes. Barring any unforeseen circumstances, I'll come on All Saints' Day."

"Good. Then I shall be waiting." Her smile came out in full force, as beautiful as the sunshine slanting through the changing leaves.

Seeing that we were alone, I reached for her hand. Now was my opportunity to tell her the truth about who I was and the kind of life she would have with me.

However, the moment my fingers connected with hers, she stiffened and slanted a look first at the cottage and then the path leading to the kilns.

"Rory." I tried to work up the courage to do the right thing.

Before I could express myself, she pulled ahead of me and dragged me into the woods. I was too surprised by her bold move to do anything but follow like a docile steed.

When we'd gone no more than a dozen paces, she halted, then peered back at the clearing that was still very much in our view. Then, to my surprise again, she tugged me into the shelter of a towering maple, the width of the trunk shielding us from the view of the cottage.

She tripped over a root and tumbled against me. I dropped my sack and the other items to catch her. The rogue inside me couldn't pass up an opportunity to hold her one last time before we parted. And instead of merely steadying her as I knew I ought, I wrapped my arms around her and drew her near.

She didn't resist but raised her face, her eyes wide and expectant.

"Rory. I must tell you something—"

She pressed a finger to my lips and silenced me with her merest touch. "We do not have much time for our farewell."

"No, we do not—"

This time she silenced me by rising to her toes and brushing her lips against mine for the briefest instant before pulling back and studying my reaction.

If I showed the least surprise, she'd probably grow embarrassed and dart away. Instead, I remained motionless, except for allowing a slow grin, and waited for her to make the next move.

She hesitated, clearly uncertain whether her initiative was proper. I relaxed against the tree, hoping she could sense that I welcomed—no, craved—her affection.

An instant later, she leaned in and pressed her lips to mine again, this time with more force.

I needed no further invitation. I dipped in and fused my lips to hers. She'd been the one to corner me and initiate the kiss. Did that mean she'd been thinking about our kiss from the previous day?

Maybe she hadn't been able to stop reliving the kiss any more than I had. Regardless, I let myself indulge in this moment, in the sweetness of her lips and the delicacy of her taste. It stirred the love and passion that had been growing, so that I knew I had to marry her and be with her forever. If I'd had any lingering doubts, they'd disappeared.

As she began to pull away, I tightened my arms around her, not ready for the moment to end. Though I needed to be on my way, I pressed a kiss to her cheek, to her ear, then to her neck.

She gave a soft gasp of pleasure, and her hands fisted with my tunic.

"I shall miss you," I whispered against her neck, breathing her in and grazing the softness of her skin.

"And I, you." Her whisper was laced with longing.

"I wish I didn't have to go."

"Then stay."

For an eternal second, I contemplated the possibility of giving up everything for a simple life with her in Inglewood Forest. It would be the ultimate fulfillment of my Testing, wouldn't it? *Deny thyself.* I would deny myself the possibility of ever returning to a life of luxury and power and instead live in poverty and obscurity.

I could do it. The past months had shown me I was capable of forsaking all the things I'd once considered important. I'd gladly spend the rest of my earthly life going without as long as I had Rory.

Yet, a deeper facet of my Testing pressed against my heart. Could I deny myself *her*? I might be able to deny the desires of my flesh, but what about denying myself the woman I loved?

My pulse pounded a protest against sacrificing her and our relationship. But if my country needed me to become the next king, could I forfeit what mattered most in order to serve the greater good?

I brushed a kiss against her forehead, my heart thudding a different tempo—this one of dread.

Releasing a sigh, she slipped her arms around me and rested her head against my chest.

I ran my hand down her long golden braid, letting the silkiness soothe me. I didn't need to relinquish her. I would bring her home and prove to my father and the Lagting that she would make the perfect wife and queen. They would meet her and see for themselves just how beautiful and elegant and educated she was. I needn't worry.

"I love you." I couldn't keep the desperation from my tone.

She pulled back and studied my face as though trying to make sense of that desperation. I needed to tell her the truth about who I was. Now. But at the crease forming between her brows, I dipped in and seized her lips, needing to reassure her and myself that everything would work out.

I kissed her deeply, as if the morrow would never come, and she pressed back as if to reassure me it would.

A roar filled the air at the same time Rory was ripped away from me. I caught a glimpse of Chester's broad shoulders and his face contorted with rage before a fist slammed into my head, sending pain rippling through my cheek and into my skull.

It knocked me backward, slamming me into the trunk with such force that blackness swept over me. A second punch into my stomach, along with Rory's scream, dragged me out of oblivion.

Chester had caught us in our impassioned kiss and intended to kill me.

He released another roar and swung at me again, aiming for the other side of my face. Though he'd knocked the wind from me with his strike to my stomach, I managed to dodge and take a swing at him, landing a punch in his midsection.

His reflexes were quick, and he struck me again.

"Chester!" Rory slapped at him. "Stop this instant!"

He easily held her back and, at the same time, shoved the front of my thigh. The momentum was powerful enough to push me backward into the trunk and hit against my wound. While I held myself upright, the pain nearly brought me to my knees. In the next instant, Chester had a knife angled against my throat.

"No!" Rory ceased her struggle and took a rapid step back. "Please, Chester. Please do not hurt him."

The blade bit into my flesh.

From behind Chester, I caught a movement. Jorg was approaching cautiously, his weapons drawn and his expression lethal. I didn't want Jorg to hurt Chester. But his first duty was to protect me, and I had no doubt he'd plunge his sword through Chester's back in an instant if he needed to.

I tilted my head and tried to ease the prick of Chester's knife. "Let me explain—"

He pressed his blade deeper, cutting me off with the sting and the warm trickle of blood.

"I order you to cease at once!"

The knife wavered.

Jorg was almost upon him, and I prayed Chester would listen to Rory before Jorg hurt him.

Chester glanced sideways to where Rory stood, arms stiffly at her side. Though her face was deathly pale, she lifted her chin and pinned Chester with an icy glare.

"*Now.*"

Chester let the knife fall away and took a small step

back, enough that Jorg was upon him in an instant. I didn't think Chester would be a match for Jorg's skill and stealth and was surprised when Chester spun and met Jorg's thrust.

"Jorg, wait," I said.

But Jorg was already swinging at Chester again, his knife in one hand and sword in the other. His jaw flexed with determination, and his eyes filled with deadly calm.

Chester deflected both blows and parried with a knife in each hand. From the agility and swiftness of his movements, I could tell he'd been well trained, perhaps as much or better than Jorg.

"Leave him be," I said, this time louder and with more authority.

Jorg broke away but kept his weapons outstretched and his attention fixed upon Chester.

Rory was in the process of slicing her tunic with a small knife she'd produced from her boot. With a final rend of cloth, she crossed to me and touched the linen to my cut, but not before I witnessed the trembling in her fingers.

I flinched at the pain.

"I'm sorry." She flattened the linen and pressed it harder. "But I need to staunch the flow of blood."

"'Tis but a surface wound."

"Thankfully." She shot a glare toward Chester, who, like Jorg, was still poised and ready to fight. From the dangerous glint in both men's eyes, I had to do something before they killed each other.

I gently took the linen from Rory. "I should leave now before anything more happens."

She gave a reluctant nod.

I stooped and picked up my bag and cane. The extra

baked goods from Aunt Elspeth were crushed, flattened into the earth and inedible. As I straightened, I caught a glimpse of the worry in Rory's eyes before she could hide it.

I reached out to stroke her cheek, but then at Chester's growl, I let my hand fall away.

Rory backed away as if that would shield me from another one of Chester's attacks.

I dug into my bag, located the item I wanted, and held it out to her. "A token of my pledge to you."

She hesitated, grazing the fine, colorful scarf.

"It belonged to my mother, and I want you to have it." I thrust it into her hands, then hefted my bag over my shoulder. "I'll see you in a month."

"Will you be alright?"

"Yes, don't worry about me. I've fared much worse and lived to tell about it." Though I meant the words as a jest, she didn't smile.

As I started off, Jorg remained behind in the standoff with Chester. I didn't wait for him. He'd soon follow once he deemed the situation safe enough. I could feel Rory watching me, and I didn't want to glance back for fear that one glimpse of her would be my undoing, that I'd return to her and never leave.

But when I could no longer stand another moment, I paused and looked over my shoulder. She stood where I'd left her, her attention unswerving upon me. She was as beautiful, with her flushed cheeks and bright eyes, as the day I'd first met her in the clearing—maybe even more so.

Something in my chest ripped. Had Chester cracked one of my ribs? But the pain was up higher, and it was different and deep. It was the pain of a man leaving part of his heart behind with the woman he loved.

My steps faltered, and I suddenly didn't know if I could go through with this. But Jorg ushered a sharp command and bolted away from Chester and Rory. He bounded toward me, waving at me to hasten onward.

I had to leave. It was time. With a final long look at Rory, I spun and forced my feet to move as fast as they would take me with my cane.

Once again, my Testing took on new meaning. *Deny thyself.* This denying myself of Rory was harder than anything I'd done heretofore.

One month. I could surely withstand one month away from her. One month, and then I vowed I'd never leave her again.

Chapter
14

Aurora

I followed Chester into the clearing, waiting for him to turn and chastise me. Every heavy step he took was filled with rage—his shoulders were stiff, his breathing labored, and his body tense.

As we crossed toward the cottage, I hurried to keep up. "We need to talk."

His stride lengthened.

"Please, Chester."

He sheathed his knife and then his sword but didn't acknowledge my plea.

"Very well, if you have no wish to discuss the matter, then I bid you to refrain from saying anything to Aunt Elspeth and Aunt Idony. I should not like to trouble them."

As he reached the door, he threw it open with a bang and stalked inside. "Begin packing." His command filled the cottage and echoed outside.

Packing for what? With a strange urgency, I picked up my skirt and ran the last steps, halting inside at the sight of Aunt Elspeth and Aunt Idony watching Chester with wide, frightened eyes as he stomped through the living area, slamming his hand against things like a child having a temper tantrum.

"What happened?" Aunt Idony glanced first to me and then to Chester before she returned to me, staring at the exquisite scarf Kresten had given me.

I hid it behind my back and swallowed hard. "Nothing—"

"Nothing?" Chester paused in his rampage. "Are you going to tell them, or shall I?"

"Tell us what?" Aunt Idony stood at the table, where she'd been in the process of crushing dried herbs with a pestle and mortar. Aunt Elspeth, as usual, was at her loom, but the bobbin dangled idly from her fingers.

"I do not wish to speak of the matter today." I directed my response to Chester. "I shall speak of it on another occasion when you are calmer and more rational."

Chester tossed an empty grain sack on the table. "I'm calm . . ."

"You most certainly are not—"

"As calm as I can be after finding you in so intimate a position with that—that woodcutter." He spat the words as if each one were a curse.

"Intimate position?" Aunt Idony's brows rose at the same time Aunt Elspeth's cheeks flamed.

"Chester!" I hissed.

His eyes flashed with indignation. "I caught Rory with Kresten. She was in his arms and kissing him."

Aunt Elspeth gasped and fanned her face with her fluttering hand. Aunt Idony seemed frozen in place.

"And it wasn't a chaste kiss," Chester continued before I could defend myself. "It was obvious the two of them have been sharing intimacies for some time."

"'Tis not true. Not in the least—"

"I saw you!" The hurt and betrayal in Chester's yell filled the small cottage and spread down deep into the crevices in my heart. "I saw the way you were with him!"

His eyes radiated with such heartache that my shoulders deflated. I hadn't wanted to hurt him. "This is not your fault, Chester. You did all you could to protect me—"

"But you snuck around behind my back and met with him in secret anyway?"

"No! I mean, yes, just once. Yesterday. I followed him into the woods. But Jorg was nearby, and I did not stay for long."

"I don't believe you."

"You must. And believe me also when I tell you that yesterday was also the first time that we—that we exchanged a kiss."

"I do not believe you. And even if I did, it makes no difference. You shouldn't have kissed him even one time." He tossed open the lid of a trunk and threw items on the floor. His garments.

What was he doing? Was he leaving? Surely he wasn't so angry as that. "You are making more of the matter than necessary."

He paused. "You are the queen of Mercia and must save yourself for the man you will wed. And it's my job to make sure that you do so."

"I shall wed Kresten."

"No, you will not."

"Oh dear." Aunt Elspeth was fanning herself so hard, I feared she'd faint.

Aunt Idony seemed to awaken, her forehead creasing and her lips pursing.

It was clear I had some convincing to do. "I have already given him my word that I shall wait for him to come back, and then I intend to wed him."

Chester glowered. "First of all, we're not waiting for him. We're leaving today, just as soon as we're packed. And second, you're not marrying him."

"I love him."

The moment my declaration was out, silence fell as heavy as a winter storm.

I lifted my chin, unashamed of my love for Kresten. I needed only to stroke the length of the scarf and remember his whispered words of love during our farewell for my heart to well up with everything I felt for him. He'd proven to be a man of great depth of character, displaying so many qualities I admired, including kindness, humor, tenderness, and wisdom. We could converse easily about many topics, and we enjoyed each other's friendship and company. I could picture us spending our lives together and drawing even closer.

"You may think you love him"—Chester found his voice—"but that doesn't mean you will wed him."

After the past weeks of Chester's heavy-handed guardianship, I was nearly at the end of my patience. I couldn't keep from narrowing my eyes. "I think you are forgetting one thing."

"What is that?"

"You have no authority over me except that which I give you."

"I abide by a higher authority than you, especially when you act like a foolhardy, lovesick young girl." His voice swiftly escalated until he was shouting.

"Chester." Aunt Idony interrupted. "Watch yourself!"

He stood rigidly, his arms stiff at his sides. He obviously wanted to say more but was holding himself in check out of respect for me as his queen, even though he viewed my feelings toward Kresten with contempt.

Aunt Idony nodded at the open door. "Why don't you wait outside while I speak for a moment with Her Majesty."

Without another look my way, Chester pivoted and stomped across the cottage, exited, and slammed the door behind him. When the reverberation faded, Aunt Idony pulled out the bench at the kitchen table and motioned me to the spot across from her.

With reluctance, I lowered myself. From her severe expression, I sensed she would try to change my mind. And I wouldn't be swayed. I loved Kresten and intended to marry him. Even if he was a pauper, he would adjust and fit into court life eventually. In fact, the people need never know of his poor roots and his background. After all, he was more knowledgeable and cultured than most laborers.

"Your Majesty. After our last conversation about . . . well, about men, I thought I'd enlightened you regarding the stipulations for your spouse. As a queen of a powerful nation, you will be expected—nay, even required—to make an advantageous match."

"I understand that. However, once my father and the other advisors meet Kresten, they will like him immensely and support my plans." I clutched the scarf under the table.

"He is definitely likeable."

"And quite handsome." The second Aunt Elspeth uttered the words, she blushed and bent her head over the loom, fumbling with the bobbin.

I wanted to chorus my agreement. Of course, I hadn't seen many men during my isolated life and couldn't compare him with others. But he was of the caliber of man who rose far above the rest in every way.

"I love him, Aunt Idony." I couldn't keep the ardor from infusing my words. "I never thought I would fall in love, but I did."

Aunt Idony picked up the pestle and twisted the blunt club absently in the mortar of half-minced herbs. "I already explained that your father has begun making arrangements. You are to be betrothed shortly after your return to Delsworth."

"So soon? Why the rush?"

"The advisors believe Queen Margery will have a more difficult time challenging your right to Mercia's throne if the people view you as mature and ready to lead."

"Then I shall wed Kresten right away, once he comes back at the end of the month."

"You cannot set aside their choice for you."

"I assumed they were still deliberating, that nothing had yet been decided."

Her voice softened. "Would it really make any difference if the arrangements are definitive or not?"

I knew what she was saying. Even if the details of my future husband had not yet been finalized, I couldn't disregard the wisdom of the noblest men in the land and choose my own husband, especially one from amongst the lowest strata of society.

As Aunt Idony had indicated, the goal was to ensure that Queen Margery didn't gain control of Mercia. Thus, the priority would be marrying me to a royal prince from a nation who could come to Mercia's aid if Queen Margery ever decided to attack.

If I wed a pauper like Kresten, not only would we lose a strategic and important alliance, but I'd weaken Mercia and put the country at risk. By marrying a man of my own choosing, I'd also undermine the trust of my closest advisors, possibly even cause division amongst them.

Aunt Idony had taught me that a queen or king must work for the people and put the greater good of the nation above personal gain. I'd always agreed. And I still did . . .

"What shall I do?" My throat tightened with the need to cry. "I love him."

Her shoulders deflated, and she rested the pestle. "He is a good man. And he made you come alive as I have never before seen."

The tears welled up even faster now. It was true. My existence had been so limited and everything in my life so carefully controlled, until I'd met him. Perhaps this was one of the reasons—in addition to sheltering me from Queen Margery—why my aunts and Chester had wanted to keep me away from everyone and everything, for fear that something like this might happen.

"Oh my." Aunt Elspeth rose from her loom, her face wreathed with worry. "I know exactly what my sweeting needs to cheer her. Boiled eggs and hot porridge."

I couldn't tell her I'd lost my appetite or that nothing could cheer me. As she bustled past me, she patted my head, and I forced a smile at the dear woman.

Aunt Idony's face took on a haggard, aged appearance, as if the trials of this life were beginning to catch up to her. "Perhaps we should have allowed you more opportunities in recent years. If we had, maybe you wouldn't have been drawn to the first handsome man who came your way."

"Do you think me so shallow and naïve that I would cast aside good judgment and accept just any man?"

Aunt Idony shook her head, hanging it lower. "No, Your Majesty. As I said, he is a fine man. But as you have never before been around men and experienced love, 'tis only natural you would long for such things."

Was she right? Had I fallen for Kresten simply because he was the first man to come along? Something told me I wouldn't have had the same reaction to Jorg if he'd been the one I met instead. No, I hadn't felt the slightest attraction to Jorg, just as I never had to Chester.

"My feelings for Kresten are real and true. I will never love anyone else the way I do him."

"Perhaps not. But the truth is this: You were born to be queen. As such, you must put the love of your people and country above your personal desires."

I'd never expected to have any personal desires that superseded my royal duties. Until now. Until Kresten.

Maybe if I loved the people and my country, I could

more willingly sacrifice my future happiness with Kresten. But there was a part of me that lacked empathy and devotion for a people I didn't know and a country I'd never seen, except for the occasions traveling to Huntwell Fortress.

I didn't say as much to Aunt Idony. I knew what her response would be, that I couldn't base decisions on feelings alone, that I must use sound reasoning, logic, and God's wisdom instead. And that meant regardless of how I felt about Kresten, I had to do what was best for my country.

Aunt Elspeth returned to the table carrying a bowl filled to the brim with steaming porridge. She placed it in front of me along with a hard-boiled egg. The heat and the comforting scent of the porridge didn't offer me the usual solace. Neither did her gentle squeeze of my arm.

I released the scarf and let it pool in my lap. I stirred the porridge and blew on it while Aunt Elspeth hovered nearby, waiting for me to eat.

"Once you have time to gain perspective," Aunt Idony continued, "you will come to see the situation differently."

"And what if I do not ever see it differently?"

"Time and distance almost always make us view our situations with new wisdom."

I couldn't imagine my feelings for Kresten ever changing, but what other choice did I have but to accept the course set out before me, one established for me since my birth? I loved Kresten but had only known him for a month. I couldn't destroy my future, and possibly harm my country, based on my whims.

"Very well," I said, gathering the last of my inner

fortitude, "I shall do my best to move forward and fulfill my duties."

I lifted a spoonful of porridge and took a tiny bite to show my gratefulness to Aunt Elspeth. But my conversation with Aunt Idony had left a bitter taste in my mouth. Only because she was right. About everything. And I had no wish to acknowledge it.

Deep inside, I'd known from the start that a relationship with Kresten was doomed. That's why I'd tried to end it before it could truly begin. If only I'd tried harder. Now, I'd not only brought heartache to myself but to him as well.

I took another bite of porridge, but the thick, creamy oats stuck in my throat.

The door opened and Chester stepped back inside. From the stiff set of his shoulders, he was still upset about all he'd witnessed. But the frustration was gone and compassion filled his eyes. He'd likely stood outside the door and listened to my conversation with Aunt Idony and recognized my defeat.

"Time to go," he said quietly.

"Must we leave now? We still have one month."

"Aye, we need to go immediately."

"But I should like to see him one last time and explain myself."

"That wouldn't be wise." He held my gaze, and I understood what he wasn't saying, that if I saw Kresten again, I'd make our parting harder.

On the other hand, how could I simply disappear without any notice? When he came back at the end of the month and found that I'd left, he'd be frantic with worry. If I could somehow get a note to him and explain who I really was and why I'd had to abandon him, maybe he'd forgive me. I owed him that much, didn't I?

I pushed aside my bowl of pottage and stood, letting the scarf he'd given me fall to the floor. "If we must depart, then let us be on our way."

Chapter
15

KRESTEN

BY THE TIME WE REACHED BIRCHWOOD, I WAS EXHAUSTED beyond endurance. With my identity as a prince now public knowledge, I drew attention the moment I hobbled into the village. Everyone, including Walter, wanted to earn my favor, giving me the best they had to offer. In the past, I would have enjoyed the groveling and flattery, but somehow I'd lost my taste for it.

I hadn't planned to stay long in the village, only intended to spread the word that I was mended and back in my corner of the woods, with the hope of the news reaching my brothers eventually. However, because of my fatigue, I accepted food and lodging from Walter with the stipulation that I would repay him with wood as soon as I could.

I slumbered restlessly, my dreams filled with Rory. I'd been away from her but a day and already I was weary of the parting, desiring nothing more than to be with her. Several times, I considered going back to her on the morrow and marrying her right away. But my charge from the Testing whispered in my head: *Deny thyself. Deny thyself. Deny thyself.*

Alas, my thoughts circled back to the same conclusion—no matter how difficult, I had to persevere and finish my Testing.

When I awoke the next morn in the dormer room Walter had provided, I rolled over on my pallet, stiff and cold, to find Jorg gone and sunlight streaming through the holes in the thatch above me.

Voices rose from the living space below. Many voices.

I sat up and rubbed my eyes. At the waft of roasting game, my stomach rumbled. The need for food and drink prodded me to my feet. After the few weeks of eating Aunt Elspeth's bountiful cooking, I would have to adjust again to stark rations. But for today, I would indulge in a meal.

After donning my garments and tying back my hair, I climbed down the ladder, my injury slowing my descent. At the sight of me, the room fell silent. When I reached the bottom and pivoted, I wasn't surprised to find every pair of eyes upon me. But I was surprised to see both of my brothers sitting at a long table near the hearth.

Mikkel rose first, his light-blue eyes skimming over me, likely accurately assessing everything about me in one keen glance. His expression remained passive, never giving his emotions away, as usual. His hair, the lightest of all three of us, was pulled back into a leather strip in a manner similar to mine. Other than tanner skin and shabbier garments, he remained unchanged and the handsomest of us three.

Vilmar pushed away from the table and stood as well. But his face lit up at the sight of me, his easy grin emerging. While we three brothers all had our father's light-blue eyes, Vilmar and I looked most alike with our brown hair and build. We also shared similar amiable and good-natured temperaments.

"There you are." Vilmar crossed toward me. "The woodcutter himself."

I smiled in return. "And there you are, a married man."

He chuckled, then grabbed me and wrapped me into an embrace while slapping my back affectionately. "So, you've heard the news."

I pulled back. "Can't believe anyone would fall for a dullard like you."

"I can't believe it either." His eyes turned dreamy, almost comically so. "Indeed, I'm the luckiest man alive."

"After Mikkel, of course." I directed my smile toward my oldest brother. "Congratulations to you, brother. I hear you're married as well."

Mikkel gave a curt nod. "Yes, I married Princess Pearl, Queen Margery's daughter."

"And you are happy with the choice?"

"I'd have it no other way." Though his expression remained unreadable, the adoration in his voice was unmistakable.

Only then did I notice the others in the room. The most important men of the town crowded around the periphery, Walter amongst them. A handful of other men sat at the long hearth table including Jorg and the other scribes assigned to my brothers—Ty and Gregor. A curly-red-haired man sat next to Ty, and a silver-haired man with silver teeth occupied the bench beside Gregor.

"I heard you wanted a meeting," I remarked, "but I didn't expect to have one so soon."

Mikkel returned to the bench at the head of the table and waved to the seat next to him. "For the past couple of weeks, we've been in the area looking for you, since we learned this was where you'd settled. When the messenger arrived last night with the news that you were here in Birchwood, we came with haste."

With so many of them searching, I was surprised they hadn't stumbled across the secret cavern in the ravine. Or that they hadn't spotted Jorg during his trek to Birchwood earlier in the week. At the same time, I was relieved. I wanted to keep Rory and her aunts away from prying eyes for as long as possible.

"You all but disappeared." Vilmar took a place on the bench next to Ty and the redheaded man.

I lowered myself, careful not to put pressure on my thigh wound.

"Jorg refuses to expound on where you've been hiding." Mikkel shot Jorg a look of censure.

My friend shrugged. "The tale is Kresten's to tell, not mine."

And what a jolly good tale it was. Though part of me wanted to share it all, another part urged caution. First, I needed to discover what my brothers wanted of me. Though I didn't believe they meant me any harm as Jorg had hinted, I didn't have just myself to think about anymore, not after making a promise to return to Rory.

"Not only did you disappear, but you've been injured again. Recently." Mikkel's attention shifted first to the long cut on my neck from Chester's knife and then to the bruise on my face. Though I hadn't looked at my reflection, a mere blink reminded me the flesh around my eye was swollen and black and blue.

"This is nothing." I fingered the wound. "I got it in a brawl. 'Tis all." A brawl that had nearly cost me my life. But I couldn't say anything about Chester without also having to explain my love for Rory.

"Then the two of you have given up your Testing?" I threw out the question to distract them and take the focus off me.

All traces of humor left Vilmar's face. "I completed close to two months of servitude in the mines, but yes, I left of my own volition."

"And you made no plans to return and finish?"

"There was nothing to return to, not after I set all the slaves there free." He glanced toward the curly-haired man, and I guessed him to be one of the slaves, now a loyal follower.

I shifted to Mikkel. "And you?"

He held himself as regally as always, his back straight and his chin lifted. "I left intending to return, but I have found another challenge that needs my attention first."

"Then you are both relinquishing your claims to the throne?"

"When I left the mines," Vilmar said with a nod, "I gladly gave up the throne. For it means I've also given up my pride and can live in the humility of being the slave of all."

The engraving on Vilmar's sword had read *Be slave of all*. "Then you are truly living your challenge."

"Yes, but I must be honest in saying I believed I was relinquishing the kingship to Mikkel."

My gut churned. Of course. No one had expected I'd be the one to become Scania's next king. But why would they, when I'd never given them any reason to deem I was worthy or wanted it?

Mikkel took a swig of ale, then set down his mug. "When I left the Isle of Outcasts, I was unaware of Vilmar's compromised Testing."

"So if you'd known, you would have stayed?"

Mikkel rubbed his thumb around the rim of his mug before he met my gaze frankly. "No. I wouldn't have. I have spent my life doing all the right things outwardly to please the Lagting and the king. But I've learned that I have to stop being so concerned about outward trappings and focus more on the motives of the heart."

"What he's trying to say," Vilmar added with a half grin, "is that he's doing what's right regardless of whether the Lagting and Father like it."

Mikkel's sword had been engraved with *Look on the heart*. He, too, had taken his challenge seriously and was living it out.

Could I say I was yet doing the same? Though I'd thought often of my sword's engraving, *Deny thyself*, I suspected I'd yet to learn my lesson the same way my brothers had.

"You have both proven yourself to be men of honor. And though I plan to finish the last month of my Testing, I never aspired to be king and don't feel worthy of such an honor and responsibility."

"Perhaps none of us is truly worthy," Mikkel remarked.

Just then, Walter's daughters approached the table carrying platters of roasted quail with turnips, onions, and carrots covered in gravy. They served the food, dumping large quantities on all of our trenchers and refilling our mugs with ale.

As we ate, the conversation moved to other, safer topics as Mikkel and Vilmar both shared more about their adventures and their wives. This time, the other men at the table joined in, and for a while the warmth of the meal and room, as well as the camaraderie, made the past months fade away, so we were simply brothers enjoying a meal together.

As we began to push away our empty trenchers, I nodded my approval. "I should like to meet these beautiful women who have captured your hearts."

"I bid Gabriella to stay in hiding." Vilmar cleaned the last of the meat from a leg bone. "Queen Margery has become more aggressive and moved to Boarshead Hunting Ground over the border in Warwick. She brought an army of knights and has too many spies and soldiers combing the forest."

Mikkel had taken a towel from one of Walter's daughters and was wiping the grease from his hands. "Princess Pearl is likewise hiding from the queen, albeit not as willingly or carefully."

"You have both made an enemy of the queen of Mercia. Exactly what Father's weapons master warned us against."

Vilmar nodded. "Yes, and now that we have stumbled upon the queen, she is like a basilisk that has been roused. She's angry and is seeking to spew her poisonous venom."

Mikkel glanced to the laborers still lingering in Walter's cottage, now talking amongst themselves, and then motioned to Walter. "If you would be so kind as to dismiss the townspeople, we shall require a few moments of privacy."

Within minutes, the men emptied from the room, and only our table remained, including our scribes along with Vilmar and Mikkel's companions, Curly and Irontooth, whom I learned had become invaluable friends during the course of their Testing.

Once the door closed, Mikkel leaned in and spoke in a low, urgent tone. "We need to save my wife's sister, Princess Ruby, and defeat Queen Margery. Queen Margery has agreed to give us Ruby if we deliver Aurora to her."

During the time I'd lived in Mercia, I'd learned some of

the history of the country, enough to know that the infant Queen Aurora had been placed into hiding because Warwick's Queen Margery wanted to slay her and take her kingdom, which Margery believed rightfully belonged to her. While rumors abounded about the child queen having been seen in the forest, most of the laborers in and around Birchwood thought she'd been taken to the Continent for safekeeping. Others suspected she was in Norland.

Whatever the case, nobody knew the whereabouts of the child, and Queen Margery had never been able to locate her.

"We believe Aurora is here," Mikkel said, "in the forest."

"I have heard the rumors, but nobody is certain."

"Pearl used to hunt in Mercia with her father at Huntwell. She believes the fortress could have provided the perfect location for Aurora to meet with her father throughout the years."

"I haven't been there, so I wouldn't know."

"Pearl recently went back, and the servants took pity on her since she's running and hiding from Queen Margery. Though she's certain Aurora is no longer at Huntwell Fortress, she learned that Aurora had indeed met with her father there from time to time over the years. Such knowledge confirms that Aurora lives in the forest."

"It confirms she lived here at one time," Vilmar interjected. "But we don't know if she still does."

I pushed my trencher away as it was now completely empty. In my months of deprivation, I'd learned to appreciate every morsel and to waste nothing. "Even if your Princess Pearl can find Queen Aurora when all others have failed, would she be so cruel as to trade one life in order to save another?"

Mikkel twisted his mug, the muscles in his jaw flexing. "We do not intend to actually hand over Aurora. Only to use her to lure the queen out so we may put an end to her tyranny."

With each passing moment, I was growing more suspicious of their undertaking. Something wasn't adding up. "Attack the lodge. Surround it and lay a siege."

Vilmar shook his head. "Though Boarshead Hunting Lodge has no perimeter wall, it is surrounded by a gully where she has trapped numerous basilisks. No one can get past the creatures without dying."

At the revelation, I paused a moment. "How, then, do she and her people come and go from the lodge without fearing for their lives?"

"She is cunning." Vilmar's smile was wry, as though he knew just how cunning. "She has developed a protective bridge connected to the lodge that can be raised and lowered."

"So her lodge is impenetrable."

"Yes," Mikkel spoke tersely. "That is why we must draw the queen out. And the best way to do so is to stage an exchange of prisoners. Only then will we have access to Ruby and the queen in one occasion."

Somehow I guessed he wanted to involve me in this mission, but what exactly did he want?

As if sensing my unasked question, Mikkel leaned in further. "Vilmar and the other freed slaves have agreed to join in the effort to rescue Princess Ruby and capture Queen Margery. I would like to know I can count on you and any of your companions to do the same."

"I am always at your service. Though with my leg

wound, I doubt I will be of much aid."

"Then perhaps you would be of service in another way."

"How so?" I stiffened, having the feeling this was the true reason he'd sought me out and that I wouldn't like his request.

"Since you and Jorg know the forest better than any of us, will you help us track Aurora?"

"Track Aurora and put her into grave danger not of her own making and possibly risk her life and throne?"

Mikkel didn't look away. "We will *all* put our lives at risk to destroy Queen Margery. However, doing so will put an end to her threat to Mercia, which will bring peace and security during Aurora's reign."

The conversation had grown increasingly tense. But that was always the way it was with Mikkel. I grabbed my mug and took a sip of ale, needing to bide my time and figure out how to refuse him without offense. All I wanted to do was finish my Testing, get Rory, and return to Scania. Mikkel and Vilmar's trouble with Warwick's queen wasn't my problem, and they needed to figure out how to solve their issues without involving me.

I took another swig, set down my mug, and started to push away. Vilmar reached across the table and snagged my arm. "Wait. You need to hear the full story about just how wicked Queen Margery is before you make up your mind."

I stared at his fingers grasping my sleeve and wanted to shrug him off. My brothers had never paid me much heed while in Scania. Why should I give them heed now?

"Please?" Vilmar's forehead furrowed. "Though our father and the Lagting couldn't have known Queen Margery's deep, evil secrets, 'tis entirely possible God ordained our Testing here on the Great Isle to rid the land of her darkness."

I extricated my arm from his grasp. "Queen Margery's darkness has nothing to do with me in Mercia."

"The effects of her greed and evil have spread everywhere, and her threat will only grow," Vilmar insisted. "Even the presence of the basilisks here in the forest is because of her."

I'd heard variations of such a rumor from the people who lived in the forest, but I didn't stop Vilmar as he relayed what he knew.

"Many years ago, she had the deadly reptiles brought to Warwick for use in her alchemy. She experimented with many recipes, including one that called for powdered basilisk blood. When the recipe didn't produce the jewels, silver, or gold she desired, she released the remaining basilisks into Inglewood Forest."

"Such a story may be true, but again, it has nothing to do with me. Jorg and I have done well to keep away from the basilisks."

"Unfortunately," Mikkel interjected, "the basilisks are the least harmful of her alchemy experiments."

Though I was tempted to stand up and walk away, I remained on the bench and let my brothers tell me everything they'd pieced together about Queen Margery's experimentation in alchemy. When her father, King Alfred, had died, he'd bequeathed a coveted ancient white stone to her, one mentioned in Holy Scripture saying: *"To him that overcometh will I give to eat of the hidden manna, and will give him a white stone."*

Rumored to have special transforming powers, the white stone had been placed into the safekeeping of the royals to prevent abuse. But instead of guarding and protecting the stone as other kings and queens had done before her, Margery enlisted the assistance of priests from all over the world to aid her in unlocking the secrets of the stone's power.

While everyone knew about her obsession with alchemy and her many experiments over the years, no one had guessed just how evil her practices had become. Until Vilmar's wife, Gabriella, discovered that the queen had created a successful elixir for growing jewels within the Gemstone Mountains long after the original gems were gone.

"She figured out how to make gems," I said. "Certainly that doesn't warrant her death."

Mikkel exchanged a look with Vilmar, one that told me their tale had only just begun. I sighed and settled onto the bench more comfortably.

Mikkel glanced to the door to make sure we were still alone. "Apparently, Margery's priests spent years deciphering a cryptic language in order to understand the ingredients necessary to mix with the white stone. They discovered blood from a heart was necessary and tried many different hearts, including that of the basilisk."

I sensed where the story was going and sat forward. "They learned they needed a human heart."

Mikkel nodded. "Not just any human heart. For jewels, they needed the heart of the fairest maiden in all the land—"

"And Gabriella was to be her next victim," Vilmar said gravely, "but we outwitted her, which is why she seeks our demise."

"For making gold," Mikkel continued, "the secret ingredient is the heart of the fairest *royal* maiden in the land—or so they believe. The queen meant to use Pearl's heart to test her theory, but Pearl escaped thanks to Curly, the queen's former huntsman, who refused to take the princess's life and instead set her free. She fled to the Isle of Outcasts where she hid from the queen."

Mikkel peered down the table toward the redheaded man next to Vilmar. Curly gave a curt nod back at Mikkel but otherwise remained silent.

I was growing more fascinated at the unfolding tale by the moment. "So the queen still hunts Princess Pearl, hoping to use her heart to make gold?"

"No. The queen has no need of her now that she is my wife. The elixir can only be concocted from the heart of the fairest *maiden*—an unmarried woman who has not yet reached her twentieth year."

"So she intends to use Princess Ruby's heart instead?"

"Perhaps one day. But for now, Ruby is still too young."

"Then you and your wife and her sister are safe," I said. "You have nothing to worry about anymore—"

"Queen Margery not only wants to steal Mercia from Queen Aurora, but she also intends to steal her heart. If Margery uses the heart to make gold, there will be no end to her power and wealth. She will become a threat to every nation, including Scania."

Mikkel's pronouncement settled around the table like a knell of death. Finally, I understood the depth of the queen's depravity, and I stared into my almost-empty mug, my gut swirling with a sourness that rivaled the dregs of ale.

"So now you see why we seek Aurora." Vilmar broke the silence. "The queen desperately wants her. Thus, if we find her first, we can make use of Pearl's bargain with the queen. We shall strike at Margery's weakest moment and crush her evil reign."

Now that I knew all that had transpired, I understood my brothers' desire to bring an end to the madness, the needless suffering, and the threat to all nations. But I still didn't feel right about aiding them in finding Aurora. "Why bring the child into the midst of the problem? Surely, like Princess Ruby, she is too young to be of use to the queen?"

"Child?" Vilmar's brows rose. "Queen Aurora is no child."

"She's not?"

"She's a grown woman, less than a month from her twentieth birthday."

A strange fear shimmied down my spine. A grown woman. Almost twenty. Living in isolation in Inglewood Forest.

Underneath the table, Jorg bumped my knee with his. I glanced at him sideways and caught the glimmer in his eyes. Was it possible Rory was Queen Aurora?

Chapter
16

Kresten

Suddenly everything made sense. Rory—Aurora's level of education, her impeccable manners, her polished speech, her inner strength of character. Her "aunts" were likely her teachers and Chester her guardian, which would account for how vigilant and skillful the young man had been in protecting her.

No, she wasn't merely a woman from a noble family who'd fallen on hard times. She was Mercia's queen, awaiting her twentieth birthday—the day she would be able to take the throne and rule her own country.

As silence once again prevailed over the table, I realized all eyes were upon me. Mikkel and Vilmar exchanged another look.

I was tempted to jump up and storm out of Walter's cottage, away from the men before I gave myself away. Instead, I relaxed my shoulders and schooled my features into what I hoped portrayed nonchalance. "As far as I'm concerned, you should leave Aurora alone. This isn't her fight, and she'll be safer remaining in hiding away from Margery."

In fact, now that I knew the truth, I wanted Mikkel and Vilmar to stay as far away from Aurora as possible. She'd remained in seclusion these many years without Margery finding her. She could go one more month. By the time she reached her twentieth year, Margery would have no more need of her heart and wouldn't be able to question her authority to rule over Mercia. At that point, Aurora would be able to leave the cottage and return to Delsworth without as much fear of Margery assaulting her.

Of course, there was always the chance Margery would still challenge Aurora's right to the throne and might even attack Mercia. But if that happened, she had an ally in Scania—at the very least an ally in me.

"So . . ." Mikkel eyed me as though watching my thoughts unfold. "This means you will not help us find Queen Aurora?"

"No doubt you have some of the best trackers already." I nodded at the fierce-looking silver-toothed man. "If they are not able to locate Aurora, then what makes you think I can?"

"Because I know you," Vilmar replied with an easy grin. "If there is a woman to be found, you are the one to do it. The ladies have always been attracted to you, like bees to a honeypot."

"You're right as usual." I grinned in return though I wanted to grimace. I'd had enough of the conversation and needed to get out before I said or did anything to put Aurora in jeopardy. I gulped down the last of my ale, then stood, planting my cane and using it to steady my stiff limbs.

Jorg rose and retrieved our weapons belts.

"I wish you Godspeed and good fortune in taking a

stand against Queen Margery, brothers." I wrapped my belt around my waist, my axe on one side and my sword on the other. "I have every confidence you will find a way to triumph over her."

Vilmar stood and clamped my shoulder. "Just not with your help?"

"I shall be of no use to you." I kept my focus on my belt. "My time would be better spent finishing my Testing."

The benches scraped against the floor as the rest of the men stood. Mikkel held himself stiffly, again watching me with a keenness that made me want to squirm.

Vilmar dipped his head and then took a step back. "If that is your decision, then I wish you the same. Godspeed and good fortune as you complete your Testing. Rest assured, I shall support the Lagting's decision to give you the kingship and will pledge you my fealty."

"I shall as well." Mikkel bowed his head.

A pang shot through my chest, one I didn't understand—except that their subservience didn't feel right. "I look forward to the day in the not-so-distant future when we will all be home again. Until then, I shall pray for your safety."

With that, I spun on my heels and hobbled out the door. I made a point of thanking Walter and his daughters while I waited for Jorg to collect our bags. When my faithful companion took his place by my side moments later, I nodded farewell to my brothers and the others who'd come outside, and then we started on our way back into the forest.

We walked for what seemed like hours. I wanted to put as much distance as I could between myself and anyone searching for Aurora. I was only frustrated I couldn't traverse faster.

Navigating the woodland was difficult under normal circumstances, much less while having a major wound that still pained me. When I was assured we'd gone a significant distance, I halted and searched the thick brush and windfall for signs of anyone who may have followed us as well as any basilisk that might be nearby.

Jorg did likewise, taking in every detail of our surroundings.

"Has anyone come after us?" He'd be able to glean more clues than I would with his sharp attention to detail.

He studied the woods behind us. "If they haven't yet, I have no doubt they will be on our trail erelong."

"Do they suspect my association with Rory?"

"They suspect you know more than you told them, and they'll be watching you closely."

"She is the one, is she not?"

"She has to be."

For the first time since I'd realized Rory's true identity, I allowed myself a real smile. "I should have figured it out sooner."

"I should have too."

"All the signs were there." How could I have missed them? And did it really matter? I loved her for who she was and not because of her status.

Jorg again glanced around, then lowered his voice. "When I saw Chester fight yesterday, I knew he was too well trained to be a charcoal burner. He has the skill of an elite guard."

The elite guards were specially trained to protect royalty, knights who pledged to remain single and solely devoted to their charges. They were the best of the best. "He easily could have slain me and maybe even you."

"Not me," Jorg retorted. "At least, not without a good fight."

Jorg was an exceptional fighter too, but not to the extent of an elite guard. Even so, I was grateful to have him as a friend and not a foe. "I won't rest until I'm able to warn her of all that's transpiring."

"Especially since they are so certain she's here in the forest. It's only a matter of time before they stumble upon her trail." The severity in Jorg's expression and tone added to my worry.

"She needs to get away now. Perhaps return to the royal fortress in Delsworth. Even if Queen Margery decides to attack the capital, Aurora will be safest there, behind the castle walls and with Mercia's army to defend her. Surely Delsworth can hold out a month until she comes of age."

I veered toward the direction that would take me to the ravine, but before I could take two steps, Jorg grabbed my arm. "We can't leave yet."

I was under no illusion I could safely guide her to Delsworth, but Chester could. In fact, he probably already had decided upon a means and a course of delivering her there. He'd just have to do it sooner than he'd planned.

I shrugged out of Jorg's grip. "The sooner we reach her, the better."

He stepped around me to block my way. "If you go now, you will lead your brothers right to her."

I halted, my muscles tightening. I didn't want to unwittingly give away her hiding place. "What do you suggest?"

Glancing around the thick woodland, he leaned in. "We'll depart under cover of darkness and split up. I'll take your cane and lead anyone on our trail upriver in the opposite direction while you warn her."

I didn't know if Jorg's plan would work, but we had to give it a try.

All through the long afternoon into the evening, we resumed our woodcutting duties. And by the time darkness settled, my body protested the final bundling of underwood. After the weeks of not wielding my axe while recovering, the muscles in my arms were out of practice and my calluses soft. Thankfully, the pain wasn't as great as the first week or two of my Testing when my arms had burned and my blisters bled.

After a cold dinner from the provisions Walter's daughters had given us, we rested for a few hours, then started out together toward the ravine river. The closer we drew, the more my anticipation mounted. Though we'd been apart for only two days, I was eager to see her again.

When we reached the spot in the river where I'd been attacked by the boar, we rested in a low part of the bank, exchanging our cloaks and the cane. Once I was through the hidden cavern, I'd find a walking stick so I could traverse the forest with haste. But until then, I would manage as best I could without.

As Jorg stood, imitated my limping gait, and moved upriver, I remained hidden, watching until well after he disappeared. When I'd tarried long enough for possible trackers to trail after him, I crept downriver, keeping low and hiding behind boulders, praying the river would wash away my tracks.

The sky sparkled overhead with dozens of constellations, and the waning moon was a thin crescent, providing just enough light, but hopefully not enough to give away my position. Though the water level of the river was low for early October, at least the gurgling was sufficient to mask my soft wading as I made my way toward the secret cavern.

When I reached the place, I again waited for an interminable amount of time before I crawled from the river into the brush, being careful to stay low and leave no indication of my presence for anyone who might attempt to follow me.

Once I was through the passageway and on the other side, I took a deep breath of relief, used my axe to hew a walking stick, and made my way toward the cottage. With some of the trees having already lost leaves, the starlight penetrated through the canopy of branches, aiding my attempts to trace the right path.

I surprised myself at how swiftly I was able to travel in spite of how tired and sore I was. My eagerness for Aurora drove me. And the closer I got, the more my anticipation mounted until I was nearly breathless with the need to see and hold her.

All day as I'd labored, I'd marveled over the revelation that she was a queen. I'd been so blinded by my feelings for her that I'd ignored all the clues that had been right before me, including her desire to learn to dance, her interest in the goings-on of court life, and even her authority with Chester that had surfaced from time to time.

Not that I'd been searching for Mercia's hidden queen. In fact, I hadn't given it much thought during the entire time I'd lived in the forest.

As I entered the coppiced woodland that surrounded the kilns, I slowed my steps and proceeded with more caution. If Chester happened to be outside at the late hour, he'd slit my throat before I could identify myself.

When I reached the edge of the clearing, I stopped and scanned the area. In the starlight, I could distinguish the faint outline of the cottage nestled against blackthorn and ivy. The shutters were closed and the chimney smokeless.

I didn't wish to disturb their slumber, but I needed to warn Aurora—and Chester—of the danger. I'd give him instructions and then leave. As much as I'd be tempted to linger or even to offer to accompany Aurora, I couldn't. I'd only slow them down.

My muscles tensed with undeniable eagerness. I crossed to the front door and knocked quietly. "'Tis I, Kresten."

I expected Chester to be there within moments, but as the seconds ticked by, my nerves began to knot. Something wasn't right.

I knocked again, this time louder, but was met with the same deathly silence. With mounting trepidation, I tried the handle only to find the door was unlocked and it swung wide open, unhindered by Chester's imposing frame.

The living area was dark, the usual glow from the banked coals of the hearth gone. Even so, I could see enough to know Chester wasn't sleeping in his usual spot on the floor. The quietness of the house was too permanent. And the stillness too eerie.

I crossed to the bedchamber, praying Aurora was slumbering but dreading what I'd find instead. Though I couldn't see through the blackness to the bed, the room contained a chill that told me it hadn't been heated that day.

Even before I moved farther into the room and patted at the unoccupied straw mattress, my gut told me she wasn't here.

I straightened, my heart thudding with the urgency to discover where Aurora had gone and why. In the time I'd been gone, had Queen Margery already discovered her and taken her captive?

At a squeak of a floorboard in the living area, I froze. Someone had followed me into the cottage. And it wasn't Jorg. My friend wouldn't feel the need to sneak in the way this intruder had.

I crept back to the chamber door, unsheathing my knife as I did so. Perhaps whoever had come for Aurora had left a small contingency behind. And perhaps even now they were waiting to capture me.

I paused and heard only the wavering *hoohoo* of a tawny owl somewhere on the edge of the clearing.

Had I been mistaken about the squeaking floor?

As soon as the question flittered through my mind, a thump sounded from the other room.

I tensed. I had to be careful so I didn't find myself in Queen Margery's clutches and end up useless to Aurora if she was in trouble.

"Kresten?" Someone whispered my name. A man.

"Chester?" I whispered in response.

"No, 'tis I, Vilmar."

"Vilmar?" All caution fled, replaced by irritation. I pushed away from the wall and stomped into the main living area, my knife still at the ready in case I was walking into a trap.

The faint light coming in the open front door revealed Vilmar's stocky, broad-shouldered frame at the center of the room near the table.

"What are you doing here?" My whisper was tinged with my frustration at not finding Aurora along with the fact that if she'd been here, I would have put her in grave danger by leading my brother right to her.

"We followed you here. Or I should say Ty picked up your trail." Standing beside him was Vilmar's scribe, the short, olive-skinned man who'd sat with us earlier at Walter's. I'd sensed then, as I did now, that there was more to Ty than mere appearances gave away. Clearly, he was an exceptional tracker if he'd found my trail through the darkness to the secret passageway.

"I can see that you followed me. But why?"

"I think you know why."

I stiffened and my fingers tightened around my knife. I'd never harm my brother, but I wanted to punch him. Hard. "And what if you've been followed by Queen Margery's spies?"

"We're alone. We made sure of it."

"You shouldn't have come."

"And maybe you should allow her to decide whether she wants to help destroy the one person who has hunted her down her entire life and who even now seeks to rip out her heart and use it to make gold."

I shuddered at the very thought. "I won't give her the choice. Not if I can help it."

"You know that even when she ascends to Mercia's throne, Queen Margery will continue to fight her. She'll find a way to slay Aurora either from within or without."

"I won't let it happen." A quiet desperation settled in me.

"If 'twas so easy to keep Queen Margery from destroying Aurora, then why did she need to hide all these years?"

I searched for an answer but couldn't find one.

"You don't know Queen Margery the way I do. She's a wicked woman and will stop at nothing to get what she wants."

I once again felt the chill of a room that hadn't been heated in a while. Though the familiar scents of Aunt Idony's herbs wafted aloft, the tantalizing aromas of Aunt Elspeth's tarts and custards and other baked goods were no longer here.

"Once Aurora realizes we have an opportunity to put an end to Queen Margery's reign of terror, she'll agree to our plan. I assure you."

I sheathed my knife. "No. Leave her out of it."

Vilmar fell silent. I could feel him studying me through the darkness.

I spun before he could find what he was looking for. I bounded toward the ladder and climbed up, knowing what I'd discover even before I saw the empty dormer. Aunt Elspeth and Aunt Idony had left too.

If they'd all been captured, I'd see signs of a struggle. But everything was in as much order or more than it had always been. I could only hope Chester had learned of the danger and orchestrated their escape while he still could.

As I descended, Vilmar and Ty were talking to each other and at my appearance stopped.

"From everything Ty sees," Vilmar said, "he guesses they left yesterday."

"That's my guess too." Though I'd longed to see Aurora tonight, I was relieved she wouldn't hear Vilmar's plea for help.

"We can try to track her—"

"No."

"Ty might be able to pick up her trail—"

"No!" The one word encapsulated all my anger. "I want you and Mikkel to stay away from her. I mean it."

Vilmar held himself rigid.

They didn't know Aurora the way I did. She was too

inexperienced and innocent to take a stand against so great an adversary.

"You love her." Vilmar's quiet declaration broke through the stillness of the cottage.

Why deny the truth? What purpose would it serve? "Yes, I love her and intend to wed her."

"As you are bound to become Scania's next king and she is Mercia's queen, how will such a match prevail? You cannot intend to rule your countries separately and live apart from one another."

Vilmar's words, though spoken kindly, barreled into me with such force that I pulled out a bench and dropped onto it. Aurora was the long-awaited queen of a country who desperately needed her to take her place as ruler in order to stop Queen Margery from demanding the throne in her stead.

And now that I was the only prince left in the competition for Scania's throne, I couldn't give up. Could I?

I had only to think of her smile and the way her eyes lit up for my chest to seize with protest. It had been hard enough to imagine a month without her, much less a lifetime. I couldn't do it.

Deny thyself.

I wanted to thrust the words from my mind somehow. But I'd said them too oft over the past months, and now they were so embedded into my being that they welled up within me almost as if they were alive.

The same question that had confronted me when I'd said farewell to her arose to confront me again. Could I deny myself when it came to her?

My shoulders slumped, and I leaned my elbows on the table. Knocking aside a lone mug, I buried my face in my hands. If I'd thought we had obstacles when I believed her to be a pauper, they were nothing compared to the mountain now standing between us. We were both destined to be the rulers of separate nations. And as much as we loved each other, we must love our countries and our people first. Our duty to them had to remain foremost.

The simple truth was, I wouldn't be able to wed Aurora. The best thing for us both was for me to let her go and never see her again.

Chapter 17

Aurora

The night air swirled around me with a chill that hadn't previously been present, one that signaled the changing of seasons but had helped to keep me awake during the long hours of traveling.

The choppy ride on the mount also prevented any slumber—not that I wanted to sleep. Instead, I was curious to survey the changing landscape and take in all I could of the thinning Inglewood Forest and the rockier terrain. The sliver of moon provided scant light for my first real sighting trip of Mercia, but I was pleased with what I saw nonetheless, especially now that the rugged heathland began to take shape.

"How do you fare, Your Majesty?" Chester asked from the saddle directly behind me. He held himself aloof, giving me a measure of privacy while also keeping me safe and secure. Aunt Elspeth and Aunt Idony each had their own mounts and followed behind us. Every time I glanced back, Aunt Elspeth was nodding off.

"You need not call me by my title, Chester," I admonished as I had already several times.

"I aim to do it whether you want me to or not, Your Majesty." Though his tone was somewhat belligerent, I sensed a note of humor and was glad we weren't feuding anymore. I'd been upset at him yesterday for harming Kresten. And perhaps I hadn't liked his decision to leave the cottage so soon, but I was trying to understand his concerns.

Besides, if I couldn't be with Kresten, then what was the use of staying any longer in the forest? I was ready to go and had been for many months. Now I was eager to explore the kingdom. If only Chester hadn't decided to travel by night instead of by day.

I understood his determination to stay hidden as best as possible. Yesterday, after we'd packed the necessities, Chester had led us on the loneliest and most secluded trails to reach Huntwell Fortress, just as we used to do when I'd gone there to visit my father.

He'd guided us through the secret tunnels into the fortress. I'd stayed secluded from the servants, but I had no doubt many of them suspected that their secret guest was someone special when baths were drawn and a lavish meal prepared.

We'd stayed but a short time, especially after learning Queen Margery had taken up residence at Boarshead Hunting Lodge, not far away in Warwick. With less than a month remaining before my twentieth birthday, Chester suspected she was increasing her efforts to locate me as well as hunting down Princess Pearl and the Scanian princes hiding in the forest.

The steward had informed us that Princess Pearl

had visited Huntwell Fortress over a fortnight ago, hoping for refuge. He'd taken pity on her and allowed her to stay for a few days.

With the news of so many of Queen Margery's men roaming throughout Mercia's southern land, we debated the wisdom of traveling to Delsworth. And yet, we couldn't stay at Huntwell Fortress, as it wasn't equipped to withstand an attack.

Chester had hoped to gain a contingent of knights to accompany us, but our unplanned arrival at Huntwell Fortress hadn't allowed for the calling of reinforcements. After much discussion, we decided our best course of action was to travel by night and stick to the hidden trails that Chester and Sir William had long ago plotted to use for my return to Delsworth.

After nightfall, Aunt Elspeth, Aunt Idony, and Chester had left on the horses given to them by the steward, while I waited at the tunnel entrance for them to come after me. We'd ridden for hours, and from my study of geography as well as everything Chester had already told me, we still had several days of riding to the northeast before reaching Delsworth. We would rest at well-armed estates and hopefully gain additional forces before we made the last part of the journey up the coastal road into Delsworth.

Anticipation had built inside me, and I drew in a deep breath. My future spread out before me as rugged and uncertain as the heathland.

A future without Kresten.

At the thought of him, pain speared my chest. What would he think when he returned in a month to find nothing but the note I'd left behind? He'd be disappointed to discover I was gone.

I pressed a hand against my chest and felt the soft linen of the scarf he'd given me. I'd tied it under my tunic near my heart. Though I'd debated leaving it at the cottage with the note, in the end I hadn't been able to let go of it. Perhaps I wouldn't be able to have him, but I could cling to the memories—at least for now—couldn't I?

Chester slowed our mount. "If you need to stop, we should do so now before we are out on the open heathland."

"Very well." I wasn't accustomed to riding and was already saddle weary. "I should think Aunt Idony and Aunt Elspeth would appreciate a break as well."

Chester reined the horse near a clump of sweetbriars and assisted me down. My legs refused to hold me, and I grabbed on to Chester to keep from falling. His cloak shifted to reveal a sheet of parchment sticking out of his inner pocket—a sheet exactly like the one I'd torn from the front of one of my books when I'd scrawled a note to Kresten.

Surely he hadn't taken the note from the kitchen table where I'd placed it. I jerked the parchment free from his pocket. "What is this?" I couldn't keep the accusation from my voice.

He attempted to wrest the paper from me, but I pressed it against my chest where he dare not reach.

"Did you take my letter to Kresten?" From the corner of my eye, I could see Aunt Idony hastily dismounting, likely sensing another feud brewing between Chester and me. Had she known Chester had taken my note? What if she'd conspired with him to sneak it away?

I took several more steps away from Chester, frustration rushing through me and crashing into the walls I'd constructed around my heart to keep myself from mourning too deeply for Kresten.

"You couldn't leave a note like this on the table, Your Majesty," he replied with too much calmness. "If the queen's spies had happened upon it, they would have easily picked up our trail."

"How dare you!" My heartache had no barriers to contain it, and it rose swiftly into my throat.

"'Twas for your safety."

Arching her back, Aunt Idony wobbled over and stood next to Chester. Aunt Elspeth struggled to dismount, and when her feet finally touched the ground, she promptly sat down and released a loud groan.

The letter crumpled beneath my fingers. Now Kresten would never know what became of me. When he returned, he would be sick with worry and heartbroken. At the very thought of his turmoil came the sudden need to weep.

"Your Majesty," Aunt Idony said. "Once you are safely settled at Delsworth, you'll have plenty of opportunities to write and inform the young woodcutter of your whereabouts."

"What if he returns before the month's end?" The question tore from my throat, laced with all the agony I could no longer ignore. "He will be devastated."

Chester released an exasperated sigh. "It makes no difference. He'll be devastated note or not."

Tears stung my eyes, the tears I'd wanted to shed at the loss of the man I loved but that I hadn't allowed in our hasty departure and flight to Huntwell Fortress.

Now several spilled over. I swiped at them, unwilling for anyone to see how deeply I would miss Kresten.

As more trickled down my cheeks, I spun and stalked away, needing a moment of privacy to grieve.

"Where are you going?" Chester called.

"Let her have a few minutes," Aunt Idony said, likely with a restraining hand on his arm. "We can surely allow her that."

"She can't run off right now."

"I need just a moment, Chester," I called. "Please. After taking away the letter, you can spare me a moment, can you not?"

He mumbled something urgent to Aunt Idony that I didn't hear as I pushed past the briars and into the covering of thick foliage. My footsteps crunched against the fallen leaves and brittle branches, and as the darkness enfolded me, a sob welled up.

"Elspeth will attend her," Aunt Idony replied. "Won't you?"

"Of course I will, dear heart." A moment later, Aunt Elspeth grunted as she rose from the ground. I didn't wait for her but plunged deeper into the brush, needing to hide my sorrow.

The tears fell faster the farther I went, until I stopped, knowing I couldn't stray too far.

"Sweeting?" Aunt Elspeth's cheerful call came from near the edge of the brush. She was too easily spooked and wouldn't follow me all the way into the thick growth, especially in the dark.

"I shall be fine. I just need a few more seconds. Please." I sniffled, the burning in my throat and chest too raw.

"I'll wait right here, dear heart. You take all the

time you need."

"Thank you." I could no longer pretend leaving Kresten behind hadn't mattered. And suddenly all I could think about was going back and pleading with him to come along on this new adventure. Was there any way I could convince Chester to do so?

But even as the thought came, I thrust it away. Chester would never allow it. As Aunt Idony said, I could write another note and have it delivered to him. It was the best I could do.

My chest swelled with sorrow—sorrow over the loss of a future with him, sorrow in missing our friendship and the closeness we'd developed, sorrow at the thought of never sharing any more laughter or smiles or banter, sorrow that we wouldn't have adventures together—for life with him would never be dull.

I brushed at the wetness on my cheeks. At the soft crunch of a step nearby, the hairs on the back of my neck prickled. But I had neither the time nor the presence of mind to call out before something heavy banged into my head. Pain reverberated through my skull and down into my body. I felt myself crumpling, and then everything went black.

Chapter 18

KRESTEN

I HAD TO LET AURORA GO. I REPEATED THE WORDS TO MYSELF over and over during the hike away from the cottage. When Vilmar had suggested I return to Birchwood with him, I was readily swayed, since I was weary from my wound and wallowing in my loss.

The next morning, when I exited Walter's home, I halted abruptly at the sight of so many men amassed. They were in the process of saddling horses, donning weapons, and packing saddlebags with supplies they were purchasing from the townspeople.

With a nod at me, Vilmar broke away from the group and headed my way.

"You'd better not be going after her," I growled as I stalked toward the rain barrel.

He followed me. "Good morning to you too."

The water level in the open barrel was low, but I cupped my hands and splashed the cold water on my face anyway. Faint morning light glistened on the rippling surface, and I wished I could somehow drink the light and find that it would take away the ache in my chest. It had resided there all night, growing only heavier as the restless hours passed.

Vilmar waited until I'd finished before speaking. "She could be in danger. Queen Margery is anticipating Aurora coming out of hiding and has set snares all throughout southern Mercia."

I dried my face with my sleeve. "Her elite guard will guide her safely to Delsworth." I was counting on Chester more than he knew.

"If we follow her, we can ensure her safety."

The frustration that had festered since seeing him in the cottage turned into a burning wound. I shoved his chest, sending him toppling backward so that he landed in the dirt street on his backside. "Cease this endless hounding! You shall have her only over my dead body."

The others stopped their preparations and stared. Mikkel began to cross toward us, his expression full of confidence and determination that made me angrier. He ought to be the next king of Scania. It was in his bones and his bearing. I was a poor substitute, and the realization added to my frustration.

Vilmar accepted Mikkel's outstretched hand to aid him back to his feet. "You don't realize the scope of the issue, Kresten—"

"I realize you wish to involve her in a war that isn't hers to fight."

"But it is hers, and it will be until the queen is vanquished." His voice contained a note of passion that surprised me.

Was Aurora in greater peril than I realized? Or was Vilmar simply looking for another way to persuade me to go after her?

One of Walter's daughters approached with a mug and trencher. I accepted it with a nod of thanks and waited until she walked away before divulging my thoughts. "We were sent to the Great Isle for our Testing. We didn't come to solve all of their problems. Our duty is to our country alone."

Mikkel spread his feet and crossed his arms, his gaze imposing and hard. "We are small-minded to believe our Testing can only occur in the places assigned to us with the specific challenges we were given. Rather, the Testing happens whenever we allow our circumstances to push us to grow in the areas we most need it."

"Are you telling me I'm small-minded?"

"I admit to my own narrow view of the Testing at first. I have since learned the Testing is intended to push much deeper and wider than we can imagine."

Mikkel never failed to rankle me, perhaps because of my own insecurities or the differences in our temperaments. Whatever the case, I guzzled my ale, ready to be on my way into the forest and away from my brothers.

As I was draining the last frothy drop, the pounding of hooves and shouting from the northern edge of town drew our attention. At the sight of several hooded and cloaked figures riding toward us at high speed, Mikkel's brows wrinkled, and he jogged toward the newcomers.

"Mikkel!" one of the riders called in a distinctly feminine voice.

As the rider reined in, he grabbed the bit to steady the creature. The rider hopped off with a litheness I didn't expect. In an instant, Mikkel was drawing the newcomer into an embrace.

The hood fell away to reveal a stunningly beautiful

woman with ebony hair that rippled in long waves over her shoulders. Her features were exquisitely perfect and her creamy skin unblemished.

She stood on her toes while Mikkel bent in and eagerly captured her upturned lips in a kiss. His passion for the woman was unmistakable. And she responded in kind.

This had to be his wife, Princess Pearl. I'd heard rumors of her beauty, but she far exceeded them. Of course, she wasn't as beautiful as Aurora, but she was the only woman I'd met who could come close.

Their reunion was poignant, and I couldn't begrudge them this moment of happiness. But the grief of my own lost love swelled up so sharply I had to look away. Mikkel had found a treasure in this woman. I thought I'd found that in Aurora. But now I understood how futile our love had been.

"We have come from near Huntwell Fortress." Pearl pulled away from Mikkel. From the way he strained after her, clearly he wasn't ready to relinquish her, although he did so, but reluctantly.

For the first time, I took notice of her two traveling companions. One had an overly large head with big ears that couldn't be hidden beneath his hood. The other had skin covered in thick black hair, almost as if he were a beast instead of a man. These men were no doubt from the Isle of Outcasts and friends of Mikkel's.

"The news is not good." Pearl spoke not only to Mikkel but the rest of the gathering. "Queen Margery's elite knights have captured Aurora."

My blood turned to ice.

"We cannot know for certain where they are headed," she continued, "but we believe they are taking her south into Warwick. Likely to Boarshead Hunting Ground."

The ale I'd just swallowed roiled in my stomach. For a moment, I thought I would be ill.

Mikkel and Vilmar both cast their gazes upon me.

Pearl did likewise, her beautiful green eyes narrowing as she took me in. "So, you have located the youngest prince?" She strode toward me, her cloak flapping open to reveal men's garments as well as men's boots, again taking me by surprise. "'Tis regretful he could not lead you to Aurora first."

"He could have." Mikkel followed after her. "But he withheld it from us until too late."

I bent over and closed my eyes, sick at myself and sick with worry for Aurora. This was my fault. I hadn't wanted to admit it, but deep inside, I knew Chester had forced Aurora to leave the cottage because he'd caught her kissing me. He'd likely discovered our plans to get married. And as an elite guard with her utmost protection at heart, he'd decided to take her to Delsworth early rather than risk our reunion.

He saw me as nothing more than a pesky intruder, a peasant man who had no business winning the heart of a queen. If only I'd spoken sooner and revealed my identity the way I'd intended to. Perhaps then Chester wouldn't have been so angry at my presence there—although I suspected he wouldn't have liked me even if he'd known I was a prince. He was bound to protect Aurora, and that included keeping her pure for the man she'd one day wed.

"Prince Kresten?" Pearl's tone softened.

From my bent position, I took several deep breaths before I straightened. I bowed my head in respect to her. "Your Highness. I wish you happiest felicitations in your marriage to my brother."

She tilted her head in acknowledgment, studying me

with a keenness that mirrored Mikkel's. "What do you know of Aurora?" Her bluntness matched Mikkel's as well. They would be a good fit for each other.

"He fancies himself in love with her." Although Mikkel's voice was without judgment, it needled me so that once again, I glanced to the forest and wished I had no more need of him and could simply walk away. The trouble was, now I did need him. I needed all of them if I had any hope of rescuing Aurora.

I flexed my jaw and fisted my hands. But I forced myself to remain calm before I answered the princess. "My feelings for Aurora are of no consequence. What matters is finding a way to free her from Queen Margery."

"I agree." Her eyes flashed with something. Pain, perhaps? Did this have to do with her younger sister? Whatever her motive for wanting to help Aurora, it didn't matter. The only necessity was that we work together against the queen.

"Can we find the trail of those who captured her?" I asked.

"We will no doubt come upon it," she replied. "But the true test is whether we can catch her before she reaches the lodge. If the queen sequesters her there, we shall have no chance of getting past the basilisks to rescue her. At least, not before the queen slays her and cuts out her heart."

Again I felt ill. If I'd behaved with more restraint, if I'd kept the boundary of friendship between us, if I'd honored her wishes to stay away in the first place, she'd still be securely ensconced in the cottage.

I fought down my nausea. "We have no time to spare. Let us be on our way."

I didn't wait to discover the princess's reaction to my

command, nor did I care what my brothers thought. Instead, urgency prodded me into action. I instructed Jorg to locate mounts that we could use for our travels. While he did so, I gleaned as much information as I could from Walter and the other men of the town regarding the swiftest route to Boarshead Hunting Ground. Walter, having lived in Inglewood Forest his whole life, offered to lead us to the most direct paths, which he claimed would reduce hours—if not an entire day—from our race to cut off the queen's men who had Aurora.

We started on our way less than a quarter of an hour later. Ty rode at the front with Walter. In the months of living in Inglewood Forest, Vilmar's scribe had grown familiar with the forest, learning its trails, and was especially keen in spotting evidence of basilisks and steering us away from their territory.

Jorg and I took up position behind them, while Mikkel, Pearl, Vilmar, and the rest of the men rode closely on our heels. We pushed our horses hard, staying to the coppiced woodlands where the trees weren't as thick, and the brush didn't slow us down.

At midday, we stopped to rest at a brook and water our mounts, although I agreed to the break only reluctantly. With every passing hour, our time was running short. I couldn't bear to dwell on the possibility that we might fail to intercept Aurora before she reached the queen.

"Let us be on our way," I called as I finished kneeling and drinking from the brook. Noon sunshine slanted through the remaining leaves overhead. Though the woodland wasn't as thick as other parts of the forest, it was dense and hilly enough that we couldn't see far ahead, which added to my feeling that we weren't making enough progress.

"Make haste." I started to lead my horse forward.

"Everyone quiet." Ty stood suddenly and narrowed his gaze upon the path we'd just ridden. "Riders are coming and will soon be upon us."

Chapter 19

Kresten

I STUDIED THE LANDSCAPE, SEEING NAUGHT BUT THE STILLNESS OF the sunlight warming the leaves scattered over the forest floor.

"You've heard someone?" Mikkel searched the trees and boulders we'd just passed.

"I feel the rumbling in the ground," Ty replied. "Someone is following the same path and will soon overtake us."

Mikkel grabbed his steed's reins. "We shall take cover until we determine if this newcomer is friend or foe."

"'Tis only more time wasted," I countered. "I say we proceed as planned."

Mikkel frowned, irritation in his eyes. "Do not be naïve, Kresten. Now that the queen has her prey, she will anticipate opposition. She'll have her forces out to stop anyone who comes after Aurora."

At the incoming thud of hooves, we had no time to argue. Mikkel and Vilmar pulled me into the shrubs while the rest of our party scattered with the horses.

192

A moment later, a half dozen horses and riders crested the rocky rise to the north of us. Their beasts kicked up leaves and dirt, pounding down the hill and bearing upon us. In the lead was a man of stocky girth whose outline had become all too familiar over the past weeks.

I relaxed my grip upon my axe and knife and stepped out of the shadows into a patch of sunlight, praying Chester's wrath toward me had diminished. Without Aurora to stop him, he might decide to finish what he'd started the day I'd left.

From the brush behind me, Mikkel hissed a warning, but I shook my head to silence him.

Chester rode several more paces before he shouted to his companions and slowed his mount. With his knife poised to throw, he'd have no trouble impaling the blade into my neck if he chose to do so.

He was no longer attired as a humble charcoal burner and was instead wearing chain mail and numerous weapons on his belt. He made an imposing knight, one I didn't want to battle again if I could help it.

I wasn't surprised he was taking the same route, as he likely knew the forest trails as well as Walter. My only wish was that he was nearer to catching Aurora than we were. But in order to secure reinforcements, he had lost time.

I waited, my back and shoulders rigid. "Chester."

"Kresten." He glanced to the woods around me, likely spotting each person where they'd hastily hid. His hand went to the hilt of his sword as though he intended to fight his way through us if need be.

I cocked my head in their direction. "We mean you no harm."

"What are you doing here?" Anger edged his tone.

"Are you in league with the queen?"

"You know I'm not. And you know I'd do anything for Aurora."

He didn't blink at my use of her true name. He'd clearly already guessed that I knew her identity.

"I love her."

"You have no right to love her." His fingers didn't leave his sword.

"I know that now. I was selfish."

His glare was as menacing as always. But the shadows under his eyes were new and deep. When was the last time he'd slept? I could only imagine the agony he was experiencing in knowing he'd failed in his one task, to protect Mercia's queen.

"I understand I can never have her, but I'm still going after her." I waved toward the woods. "We all are."

I hadn't realized Mikkel and Vilmar now stood directly behind me with their weapons drawn. The silver-toothed man was holding Princess Pearl back, but from the way she was struggling, I doubted he'd be able to restrain her for long.

"Who are you?" Mikkel stepped to my side. "And what business do you have with Queen Aurora?"

Chester scowled. "What business do you have with her?"

"She is my wife's cousin."

Chester's retort died on his lips. His attention shifted to Vilmar, back to Mikkel, and then to me. I had no reason to keep my identity from him any longer. "I am Prince Kresten of Scania. I have resided in Inglewood Forest for nigh six months undergoing my Testing."

"I heard the rumors regarding Prince Mikkel and Prince Vilmar." Chester studied my brothers more carefully, obviously having learned enough to know their names. "I didn't realize Scania had a third prince on the Great Isle." His gaze alighted upon me with new interest, as though seeing me for the first time.

"I regret I did not inform you and Aurora." I let my hand fall away from my weapons.

He dropped his away as well. "I should have realized your identity sooner. As it was, I believed you to be a man of some means who'd been rejected by his family."

Of course a knight of his training wouldn't believe my woodcutter ruse indefinitely. "Now that I am aware of Aurora's status as Mercia's queen, I fully understand we cannot be together. You need not worry any longer on that score."

"Good." He nudged his horse. "Then let us pass. I shall not rest until I have her back in my possession."

"We shall ride with you. We can accomplish more together and shall be stronger in number against the foe." I beckoned Jorg to bring me my horse.

Chester shook his head. "No, you'll only slow us down."

"We believe Queen Margery is taking Aurora to the Boarshead Hunting Ground over the border into Warwick."

"I believe this as well. She wouldn't leave Mercia's queen exposed and susceptible to recapture any longer than she has to, especially for so great a distance to Kensington."

Jorg neared me with my mount, and I took the lead line from him. "You know the woods better than anyone. Do we have any chance of regaining Aurora before she reaches the lodge?"

The shadow of sorrow that rippled across Chester's

features was my answer even before he straightened in his saddle and scowled at me again. "If you let me pass, I'll get her."

"Once she reaches Boarshead, all will be lost. Princess Pearl assures us the basilisks will prevent us from attacking the lodge."

"I have already sent a messenger to Delsworth. King Stephan will discharge ambassadors to bargain for her release, and Queen Margery will return her once she has the keys to the ancient treasure."

I didn't know anything about keys and an ancient treasure. But I did know Chester was wrong. "My brothers have informed me that Queen Margery will slay Aurora in order to use her heart in her alchemy."

Chester wrapped his reins around his hand, and his steed snorted and shied sideways. He showed no surprise at the mention of alchemy or the queen's design for Aurora's heart. "Queen Margery has always aspired to have the keys, even more than her desire to rule Mercia. She'll exchange Queen Aurora for the keys."

"You are wrong," Princess Pearl said, wrenching away from the silver-toothed man and striding toward me, her gaze trained on Chester. "Queen Margery has discovered she needs a royal maiden's heart for making gold. And she will stop at nothing to ensure her years of experimenting come to fruition."

"She'll have no need for alchemy when she unlocks the treasure and has all the gold she could ever want."

Pearl stopped next to Mikkel, and again I was struck by how regal and beautiful she was. From the admiration in Mikkel's eyes, it was clear he was thinking the same. "My mother will lure Mercia into giving her the keys. But have no doubt, Mercia will never have Aurora as its queen as my mother will take Aurora's heart first."

"You don't know that." Chester's tone filled with frustration more than anger.

Pearl lifted her chin. "I do know it. If she was willing to slay me—her own daughter—to attain my heart, then she will most definitely butcher Aurora without delay, for she must have the heart before Aurora turns twenty."

Chester swallowed hard. His anxiety only made mine worse. I hoisted myself into the saddle, ready to resume our frantic chase.

Pearl grabbed my horse's bridle and prevented me from leaving. I wanted to shake off her hold and spur my horse onward, but in my haste, I wasn't willing to chance hurting her.

She hadn't taken her narrowed gaze from Chester. "You must believe me that we cannot count on Mercia's ambassadors to negotiate her release. The queen is duplicitous and will say one thing but do another."

Chester pressed his lips together and stared into the forest. Once again, his lack of protest stirred my despair.

Mikkel spoke before I could. "We must work together to rescue her. 'Tis the only option if we hope to defeat the queen."

Chester shifted in his saddle. "I will not stop you if you wish to accompany me."

The determination in his eyes was like flint and sparked a fire inside me. "Wait." My command rang out. "If we fail to intercept Aurora, then we must have a way to get past the basilisks and into the lodge."

"How do you propose we do so?" Mikkel asked.

"Weasels." I met Chester's gaze, hoping he'd understand my proposal.

Chester paused, then gave a curt nod. "'Tis possible."

Mikkel leveled a stern look at me. "Explain yourself."

"Chester has the expertise in weasels, and I give him leave to explain."

Chester bowed his head slightly at me before speaking. "In studying the old texts, my father learned weasels are the sole creatures able to slay a basilisk. He populated the forest surrounding Queen Aurora's hiding place with weasels, and we never once had a basilisk trouble us."

"He speaks the truth," Vilmar said. "During the hike past the ravine, Ty and I saw no evidence of any basilisks. It was as if we'd stepped into another part of the forest altogether."

Mikkel studied Chester and then me, clearly weighing the options. "You suggest bringing weasels to the lodge?"

"Aye," Chester said. "The weasel is immune to the basilisk's venomous vapors. The basilisk also cannot abide the scent of the weasel's urine. The weasel uses the noxious odor to trap the basilisk before biting it. Most often the basilisk also bites the weasel, and both creatures die."

"So, if we have any hope of being successful, we must have an equal number of weasels to match the number of basilisks surrounding the lodge?"

"I cannot say whether or not releasing weasels into the basilisk pit will work to give us a way inside the hunting lodge, but I agree with Prince Kresten that we must try."

"And does anyone know how many basilisks surround the lodge?" Mikkel glanced at the others of our party who'd now gathered around us.

"At least a dozen," Princess Pearl said. "I have not been there in recent years, but I hunted there oft with my father. I know the grounds well and can lead us wherever we need to go inside—if we are able to pass through the basilisks."

Mikkel nodded. "Then we must capture a dozen or more weasels. How shall we accomplish it?"

"At the cottage?" I addressed my question to Chester. "Is it possible there?"

"Aye." Chester guided his horse back a few steps. "My men will ride with you to continue the chase after Queen Aurora, and I'll go back to the cottage to trap as many weasels as I can. They're accustomed to my presence and will not frighten easily at my approach."

Though the plan wasn't solid or even viable, it was the best we had.

"You'll need help." Vilmar was mounting his horse. "I'll come along—"

"No," I interrupted. "Jorg and I shall go with Chester. We know the forest there better than any of you. Thus, we are better equipped to aid him in tracking the weasels and in transporting them to the lodge."

Chester didn't protest my offer, which I took for his acquiescence.

I didn't want to stop chasing after Aurora. But my brothers and the rest of the men would be able to track her without me. They didn't need my help. However, Chester did if he had any hope of capturing enough weasels and making it to the lodge before the queen killed Aurora.

I pinned my most serious gaze upon my brothers. "If you cannot rescue Aurora before she is locked away inside Boarshead, you must begin Mercia's negotiations for her life. Stall Queen Margery. Do whatever you must to ensure she doesn't slay Aurora."

Chapter 20

Aurora

A throbbing in my temple woke me. For long seconds, I couldn't think and could hardly breathe. At a jarring motion, I tried to turn my head, but instant pain made me cry out—except my cry went nowhere. It stuck in my throat, lodged there by a rag tied tightly across my mouth.

I became conscious of ropes binding me so securely my feet and hands were numb. I was upon a horse, sitting sideways in front of a rider, and we were galloping at a punishing speed. The pounding of multiple hooves told me there were several horses.

What had happened?

The last thing I remembered was starting to cry and rushing off into the shrubs. Had someone snuck up behind me and knocked me over the head? If so, who? Wetness on my scalp and the sticking of my hair told me the hit had been hard enough to cause bleeding.

From the angle of my position in the saddle, I couldn't see any of the other riders. But I could see that we were back in Inglewood Forest, the heathland nowhere in sight, not even through the distant trees.

How long had I been unconscious?

From the way the sunlight slanted through the branches overhead, I guessed 'twas afternoon, which meant many hours had passed since I'd been taken captive. Not only did my head ache from where I'd been hit, but my body was sore from the endless riding.

As the horse leaped over something and landed, I jostled against my captor. He was wearing a chain-mail hauberk and gauntlet gloves. He smelled of metal and horseflesh and seemed to take no care that I was sitting awkwardly in the saddle.

I stiffened and bumped the reins to get his attention. But he kicked his mount harder and lifted the reins away from my reach. I tried to speak but couldn't utter a single coherent sound. I wiggled my hands and feet, but the rope cut into my flesh.

An eerie disquiet swelled within me. I'd been captured, bound, and taken away. Only one person would do this. The one person I'd been hiding from my entire life. Queen Margery.

Were these knights even now taking me to her? Riding overland into Warwick would likely take several days. If they were intent on delivering me to Queen Margery's royal residence in Kensington, the journey would be even longer.

I strained to see the riders again, but the movement made my head throb. I wanted to release a frustrated cry. This was my fault. I shouldn't have started weeping over Kresten, shouldn't have been feeling sorry for myself, and shouldn't have walked off. If I'd acted responsibly and maturely like a true queen, I wouldn't have made myself such easy prey.

Now I needed to escape from my captors and find my way back to Chester. If I didn't, I would face certain death. Unless . . .

What if I gave Queen Margery what she wanted— Mercia and the desire to reunite the country into Bryttania? I could relinquish my throne to her and put an end to the madness.

After all, I wasn't sure I'd really make a good and wise queen, at least not one like my mother.

Could I bargain with Queen Margery? Tell her to send me far away to live in exile? In doing so, would I be able to find a way to reunite with Kresten and convince him to come with me?

Even as I entertained the possibility of a future with him, guilt pricked me. My desire for a simple life without riches and power couldn't be considered selfish, could it? All I wanted was to be happy. There wasn't anything wrong with that, was there?

Queen Margery was the selfish one, never satisfied, always seeking more. From everything I'd learned from Aunt Idony's lessons as well as the news Chester brought back from the outside world, Warwick's citizens had faced increasing poverty and hardship while the queen paraded around in lavish jewels.

The simple truth was, Queen Margery cared more for her own interests and gain than for those of the people.

Her own interests.

Would I be guilty of the same if I chose to abdicate Mercia's throne and live as a common woman? Caring for my own interest rather than the interests of others?

Thinking only of what I wanted and what was best for me instead of what was in the greatest good for my people?

Whether highborn and wealthy or lowborn and poor, the plague of selfishness could afflict us all. Was it possible, no matter our status, that we had to choose how to live? For ourselves or for others?

As much as I longed to embrace happiness with Kresten, a truth Aunt Idony had taught me from Scripture resounded in my head: *"It is more blessed to give than to receive."* I might initially find contentment with Kresten, but in the long term, I would obtain more satisfaction giving of myself, my love, and even my life rather than clinging to my selfish desires.

Perhaps I wasn't yet a strong queen. And perhaps I still had much to learn about my country and her people. Nonetheless, I couldn't deny my birthright or the path God had bestowed upon me.

I closed my eyes and whispered a silent prayer for the strength and wisdom to somehow free myself from the danger I'd brought upon myself.

We rode until well over nightfall. By the time we stopped and my captor lowered me to the ground, I collapsed, unable to hold myself up. My bindings had chafed my wrists and ankles, causing my skin to blister and bleed. My mouth was parched, making me almost delirious for want of a drink. And my body was bruised so that I ached in every conceivable place.

I was too weary to take note of my surroundings,

except that we'd come upon a camp with more soldiers and horses milling about. From the way the men greeted one another and the wary glances they cast my direction, I guessed these were more of Queen Margery's men.

Though I was both cold and hungry, no one thought to position me by the blazing flames of a bonfire or give me a portion of the roasting game. From their callous treatment, they clearly had no incentive to treat me kindly, had likely been tasked to bring me before the queen alive and naught more.

When one of the soldiers finally untied my gag and tipped a cup of water to my lips, I drank greedily and to my fill. After I finished, he tied the gag back in place, but thankfully, it wasn't as tight. I lowered myself into the dry leaves, exhaustion overtaking me.

Shouting awoke me. Before I could make sense of what was happening, one of the queen's knights was yanking me to my feet. The camp was in a commotion, with men calling to one another and mounting their horses. A second later, I felt myself being lifted onto a saddle in front of a soldier. I couldn't tell if this was the same knight as previously. All I knew was that I was weary, sore, and in more trouble than I'd ever been in before.

I should have used the break to attempt an escape, and I vowed to make a getaway at our next stop. That meant during this leg of the journey, I needed to wrestle more diligently to free my hands of the fastenings.

Once again, I found myself in a small contingent of soldiers riding hard. My captor continued to glance over his shoulder, kicking his horse and urging it ever faster. Was someone following us? Perhaps Chester? Why else would Queen Margery's men be worried?

I prayed fervently that someone would reach me and be able to rescue me. I attempted to think of something—anything—I could do to slow our horse and allow the pursuers a chance to reach me. But the helplessness of my predicament constricted me every bit as much as my bindings.

Chapter 21

KRESTEN

DARKNESS HAD FALLEN BY THE TIME WE MADE IT TO THE COTTAGE. My wound ached from the many hours in the saddle. When I dismounted, I would have buckled if not for my cane. Jorg came to my aid, but I pushed him aside, needing to punish myself.

Chester entered the cottage, and a moment later, light flared from a candle. I limped inside to find him hefting down two wooden boxes from the dormer room. He placed the traps on the floor, ascended the ladder once more, then returned a moment later with two more.

The traps were identical in size and crudely constructed, the boards weathered, and the metal rusty. If Chester's father had built them when they'd first moved to the cottage, then the traps were close to twenty years old.

"Do they still work?" I examined them more closely, noting that a trapdoor was attached to a lever and a hook inside the cage. Although the hook dangled aimlessly now, I guessed it would lodge in the bait so that when the prey nibbled at the bait, it would wiggle the lever above, causing the door to shut, trapping the creature inside the box.

"I'll get them working." Chester was already kneeling beside one and lifting up a trapdoor. He had a skein of Aunt Elspeth's thick thread and sliced a long piece, which he fastened to the door. "While I do this, you and Jorg collect bait."

"What kind?"

"Whatever you can catch. Weasels will eat almost any kind of meat. But you'll have the most luck finding badgers."

Jorg was outside tending to our horses. I helped him finish, and then we hiked out into the thickest part of the woods, searching for setts—the mounds of excavated soil that indicated underground tunnels were nearby. We kept the trees and shadows behind us to blend in and stayed downwind so our scent wouldn't alert any badgers to our presence.

We had the waning moon to aid our hunting. Once our eyes adjusted, we could see well enough, especially since only a smattering of leaves remained on the branches. Without a bow and arrow, we relied upon our knife and axe-throwing skills to make our kills—something we'd become experts at over the past months.

By the time we returned to the cottage with the game, Chester had fixed the traps so they were in working order. We butchered the meat and placed bloody pieces into each trap, then carried them out to the areas most populated by weasels.

As we sat in the dark and waited, I couldn't keep from thinking again of the kisses I'd shared with Aurora here in the woods. Now that I knew the future laid out for us both, I realized just how forbidden our kisses had been. Even though part of me wished I'd never met her and brought her this trouble, another part of me cherished the memory of every second I'd spent with her.

By the break of dawn, we'd captured a dozen weasels. When they were separated into three of the boxes, we each held one upon our mounts and started on our way. We had no thought of slumber, only of traveling as rapidly as possible.

We rode hard, although we had no hope of catching up to the others. By the end of the day, we stopped to rest our mounts and sleep for a few hours. The scent of roasting game awoke me, and I sat up to find that Chester had started a fire and was cooking a hare he'd caught.

"We need our strength." He slowly turned the meat that he'd thrust onto the end of his spear. "We'll eat and then ride through the night." Though the danger of stumbling across a basilisk was greater in the darkness, we rode with torches, and so far our vigilance had kept us safe.

Jorg still slumbered, the firelight reflecting the weariness in his thin face. I had no doubt my face was just as weary. Even so, I was anxious to resume our journey. Every minute of our delay could mean the difference between Aurora's life and death.

Chester stared into the fire, his eyes sparking with their usual intensity. "When we arrive at Boarshead, we must have a plan of attack."

"We'll release the weasels and wait for them to destroy the basilisks." I held out my hands toward the flames to warm them from the chill of the night.

"Aye, but after that, we must have a strategy for getting to Rory with all haste."

"Pearl will give us directions to the places inside the lodge where the queen is most likely to hold her."

He drew his spear from the fire and used his knife to test the readiness of the meat before he stretched it over the flames once more. "You'll need to create a diversion to pull the majority of the guards away from Rory so my men and I can go in and rescue her."

"I shall be the one to enter and rescue her."

"No, 'twill be too perilous crossing the basilisk pit—"

"I'll do whatever it takes to free her."

"Then you will stay with your brothers and cause a diversion."

"I'm going in for her, Chester, and there's naught you can say or do to convince me otherwise."

He stared at the roasting hare, his expression a stony mask. Now that he knew I was a prince, he was using a measure of restraint that hadn't been present when I'd been a guest at the cottage. I rather preferred the honesty of our previous interactions.

"I'm to blame for her capture." I focused on the dancing flames. "And now I must atone for my mistakes."

I could feel his attention shift to me, his keen gaze searching and testing me. "If anyone is to blame, 'tis I." I shook my head, but he continued before I could speak, his voice low and raw. "She was upset at me because I took the letter she left for you that explained our departure."

As much as I liked knowing she'd been thinking about me, such a note would have been dangerous if it had fallen into the wrong hands. "She shouldn't have left it. You did the right thing in taking it so no one would trail you."

"I could have told her instead of sneaking it away. And I could have been more sensitive to how hard the parting was." Regret etched every line of his rugged face.

"You had her best interests at heart, and I respect you for that."

"I should have known someone at Huntwell Fortress was working for Queen Margery and feeding her information. Should have known the queen's men would be right on our trail. Should have waited for more knights to join in the escort before going."

"You couldn't know—"

"I was a fool."

"If not for me, you would have waited at the cottage where she was safe."

"No, I'd already contemplated leaving. I'd seen evidence of soldiers having entered from the western ridge. Our time there was running out."

"You did what you thought was best."

He expelled a sigh. "I should have trusted her judgment. She's intelligent and strong and careful. If she'd sensed something about your character that didn't measure up, she wouldn't have fallen in love with you."

Such a statement coming from Chester was indeed high praise. "I'm no saint. Clearly I was too weak to walk away from her when I should have. Although you should know, I never intended to come to the cottage. With the severity of my injury, Jorg felt we had no other choice."

"He was protecting you as he ought to."

"Perhaps." Regardless, I understood Chester's reservations so much better now that I knew Aurora was royalty. "You were doing your duty and were right to question my motives and purpose. I would expect nothing less of you."

"But I shouldn't have questioned her motives, should have supported her."

I didn't know how to respond to his admission. Even if

he had supported her, what good could have come from it? Our love was destined to end in heartache, and surely he knew that.

He withdrew the hare from the heat again, tested it, then sliced off a slab and handed it to me on the tip of his knife. I stabbed the piece onto my knife, then bit off a chunk. It was hot and tender and juicy, and would hopefully renew my energy to ride the rest of the night through.

"Her husband has already been chosen for her," Chester said after swallowing a bite of the meat. "But it might be possible for you to go before her father and advisors to present yourself as an option. They wouldn't shun a match with one of Scania's princes. In fact, maybe such a match is already arranged."

"'Tis possible." I chewed but couldn't taste the meat any longer. I twisted my knife around and stared at the remaining portion.

The fire crackled in the ensuing silence, and I could feel him watching me and waiting for me to say more.

"The truth is"—I spun the knife again—"if I live through the upcoming battle for Aurora, I expect I shall become the next king of Scania. Mikkel and Vilmar deserve the throne more than I do and have prepared for taking the leadership of Scania. But the rules of our Testing state that we must complete the six-month challenge to be eligible for consideration."

"They are still here. Everything that is happening is still a testing, a challenge, is it not?"

"We were each given specific places to live for our Testing as well as specific challenges. If they abandon their place and challenge, they forfeit any claim to the throne."

"So now you are duty bound to take Scania's throne even though you have no desire for it?"

I hesitated in my response but finally met his gaze directly. "Before beginning my Testing, I would have done whatever pleased me without regard to anyone else. But I have been trying to live out my challenge to deny myself these past months. I may have failed to deny myself Aurora in the short term, but I know I must sacrifice my desires for her in order to rule my country. It may kill me to do so, but I shall accomplish this duty."

Chester held my gaze for a long moment. When he nodded, I sensed not only his acceptance but his respect. "You both have duties to your countries that you cannot set aside. I pray God will someday reward you both for your sacrifices."

Jorg stirred and sat up. As he joined us by the fire, we finished our meal quietly, for I had nothing more to say about a future with Aurora. Though I couldn't bear the prospect that another man would wed her, we had more urgent demands at hand.

No one would have her if we couldn't rescue her in time.

Chapter
22

KRESTEN

WE RODE THROUGH THE NIGHT AND WELL INTO THE NEXT DAY before we took another short break. We'd easily picked up my brothers' trail, and from what Chester could surmise from the horse droppings as well as embers of their campfire, they were eighteen hours ahead of us. At various points along the way, the heavy prints and wide tracks showed a frantic pace, leading Chester to believe they may have gotten close to Aurora.

But there was also no indication they'd secured her. As the day passed into another night, I despaired we would be too late, that our effort to capture the weasels would amount to naught if Queen Margery was as anxious to have Aurora's heart for her alchemy as Pearl had claimed.

"You seem to know much of Mercia's ancient customs," I said to Chester through a yawn as I struggled to stay awake at the break of dawn on the third day of traveling through Inglewood Forest.

He released one of his scoffing laughs. "Of course I know much. During my training, my father made sure I knew everything there is to know about Mercia."

We'd talked off and on during the long hours of traveling, especially when we slowed our pace to skirt more vigilantly around an area with signs of a basilisk. I'd learned much about Chester and the training he'd received from his father, Sir William, who had once been a renowned elite knight, one of the best in the land. Though elite guards took vows to remain unmarried, Sir William had secretly fallen in love and married a noblewoman betrothed to another man of some importance.

The nobleman had demanded Sir William's death. But because Sir William uncovered a plot to kill Queen Leandra, the queen pardoned him. The slighted nobleman held a grudge and eventually attempted to slay Sir William's wife and newborn child.

Though the plot succeeded with Sir William's wife, the babe remained alive, leaving Sir William a widower with a child to raise on his own. About the same time, Queen Leandra died giving birth to Aurora. With Queen Margery seeking to slay Aurora and take Mercia's throne, Sir William offered to take Aurora away and keep her safe along with his own son.

With two nuns to act as nursemaids, Sir William led the group deep into Inglewood Forest. There they raised the two children, hoping Queen Margery would soon give up her search. They'd never expected to remain in hiding for so many years.

"My father was a strict teacher." Every time Chester spoke of Sir William, he did so with admiration. "He gave me the same training he'd received, perhaps more since he concluded I'd one day need to battle Queen Margery to protect Aurora."

I stifled another yawn. "What did he teach you about the white stone and alchemy?"

"Like other elite knights, he was taught the white stone can create an elixir with the power to transform rock into jewels, silver, or gold. However, the elixir ingredients are written in an ancient code that has been nearly impossible to decipher over the centuries. Those most serious about alchemy have only been able to experiment with the stone, never knowing what it truly requires. Many speculated a human heart was necessary for riches, but no king or queen was willing to make so great a sacrifice to discover the truth. Instead, they considered themselves to be royal guardians of the white stone, making sure to protect and use it wisely."

"And how does one use it wisely?"

"Legends speak of the stone's ability to create metals using blood rather than hearts. I've heard it said the blood of a mighty warrior can form impenetrable iron."

"So rulers of the past have used the white stone for strength and not greed?"

"Something like that."

"Until Queen Margery."

"Aye. King Alfred, God rest his soul, shouldn't have bequeathed the white stone to his elder daughter."

"Once we have freed Aurora, we shall destroy it. Then the queen will never be tempted to harm anyone else." The honking of geese drew my gaze skyward. Although the day was cloudy and contained the damp chill of approaching rain, the blazing color of the leaves overhead and the majestic formation of geese soothed the ache in my soul that had deepened with each passing day Aurora was in danger.

And with every passing day, I was beginning to realize

my brothers had been right. I'd been shortsighted. Though I hadn't wanted to join the fight against Queen Margery, I no longer could deny the need to defeat her. Her cruelty and greed had seeped beyond the borders of her country to ensnare Mercia and Aurora. If Margery succeeded in her ability to make gold, she'd become unstoppable. She'd be able to build her army and pay mercenaries to fight for her. Where would she attack next? Norland? Scania?

With the white stone and her quest for gold, she would seek out additional royal maidens whose hearts she'd employ in her alchemy. The cruelty would only continue as she traded her gold with kings for the hearts of their daughters.

Chester peered overhead at the geese too. "As noble as your desire is to destroy the white stone, the legends are all the same. Its power can only be abolished if it is crushed. But anyone who touches it succumbs to the sleep of death."

"The sleep of death?"

"A sleep that never ends, except in death."

I shook my head, unable to believe a stone could contain such power. "And you believe these legends?"

"Aye. They have been passed down for centuries."

"If anyone who touches the stone dies, then how did the queen make the elixir she used in her gem mines? And how would she transport the stone from her residence in Kensington to the Boarshead Lodge? For surely with so little time left to use Aurora's heart, she has carried the white stone with her."

"The white stone is kept in a chest made of the purest unblemished gold. My father once saw the chest before King Alfred died and said only the bravest souls dare to carry it."

"Perhaps she mixes the elixir in the chest itself?"

"Perhaps. Either way, no man who touches the stone lives."

"Then there is no way to destroy it?"

"At least no way to destroy it and live."

"Then I shall take it to the East Sea and drop it into the deepest part where no one will be able to recover it."

Chester barked a humorless laugh. "If it were that easy to get rid of, someone would have tried such a method already. But, no, the stone will not sink, stay buried, or burn."

I shifted my sore backside in my saddle, my mind racing to find another solution, to uncover some other method. "Then the only thing to do is to lock it away where no one can have it."

"And that is exactly what the kings have done through time. They've attempted to conceal it where no one would be lured by its promise of riches."

"Clearly that wasn't enough."

"And as I said, King Alfred, God rest his soul, shouldn't have given it to his daughter, or at the very least should have given it to Leandra instead of Margery."

"So, you believe Aurora's mother would have safeguarded it rather than use it for her own gain?"

"From the way my father spoke of Queen Leandra, she was content to be a keeper of the keys to the ancient treasure and had no plans to seek it out. She would have done the same with the white stone."

"Then we shall not only rescue Aurora, but we shall take the chest with the stone and make her the keeper of it."

"And give Queen Margery all the more reason to seek Aurora's death and throne?"

Vilmar's admonition from the night he'd followed me to the cottage came back to me: *"You don't know Queen Margery the way I do. She's a wicked woman and will stop at nothing to get what she wants."*

"There!" Ahead of us, Jorg called out and nodded to the south. "I see the smoke of campfires."

Anticipation charged through me, chasing away the weariness that had been my companion of late. I joined Jorg and Chester in galloping the last of the distance. We broke through the woodland into a clearing to find a small army on the level plain in front of the hunting lodge. Most sat or stood around several fires, warming themselves and breaking their fasts.

I scanned the camp, searching desperately for a sight of Aurora's golden hair and beautiful face. But there was no woman amongst the camp save Pearl, who was deep in conversation with several men, including Mikkel and Vilmar.

Disappointment fell upon me as heavily as a tree toppling the wrong direction. Although I'd known catching the queen's men who had Aurora would be nigh to impossible, I'd hoped my brothers would accomplish it anyway.

At the sight of us, calls arose. Mikkel and Vilmar broke away from the others and strode toward us, their expressions grim. They didn't need to say anything for me to know the situation was serious.

I reined in abruptly and slid down, praying we weren't too late.

Jorg was at my side in an instant, handing me my cane and relieving me of the box with the weasels.

"Tell me," I demanded. "Does she yet live?"

"We believe so." Vilmar spoke first, his eyes radiating compassion.

I sagged against my cane.

Mikkel nodded in the direction of a stone complex at the center of the clearing. "The queen's ambassador, Lord Anise, was here this morn and has already returned."

Not as majestic or large as a castle, Boarshead Lodge was still an imposing fortress on higher ground with a series of connected buildings surrounding a center bailey.

A deep, dark ditch filled with blackened, gnarled limbs circled the lodge. The pit was wider than I'd expected, too long to span with a log, ladder, or some other method that would allow us to cross over. I didn't have to see inside to know it was home to a host of basilisks. The barren, scorched land on either side of the pit showed the telltale signs of the deadly creatures.

A gatehouse stood at the center of the lodge, containing a strange-looking drawbridge with high wooden sides, likely to protect those crossing it from the basilisks. The bridge was securely retracted, giving us no way to enter except through the basilisk pit.

"What news did the ambassador deliver?" I asked. "Is the queen willing to accept the keys to the treasure in exchange for Aurora?"

Mikkel shook his head. "He says the queen is willing but won't permit us to see Aurora until we deliver the keys."

Chester had dismounted and stood by my side. "Then we can't know for certain if she still lives."

"Lord Anise assured us of Aurora's safety and comfort, that the queen intends to hold her until we are able to present her with the keys."

"We cannot believe anything Lord Anise says," Pearl called as she strode toward us, her beautiful green eyes flashing with frustration. "The queen is only attempting to lull us into inactivity, thereby buying herself more time."

Mikkel and Pearl locked gazes, their bodies rigid, tension radiating between them.

"Do you have the weasels?" Pearl directed her question at me.

I nodded, but before I could speak, Mikkel interrupted. "We've discussed the matter at length, and even with the weasels, it's too dangerous. We don't know if they'll eliminate all the basilisks."

"'Tis a chance we have to take," Pearl stated.

"It's a chance I'm not willing to take with you."

Vilmar's raised brow told me this argument had been ongoing between Mikkel and his bride for some time, that they were both too stubborn to come up with a solution.

"We must attack as soon as possible," Pearl insisted. "You know as well as I do the queen cannot be trusted."

"I realize she won't give us Aurora, not without a fight. But if we hold off another day or two until the contingent arrives from Delsworth, we'll not only have additional forces, but we'll be able to see if the weasels indeed slay the basilisks."

I bent and picked up one of the weasel cages. "We'll release the weasels under cover of darkness tonight, then I'll be the one to cross over and test the safety of the ditch."

Chester retrieved the other two cages. "I'll go with Kresten."

"As will I," Pearl added with haste.

Mikkel scowled. "No."

"I know the hunting lodge and will be able to guide them to Aurora."

Mikkel shook his head fiercely. "You need only instruct

them on the layout of the complex and they'll be able to navigate without you."

"My father made me memorize the details." Chester's voice was edged with exasperation. "I need no guide."

Muttering, Chester stalked away, and Mikkel did likewise in the opposite direction.

Pearl watched her husband retreat, her features taut with frustration. I sensed her angst went deeper than she was revealing. Of course, she wanted to rescue her sister, Ruby. Mikkel had already shared the details about the first failed effort in Kensington, the attempt that had nearly cost them both their lives. But I suspected Pearl blamed herself now for losing Aurora and foiling the plans to confront the queen.

Even so, I understood Mikkel's caution in not wanting to allow Pearl to go inside the fortress. If she fell into the queen's clutches as she had previously, our negotiations with the queen would be even more complicated. I knew the pain too well of losing the woman I loved and wouldn't wish such a fate upon Mikkel.

"Your Highness," I said with a bow to Pearl, "I vow I shall not leave the lodge without Princess Ruby."

She stared after Mikkel a moment longer, then nodded at me. "If you make it across the ditch, you must find a way to lower the bridge."

If I made it across . . . that would be only the beginning of an impossible task, one I was determined to accomplish. Or die trying.

Chapter 23

Aurora

My body ached and my head pounded. But at least the incessant jostling had ceased. I pried my eyes open to discover I was inside some kind of dwelling.

I sagged with relief at being done with the torturous ride. The previous hours of pain in not only my backside but also my wrists and ankles had become so unbearable that I'd wavered in and out of consciousness until, blessedly, all had turned black.

The strong, earthy aroma of cedar hung aloft along with the bold, spicy scent of myrrh. I took a deep breath, letting the herbs comfort and remind me of home, of Aunt Idony and the sweetness of my life. Oh, how sweet and simple life had been.

From the barred opening in the upper portion of the door, scant light filtered in, permitting me to view the cell-like room with a low ceiling and simple whitewashed walls. The chamber was devoid of furnishings save the pallet beneath me and a simple crucifix upon the wall.

Pushing up, I bit back a cry at the agony that rippled through my body, as though I'd been upon the rack and had every joint dislocated. I struggled to my knees, grateful my bindings were finally gone. The blood at my wrists and ankles had dried and now crusted my sleeves and hem. I was free of my gag too and drew in a deep breath of the smoky herbal scents.

Sometime during the days of riding, my hair had worked its way loose from my plait, and it now hung in a tangled disarray, blood from my head wound matting it. My gown was muddy and stained with bits of dried leaves and dirt sticking to the linen.

Where was I?

I made myself sit up farther, trying to bring coherence to my thoughts. But all I could think about was the need for something to quench my thirst. My tongue stuck to the roof of my mouth, and my throat was parched.

With a fortitude borne from desperation, I pushed myself to my feet. Unsteady and weak, I grabbed on to the wall and pressed against it to brace my body. For several seconds, I breathed deeply and fought away the dizziness that threatened to send me back into the world of oblivion.

I couldn't go there again. I had to stay awake and determine where I was and how I could get out. Although I'd been praying and hoping Chester would rally knights to rescue me—and perhaps already had been on my trail—I guessed he was no match for the queen's men. At the very least, they'd had too much of a lead.

Gathering strength, I limped to the door and tried the handle. Of course it was locked. Standing on my toes, I peered through the bars. One knight stood directly outside my chamber and another at the end of the corridor.

At the sight of my face, the closest knight motioned to the other guard, who spun and disappeared down a different hallway.

Perhaps if I could trick this guard into opening the door, I'd be able to push him into the room and lock him inside in my stead. Though I didn't know how I'd escape beyond that, it was a start. And I needed to do something.

"I would like a drink," I managed through my parched lips.

He stood stiffly and unmoving, without even the slightest twitch to acknowledge my request. I guessed no amount of pleading would rouse his compassion.

With a sigh, I nearly allowed myself to sink to the floor and wallow in despair. But I held myself erect, even though every bone in my body protested. I wouldn't allow Queen Margery to reduce me to a helpless, quivering simpleton. If I must face death at her hands, I would do so with dignity.

My stomach rumbled with the pangs of hunger, and I pressed my fist there, wishing I could block out the hunger, not only for food but for Kresten. He'd never been far from my mind during the long past few days. Though I'd resolved to do my duty and put thoughts of a future with him aside, I couldn't so easily dismiss my love.

What would he say when he discovered I'd been captured by the queen? Would he blame himself? I hoped not. He had to know I'd consented to seeing him. And at the end, when he'd tried to distance himself from me so we could part ways, I'd been the one to seek him out.

I prayed he wouldn't discover what had happened to me until it was too late. Otherwise, he'd put himself into mortal danger coming after me. And I didn't want him to do that.

Footsteps echoed in the corridor along with voices. I held myself up rigidly, though my knees threatened to buckle. A moment later, keys rattled in the door, and then it swung open to reveal the guard.

Behind him stood a beautiful woman and several more soldiers, servants, and monks. The guard stepped aside, and the woman glided inside the cell. A servant scurried past her, holding up a candle.

The amber light fell across the woman, highlighting her features. Queen Margery, my mother's twin sister. Margery looked nearly identical to my mother, except instead of having fair hair and blue eyes, Margery had waist-length, raven-black tresses and stunning emerald eyes. She wore an emerald gown that matched her eyes, along with emerald bracelets, emerald earrings, and emerald-studded ribbons.

While she was every bit as beautiful as my mother, something in Margery's eyes was cold, almost cruel. Nothing like the strong, purposeful, and courageous eyes that had always peered at me from my mother's portrait at Huntwell Fortress. I tried to picture my mother standing beside this woman. What would Leandra think? What would she do in my situation?

I guessed she would have exuded strength and self-confidence. "Your Majesty, I regret that I am not at my best to receive you, but I am pleased to make your acquaintance."

She tilted her head and studied me further, her lips curving up as though she somehow found me or my predicament amusing.

At her mockery, I was all too conscious of how inadequate I was and how little experience I had at interacting with people. While Aunt Idony had prepared me for many things, she couldn't make up for all that I'd lost in being sequestered for so many years. Was I fooling myself into thinking I could be anything like my mother?

I straightened my shoulders and lifted my chin. No matter what might happen here with Queen Margery, I would face it with grace.

"You look like Leandra," Queen Margery said with a note of spite, as if my resemblance to my mother was objectionable.

"You look like her too."

"Our father always thought Leandra, with her fairer coloring, was more beautiful."

"Is a raven any less beautiful than a sparrow?"

Margery's mirth faded, and her gaze narrowed upon me. "Our father also thought Leandra was kinder and wiser and would make a better queen than I would."

So the speculations were true—Leandra had been King Alfred's favorite daughter, and he'd intended to give the kingdom in its entirety to her. If so, surely Margery would have felt slighted, even unloved. Perhaps those pains lingered with Margery her whole life and shaped her into this cruel woman she'd become.

Even if the king hadn't favored Leandra, maybe Margery had compared herself to her twin and always found herself lacking. Wasn't that what I'd been doing? Comparing myself to my mother and seeing only my shortcomings?

Perhaps that's what comparison did. Fostered inadequacy.

"Indeed," I said, "my mother was renowned for her wisdom, purpose, and fortitude. But that cannot diminish the fine qualities you have that could make you into a kind and wise queen."

"I am nothing like her."

"And neither am I." 'Twas the truth, and I could no longer deny it. I had to stop believing I needed to imitate her in order to be worthy. "I must discover my own strengths and gifts and let those guide me into making good choices for my kingdom."

"Then you think I have made poor choices, dear niece? Is that it?"

"I think you yet can become the queen you have always wanted to be, one King Alfred would admire."

She studied me as though she might be considering my words, and I hoped she would see the futility of hanging on to grudges against her father and Leandra. In failing to win her father's approval, had she given up trying to please him and allowed herself to become the opposite of her sister?

"'Tis never too late for any of us," I added softly. "As long as we have today, we have the opportunity to choose rightly and walk a better path."

"And who made you the wise one?" Her tone was laced with mockery. "You must feel as though you are ready to become a queen just like your mother."

"I am ready." And at that moment I knew that I was. I hadn't realized just how ready. Of course, my inadequacies still lurked beneath the surface, but I couldn't allow them to make me feel less about myself as Margery had done. I had to push forward and discover my own unique strengths and abilities.

"I shall not be the same queen as my mother. In fact, I shall be different in many ways. But that will not stop me from doing all I can to be the good and wise queen the people of Mercia need."

She scrutinized me again, her gaze halting at my wrists and ankles. "Since you are so eager to become Mercia's queen, then we must transform you so you are worthy of the part." She motioned to the servants standing just outside the doorway.

"Take Aurora to one of the guest chambers and do everything you can to make her the fairest maiden in all the land."

"That is not necessary—"

Queen Margery cut me off with a wave of her hand. "Of course it is necessary. You are a queen and, as such, must be regal and beautiful." She gave me one last look before she pivoted and issued a string of orders to the servants about baths and purifying and gowns and jewels.

I listened in confused silence. I'd assumed the queen had every intention of killing me and taking my throne. Wasn't that why she'd hunted me these many years? Why the change of heart now? And why go to the trouble of kidnapping me if only to make me presentable as queen of Mercia?

As she left the chamber, she murmured to one of the monks, "She will be perfect."

Moments later, the servants ushered me out of my cell and down the corridor. A part of me warned that I must use the opportunity to escape now while I could. But another part of me wanted to believe that perhaps I, of all people, could somehow atone for the mistakes my mother had made with her sister. That perhaps I could find a way to repair the relationship with Margery so we might each rule our countries and remain at peace.

Chapter
24

Kresten

I CROUCHED NEAR THE DITCH AND PEERED INTO THE DARKNESS. For the past several hours since we'd released the weasels, Chester, Jorg, and I had waited, listening to the hissing and scraping coming from below. Only within the past half hour had the pit grown eerily silent.

With low clouds covering the night sky, we had neither stars nor moon by which to see what was happening. And we couldn't light torches and risk the queen's guards spotting us trying to cross.

Except for the courier lurking nearby, the rest of our men, including my brothers and Pearl, waited at the path leading to the drawbridge. The section was the narrowest part of the ditch, and they planned to lay a series of platforms in an attempt to cross. We'd spent the better part of the day felling trees and constructing a makeshift bridge we hoped would span the distance.

At the very least, we hoped our flimsy platform would distract our opposition so Chester, Jorg, and I would be able to enter the complex undetected. At best, if the majority of basilisks were killed, Mikkel and Vilmar and the others could ford their bridge, fight the queen's guards, and force their way through the gatehouse, focusing the battle there while we located Aurora.

I tightened the strip of my cloak I'd ripped off earlier, and I positioned it over my mouth and nose so I wouldn't be overcome by the basilisk's venomous fumes.

"Ready?" I whispered as I lowered the crude ladder we'd also built, one we needed for climbing up the other side of the pit.

"I'll go first." Chester's voice was muffled behind his mask. He pushed past me and reached for the top rung.

I shoved him back. "Let me do it. I'm the weakest and most expendable." With my injured leg, I feared I'd slow them down. Moreover, they were both better trained at stealth and warfare than I was.

"No!" Chester hissed, starting down the ladder. "I know the movements of the basilisk the best. If any are still alive, I'll be able to detect their presence."

And do what? I left the question unasked and stood by helplessly as he descended. Since the creatures sprang with haste from their lairs, he'd have little time to react without any light to warn him. Their bites were painful and deadly. Worse, the poisonous fumes had the potential to render us immobile.

I could only distinguish his outline disappearing into the blackness. When the ladder ceased wobbling, I knew he'd reached the bottom. He was silent for an everlasting moment before we heard his whisper. "None yet. You can come down."

My pulsed picked up its pace, and I started descending. Once my feet landed, I tensed. The stench of poison in the air was heavy even through the thick wool over my mouth and nose. If we didn't hurry, we would be overcome erelong, too weak to cross.

"Here." Chester guided my hand to his cloak. "Hold my garment and stay directly behind me."

An instant later, Jorg's footsteps thumped behind me. He grabbed a fistful of my cloak in one hand and hefted the ladder across his shoulders with the other.

Chester moved with caution, using an axe to slice the blackened limbs and barren branches tangled across the pit. As an elite guard, he'd learned to use all his senses and was no doubt employing them now to guide us through the darkness without walking into a basilisk.

"Try not to breathe," he whispered.

Though we'd been in the pit but a few minutes, already my mind grew dull. I held my breath, praying that cutting off the fumes would help.

A few seconds later, Chester halted abruptly, throwing out his arm to stop us. At a jostle of dead branches ahead, I stiffened and could feel Jorg do the same behind me. Chester crouched, the axe in one hand and his sword in the other.

The soft but distinct high-pitched squeal of a weasel shattered the silence. The tension in Chester's back eased. He straightened and continued forward. My tension remained, however. If a weasel was loose in the pit, it must mean basilisks were still lurking. Had we come down too soon? Should we have waited another hour?

I let the thought pass. We'd already delayed our rescue attempt long enough. All day, while we'd felled trees and hewn logs, my mind had returned to Aurora and the possibility the queen was mistreating her, that perhaps she was cold, hungry, and maybe even wounded. While preferable than death, I loathed her enduring any suffering at all.

I had to reach her. The panic within my chest had been slicing deeper. And now it chopped hard and painfully, so that though my lungs burned with the effort of not breathing, I forced myself to go even longer than I imagined possible.

When I finally had to draw in another breath, the intake made me dizzy. I paused to fight a wave of blackness. Behind me, Jorg wavered, struggling just as I was.

Chester pressed forward, increasing his pace, hacking more frantically through the dead branches. If he was having trouble fighting against the fumes, he didn't let it stop him, and I was grateful more than ever for his strength and training that allowed him to persevere beyond the limitations of the average man.

With every passing minute, each step I took seemed heavier and more laborious than the one before it. Jorg's grip on my cloak began to loosen. He dropped the ladder several times, towing it behind him on the ground, stumbling and tripping as he struggled to maintain his footing.

I simply put one foot in front of the other, until I tripped and fell to my knees. Chester yanked me up and shoved me ahead of him along with the ladder. He pressed me against the rungs, as though urging me to climb. For an instant, I couldn't move, couldn't make myself ascend. All I wanted to do was fall over and sleep.

The sharp prick of a blade into my backside prodded me upward, and somehow I managed to pull myself rung after rung until I reached the end. I hoisted myself up and collapsed onto solid ground, unable to think or move. All I could do was breathe in and out.

An instant later, Jorg fell next to me on his knees, gasping. For long moments, only the sound of our labored breathing filled the air. With each intake, my mind became clearer until I realized Chester hadn't mounted the ladder yet.

"Chester?" I attempted to push myself off the ground but failed.

Jorg lifted his head and then crawled back to the ladder.

Drawing on a reserve of strength I hadn't known I possessed, I dragged myself to the ladder too and peered over the edge. I couldn't see Chester, but I sensed he'd used the last of his coherency to make sure Jorg and I were safely out before he succumbed to the fumes. "We have to go back for him."

"I'll go," Jorg whispered, already on the top rung.

"Let me," I hissed after him.

"No, if I can't find him"—he wheezed for another breath—"you need to give the others the signal and then go after Aurora."

I hesitated. One of us needed to survive the crossing and throw the stone to the courier, who would then relay the news to Mikkel and Vilmar, letting them know we'd survived.

In my moment of indecision, Jorg was already climbing back down. I held the ladder in place and watched the blackness, waiting and praying he'd have the strength of mind and body to locate Chester.

"He's here," came Jorg's strained whisper. "I'll lift him as high as I can, then you drag him the rest of the way."

I took in a deep breath, then climbed down several rungs. I couldn't feel my limbs, but I forced myself to move anyway. As I bumped into a body, I grabbed it and began to heave it upward, working mostly on instinct. Though I was still weak and dull minded, I had enough wherewithal to keep going. Once above the pit again, I collapsed next to Chester and was relieved when Jorg landed beside us several seconds later.

I wasn't sure if Chester was alive, and I needed to haul him away from the basilisks' poison and someplace where the air was fresher and he'd have a better chance of reviving. The only direction to go was up since the complex sat atop a mound. The climb was steeper than I'd realized, and in my weakened condition, I struggled to move Chester.

Moments later, Jorg joined my efforts, and together we crawled a dozen paces away from the ditch, dragging Chester with us. There we sprawled out, took off our masks, and gulped in the air that was mostly free of the venomous odors.

Chester didn't move, and I feared we'd drawn him out too late. After rolling to my side, I pressed my fingers against his neck and checked for a pulse. A slow rhythm told me he was still alive, but barely.

I slid my arms underneath him. "Let's lift him so he's sitting." Jorg aided me, and we were rewarded with a slight groan. I tilted Chester's head back, hoping to open his airways. Then I slapped at his cheeks, trying to revive him.

He released another low moan and then attempted to drag in a breath.

"Wake up, you big oaf." I prodded his chest.

This time he coughed and gulped in more air.

Relief rushed over me, clearing my head and giving me renewed energy. I flexed my arms and legs, the numbness from moments ago fading. I had to throw the rock.

Though the pit wasn't safe and we'd nearly died during the crossing, my brothers needed to distract the guards so we could begin our trek farther into the complex.

Earlier in the day, Pearl had drawn the outline of the buildings in the dirt and marked several places we might be able to enter. Most were windows that led into buildings least used at this time of night. Chester added his knowledge to Pearl's. And together we worked out a plan, allowing us to hunt through the many chambers where the queen might be holding Aurora.

At another grunt, this one louder, Chester pushed himself up. He held his head in his hands. "Have you thrown the rock?" His voice was hoarse and breathless.

"Just about to."

"What are you waiting for?" he snarled.

"Good to see you're back to yourself and that the fumes didn't hurt that sweet nature of yours."

"Throw it," he growled.

I couldn't suppress a grin as I extracted a stone from my pocket. We'd each carried one over, not knowing which of us would live to throw it—or if any of us would. I wanted to throw all three so the courier would know we'd all lived. But we didn't have the time to spare.

Instead, I chucked the stone in what I hoped was the right direction, praying my strength was sufficient for the rock to reach the other side.

Other than our heavy breathing, the night around us was strangely silent. The complex at the hilltop was too silent, devoid of revelry either from within or without the great hall. Even the usual noises of the nocturnal creatures were absent.

Had the queen's men discovered our plan to cross the basilisk pit tonight? Were forces even now waiting to trap us?

"Let's go." Chester hauled himself to his knees.

"We need to wait for Mikkel and Vilmar to make their move."

"They will." Chester was already crawling up the hill. I didn't know how he had the energy or ability to keep going after almost dying. Though my limbs were yet weak, I moved after him. If he could keep fighting in his condition, I could too. I had to. I had no other choice.

Just as we crested the hill, shouts arose from the drawbridge path, and I breathed out a prayer of gratitude that Mikkel and Vilmar had gained the news and were now doing their part. A moment later, shouts and the slapping of footsteps resounded in the lodge as the soldiers raced through the complex and rallied to fend off the attack.

"Here's where we split up," Chester whispered. A few new lights flared above us, adding to those already glowing in a lone window here and there. It was enough that I could now see Jorg and Chester more clearly as well as the outer walls of the stone buildings.

"Remember," I said, "we cannot leave without Princess Ruby."

"The young princess isn't my consideration." Chester pressed against the wall and slid toward the region of the bedchambers, where he planned to enter through a window.

"I vowed to Princess Pearl I wouldn't leave without Ruby."

"Your mistake, not mine."

My humor at Chester from moments ago dissipated, replaced by annoyance. Sometimes he was too stubborn for his own good. "Then if I find Aurora, you will take her to safety while I ensure Princess Ruby is freed."

Chester didn't answer, and I didn't waste any more time trying to persuade him. He might be stubborn and gruff at times, but I'd witnessed his kindness and goodness underneath. He'd never willingly leave behind someone in need, even if that meant he had to risk his own life—just as he'd done for me and Jorg in the basilisk pit.

I wanted that to be true of me as well. But was I still too selfish? Was that the whole point of my Testing? To strip away everything else so I could ultimately see just how selfish I was? If so, I was learning the lesson well.

I crept in the direction of the low buildings that housed the infirmary. My limp was pronounced since I'd had to leave behind my cane.

Jorg stepped into my path, bringing me to a halt. "I'll be nearby. If you run into any trouble, you only need to shout, and I'll hear you."

"Likewise." He was entering a window in the servants' quarters. Hopefully, they would all be asleep, although with the commotion the guards were making, perhaps they'd roused.

The danger of this mission was beyond anything he'd agreed to, and yet he was still taking his duties as my scribe as seriously as he had from the start.

"Thank you," I whispered.

"For what?"

"For being a good companion and a faithful friend. I couldn't have done all this without you."

He paused, as though he hadn't expected my heartfelt praise. "Sounds like you're saying farewell."

It might very well be farewell, but I wouldn't dwell on that yet. "We'll get Aurora out in no time and be drinking hot ale by morning."

"Don't do anything foolhardy."

"You know me," I jested. "I never do anything foolhardy."

He didn't guffaw or tease back.

I started off. If I waited any longer, he'd suspect I had every intention of doing whatever it took to free Aurora. I couldn't have him tagging along trying to stop me. It was best if we parted ways here. I could only pray he wouldn't hold himself responsible if something happened to me.

Chapter
25

Aurora

Though the guards attempted to hurry me, I walked down the corridor carefully, trying not to disturb a hair on my head. After the servants had labored so meticulously over my appearance, I didn't want to ruin anything.

A clamor had arisen minutes earlier, with shouts and the pounding of steps in the corridor outside my chamber. Guards had appeared at my door, demanding that I accompany them. Though the maidservants complained that they needed more time, the guards had insisted, urgency marking their commands.

Now as we walked, the sconces lit the way through the long passageway, revealing stone walls and the same dark log ceiling beams that had been a part of the architecture of every room. Though I wasn't familiar with Queen Margery's royal residences, I'd long since guessed she'd brought me to one of her hunting lodges, likely the one at Boarshead Hunting Ground closest to Mercia's border.

Earlier, I'd marveled when I stood in front of the looking glass and examined my reflection. Though I'd glimpsed myself in the small mirror amongst my possessions at the cottage, I'd never seen myself in full, and certainly never so grandly attired.

After wearing simple peasant garb my whole life, the cascading layers of the rich blue skirt were heavy, almost cumbersome, the bodice tight and constricting, and the jewels heavy in my ears and hair. I would grow accustomed to such fancy attire eventually, but the contrast to my previous life made me wish for Kresten all the more.

A door opened abruptly to one side, and a girl darted into the middle of the corridor, forcing us to stop. "Aurora?"

A giant-of-a-guard from within her chamber rushed after her. "Your Highness, you know you're not allowed out."

"Please, just one moment." She smiled gently up at the man, who hesitated before he bowed his head.

I examined the girl, noting the resemblance to Queen Margery in her dark hair and green eyes. Rather than a slender build, she was stockier with a wider girth and broader face. Her features were comely but not dainty.

"Aurora, I am Ruby, your cousin."

"Ah, yes." Queen Margery had two daughters—Pearl, who was around my age, and Princess Ruby, her youngest child. I guessed her to be twelve or perhaps thirteen years. Before I could formulate the proper introduction in return, she tugged me from the corridor into her chamber, slammed the door closed behind her, and swiftly bolted it.

The guards we'd left behind began shouting and pounding.

Ruby grabbed my hands and dragged me across the room. "We must escape now. Through the window."

The shutters on the window ahead were wide open. Though too high for me to see outside, I could hear the shouts of more soldiers in the distance. I resisted Ruby's hold, drawing to a stop even as she continued to tug at me. "I do not believe your mother means me harm."

Ruby's eyes were frantic. "Mark my words, she intends to slay you."

I smoothed a hand over the silky skirt. "'Tis possible she intends to bargain for me, gaining the keys to the ancient treasure she has always wanted." 'Twas the conclusion I'd arrived at for why the queen had ordered such care be taken with my appearance. When the liaisons from Mercia's court arrived, she wanted them to see me as a regal queen, one worthy of trading for the keys.

The banging against the door intensified.

"No, Aurora." Ruby wrestled with me again, but I resisted, and she only moved me mere inches. "My mother wants your heart for her alchemy."

A shiver raced up my spine. "My heart?"

"She could not get Pearl's, though she desperately tried. And now you are her last hope."

The news of Queen Margery's attempts at alchemy didn't surprise me. My whole life I'd known she was experimenting with the white stone she'd inherited. However, I hadn't expected she'd become so twisted in her experimentations that she'd consider murdering her own daughter. Poor Pearl.

The ramming from the guards rattled the walls and shifted the hinges. Did the guards intend to break down the door to retrieve me?

"But why go to all this trouble if she plans to slay me?" I motioned toward myself, indicating the lovely ringlets that cascaded with jewels.

"She must have the heart of the fairest royal maiden in all the land for the alchemy to work. She is ensuring that you are indeed the fairest."

I didn't want to believe Ruby, but the earnestness in her tone and the pleading in her eyes left no doubt of her truthfulness. I needed no further urging. I didn't know all the details, nor did I need to know. My cousin was offering me an escape, and I must take it while I could.

"Make haste." She pushed me toward the window while she stopped to grab the stool at her dressing table. "We must go now. Something is happening, an onslaught of some kind. Perhaps my sister is coming for us."

I now understood the commotion and also the urgency of the soldiers in coming after me. If Pearl and her Scanian prince-husband were indeed attacking, then the queen likely feared she would lose the opportunity to claim my heart.

I shuddered at just how close I'd come to being led to my slaughter. And now I felt foolish for holding out hope Queen Margery might yet be swayed into seeing the error of her ways, that perhaps we might even learn to live at peace with each other.

With a burst of both frustration and panic, I joined Ruby in dragging the stool to the window.

"Up with you." My heart thudded with the need to

escape. "You go first."

"No, the queen does not intend to kill me tonight—"

"She will once she learns you have aided me." I picked the girl up and hoisted her onto the stool, giving her little choice in the matter. Then I folded my hands together to make a step. "Now go."

Ruby hesitated. At the crashing and splintering of wood behind us, we had mere seconds before the guards broke down the door.

Ruby placed her slippered foot into my hand, leapt upward, and grabbed the windowsill. From underneath, I pushed until she was all the way in the window. After a moment of writhing, she managed to situate herself and straddle the opening.

"Come on." She held her arm out toward me.

I climbed onto the stool and grabbed hold of her. With the first effort, I nearly toppled her from her perch. When she clasped the window frame for more leverage, I tried again, scrambling up the wall.

A final crash behind us was followed by rapid footsteps and shouts as guards entered the room. I didn't need to glance over my shoulder to know I was too late. I wouldn't make it.

"Go!" I called to Ruby, releasing her and dropping back to the stool. "Go now to the gatehouse, and maybe you can lower it so the others might reach me in time."

Soldiers grasped me from behind, but I resisted, twisting and shoving them away, hoping to distract them from Ruby, giving her a chance to drop down to the other side. When she disappeared, I lifted a silent prayer for her safety.

And then I allowed the soldiers to lead me away.

This time, I took no care with my gown or hair. I allowed them to push me along with haste, hoping that in the process my carefully made-up appearance would fall to pieces and I'd no longer be considered fair. 'Twas wishful, but I was desperate.

Much too soon, we arrived at an arched door with intricate engravings of biblical stories etched throughout. The guards opened the door to reveal a simple chapel with a few benches, a prayer rail with a cushion, and an altar at the front of the chancel. A cross made of ornate jewels hung on the wall above the altar, out of place in the otherwise rustic place of worship.

I wasn't surprised to find the queen there. She was kneeling at the railing, her head bent, and her long hair falling in a curtain around her. As the soldiers pushed me to the front, she didn't look up, seemingly unaware of my presence although, with the commotion, she had to know I was here.

Two monks who'd been standing in the shadows stepped forward, their hands tucked into the wide sleeves of their habits. "Tie her to the altar." The older monk with a gray tonsured ring nodded at a wooden table with the same type of engravings as the door.

I shuddered. Would I die upon the altar? Was this, then, my fate? To become an offering to the queen after so many years of trying to avoid her?

The cold fingers of panic gripped my throat, choking me. As I passed the queen, I had to make one last effort at bargaining for my freedom. "Stop this now. How will you be able to live with yourself if you follow through on slaying me to gain gold?"

She didn't lift her head.

I struggled against the guards again. "You may gain riches, but in the process you will lose your soul."

An engraved pedestal table was positioned near the prayer rail, a shining gold chest displayed on top. The lid was open, and inside I glimpsed a silvery-white stone no bigger than a human heart that almost seemed to glow with an otherworldly aura.

The cursed white stone.

I flailed against the guards with renewed energy and panic, but they were much stronger. Within moments, they laid me out on the table and tied my hands and legs to the table posts. Once I was secure, they stood back.

The queen finally arose. She shook back her long raven tresses and drew a fur cloak over her shoulders. "You are dismissed." She waved her jeweled fingers toward the soldiers. "Go join the others and make sure the Scanian princes and Princess Pearl do not cross the bridge into the fortress."

Ruby had been right. The lodge was under attack. Were they coming to my aid? If so, I feared they would be too late.

With a bow, the soldiers left the chapel, their heavy steps clanking an urgency that matched the tempo of my heartbeat. When the door closed behind them, I wanted to cry out, scream, plead, do anything to call them back. Instead, I forced myself to speak calmly. "My mother. What happened to make you hate her?"

"And who said anything about hate?" Her expression serene, the queen stepped into the chancel past the gold chest.

"What happened?" I persisted. If naught else, I would buy myself more time and pray that Pearl broke into the complex soon. "You were close growing up, were you not?"

"We were the best of friends." The queen rounded the table.

"You must have many fond memories of your times together."

"We were happy together ... until she turned against me."

"And how did she do that?"

The queen stopped beneath the jeweled cross. "She vowed we would let fate determine our inheritance, that no matter what our father decided, once he died, we would toss dice to divide up our share."

On the altar beside me, one of the priests unrolled a bundle containing knives in all shapes and sizes. I struggled against the ropes binding me, but they bit into my flesh where I was still raw from my previous binding.

The queen drew back a strand of my hair and positioned it by my cheek. "She knew as well as I did that our father favored her. Rather than getting the best, she agreed we would divide it equally."

"So my mother did not carry out her vow to you, and that is why you hate her—hate me?"

"She chose Father's wishes over mine."

The priest pulled out a long knife with a thin blade. It gleamed in the lantern light, and I shrank at the sight of it, pressing myself farther into the table.

I had to keep the queen talking. "Surely she had an explanation for why she chose to carry forth with your father's wishes."

"Of course, she claimed Father had divided the land and inheritance fairly and had wisely given us each what we needed. But in the end, she proved she cared more about him than me."

"And why is Mercia better than Warwick? Are they not both rich in resources?"

"Everyone has always known that nothing good ever comes from Warwick." The queen motioned for the priest to step forward. "I shall take Mercia and reunite the country, and in so doing, I shall prove to everyone, including my father, that I am a greater ruler than anyone who has ever come before or will come after. He will know I was the one most worthy of his love."

"How will he know this when he is dead? Your efforts are futile. You think that in proving yourself, you will find happiness? Alas, we can never truly be happy if we seek our own pleasure."

"I shall be happy enough."

"When you have alienated yourself from all of your family and anyone who cares about you? How can that bring happiness?"

She laughed, but the sound was cold and bitter. "And what do you know about real happiness? You, a mere child, who have been sheltered your whole life."

"I know enough to realize 'tis not the things we own or the places we live that give us meaning. 'Tis the things we do for God and for each other that matter most."

"Enough!" The queen motioned toward the priest, who raised the thin knife above me. "Nothing you say will sway me against my alchemy. I have been working toward this moment my entire reign. And from here on out, the world will remember me as the one who finally learned how to make gold."

I pinched my eyes closed and prepared for death.

Chapter
26

KRESTEN

THE INFIRMARY WAS DESERTED SAVE A LONE OLD SERVANT ASLEEP on a pallet. The noises from when I opened the window and dropped through hadn't awoken him. Or perhaps he was too ill to care. Whatever the case, I'd been able to make my way easily into the lodge. It was the traversing of the hallways that proved to be more difficult as servants and soldiers alike scurried everywhere.

The attack efforts at the gatehouse had thrown the queen's men into confusion. I hoped it was enough distraction that no one would stop to question my presence.

I crept along the west wing of the compound, checking each room, while Jorg and Chester were each in their hallways doing the same thing. One of us would find Aurora. She was here somewhere.

I just prayed we weren't too late.

At the slapping boots of another guard on the run, I ducked into the closest open doorway and hid out of sight, hardly daring to breathe. When the steps faded, I resumed my search through the deserted chambers. From the plainness of each one, I guessed the monks resided in this part of the lodge, where they could act as caretakers to the sick.

I paused before an ornately carved arched door. Was this the chapel? Of course, the monks would reside near a chapel to perform their duties there as well.

Carefully, I opened the door and peered inside. At the sight before me, my blood turned to ice. Aurora was tied on the altar, a priest standing above her, a knife poised above her heart.

"Stop!" I cried out.

The priest fumbled with the knife, his eyes widening at the sight of me. Next to him stood a second priest and a beautiful woman I assumed was the queen, and they, too, startled at my shout.

With my axe in one hand and my knife in the other, I sprinted down the aisle, the chill racing through me giving me an extra burst of speed and strength.

"Kresten?" Aurora strained her head to see me. "What are you doing here?"

I made it to the prayer rail before the queen reacted, grabbing another knife from the table in front of her and pressing the blade to Aurora's throat. "Halt! Or I'll slit her throat."

I froze as the blade pressed into Aurora's throat and drew blood.

"Drop your weapons," the queen commanded.

"Please. I beg of you." I lowered my knife and placed it on the prayer cushion. "Let's talk rationally about this."

"Kresten?" The queen held the blade so tightly that Aurora winced and closed her eyes.

"Yes, I am Kresten."

"I have had the delightful opportunity to meet your brothers." Her tone was derisive. "And now I am fortunate to meet the youngest Scanian prince."

Aurora's eyes flew open to meet mine. Confusion swirled in the beautiful violet-blue depths. While I'd discovered her true identity, she'd yet to learn mine.

"I am Prince Kresten, third-born son of King Christian of the Holberg kings." I didn't let my gaze waver from hers as I announced the truth. "Aurora, I'm sorry I did not tell you sooner."

The queen raised one elegant brow. "Then the two of you know each other?"

"I love Queen Aurora and will do anything to free her, even become your slave."

The queen's lips curved into a small smile. "How sweet of you."

I gauged Aurora's reaction and could see she understood what I hadn't told her, that I knew her identity already and was there to rescue her. Yes, I had a duty to my country to become the next king. But Aurora's life was more important than anything else, and I had to find a way to save her.

The knife against her throat didn't waver.

I tightened my grip on my axe, trying to decide if it would reach the queen and knock her back before she could make the slice that would end Aurora's life.

"Put your axe and sword down too," the queen said, as though sensing the direction of my thoughts.

"For what purpose? Either way you intend to slay Aurora. At the very least I shall kill you and put an end to your tyranny, ensuring you never have the chance to make gold."

Never have the chance to make gold.

The golden chest with the white stone sat within my grasp. If I destroyed the white stone, the queen would no longer have the means for carrying out her alchemy. She'd have no need for Aurora's heart.

I glanced at Aurora, who was watching me. I couldn't read her expression or her eyes, but I sensed she would want me to do whatever was necessary to end the queen's cruel use of the white stone. In so doing, I'd not only save Warwick and Mercia but other nations from the queen's threat.

With a nod at Aurora, one I hoped conveyed my love, I swiped the gold chest from the pedestal table, tipped it over, and let the stone hit the floor with a clatter.

Deny thyself. The challenge of my Testing resounded clearer than it ever had before. And I knew what I had to do.

"No!" Queen Margery yelled.

In the same moment, I swung my axe down with all my might, aiming for the center. As the blade connected, the stone shattered. A surge vibrated through the axe up into my torso, but I ignored it, flipped my axe over to the blunt end, and swung again and again with hard blows, the practice of many months holding me in good stead.

From the corner of my eye, I could see the queen racing around the table, followed by the priests. But each slam of the axe head was sure and swift, crushing the rock into hundreds of fragments that could never be put back together.

With every swing, the strange surge coursed through me, making me light-headed. When the queen shoved me a moment later, I toppled backward and fell to my knees on the prayer cushion. She paid me no heed and knelt above the shattered stone, crying out her dismay.

Dizziness hit me again, this time in a wave that sent my senses reeling, as though I were setting sail on a voyage upon a rough sea. I tried to push myself up. I needed to get to Aurora, cut her bindings, and usher her out of the chapel. She still wasn't safe. Even if the queen no longer needed Aurora's heart, she still had every reason to kill her in order to take control of Mercia.

I tried to climb up but couldn't make my muscles work. I was too tired.

Queen Margery's cries continued to rise into the air with increasing intensity. Aurora called out for help.

With every last ounce of strength I could muster, I grabbed on to the prayer railing and staggered to my feet. But the dizziness was too blinding. The only thing I could make out was Jorg sprinting down the aisle toward me with Chester on his heels.

"Save Aurora." My voice was breathless and tight, as though the sea had swallowed me and wouldn't allow me to speak.

Jorg paused by my side, his keen gaze sweeping over me. For once, I was glad he couldn't see the extent of my injuries. "Go on. Save her," I managed. "And lock up the queen."

In an instant, he disarmed the queen and twisted her arms behind her back while the priests cowered against the wall. Chester was already at the altar cutting away Aurora's bindings.

The blackness of the depths rose within me, and I could no longer fight it off. Now that Aurora was safe, I could go to the grave in peace.

Chapter 27

Aurora

I pushed up from the altar and threw my arms around Chester. He hugged me hard in return. "Thank you, Chester." Tears spilled down my cheeks.

"None of that now." Chester drew back and ripped a piece of linen from his cloak. "We're not free yet."

I swiped at my cheeks as he lifted the linen to the cut at my neck.

Kresten took a step toward us. His cornflower-blue eyes met mine. Though clouded, they were full of love. For me. I didn't understand his revelation about being a prince, and I didn't understand how he'd come to be here at the lodge in the middle of rescuing me. But none of it mattered.

What mattered was that we were both safe.

Chester helped me down from the altar, and I started toward Kresten, needing to feel his arms about me more than anything. But he wavered, closed his eyes, and crumpled, almost hitting his head on the prayer railing.

I couldn't contain a half gasp, half scream. Chester bolted toward Kresten, laying him out and turning him on his back. He put his fingers against Kresten's neck. And as I knelt next to them, Chester slapped Kresten's cheeks. "Come on. Just giving you a little of that loving care you gave me after crossing the pit."

Kresten didn't move.

Chester glanced around and then froze at the sight of the golden box and crushed stone all around it on the floor with Kresten's axe in the middle of the debris.

Chester's shoulders sagged. "Ah lad, what did you do?"

"He crushed the stone," I answered for Kresten. His swift thinking and his distracting the queen had saved my life.

Chester's head dipped lower. He laid a hand over Kresten's heart and didn't move.

The queen's lamenting had grown silent. Jorg was in the process of binding her hands behind her back. She continued to gaze at the golden box and the place on the floor where the white stone spread out in hundreds of small pieces. "He destroyed it. The fool."

"The power of the white stone is gone?" I asked hopefully.

"It's gone," Chester replied gravely, "but so is he."

I stiffened. "What do you mean?"

"Anyone who touches the white stone dies." The queen spat the words, bitterness punctuating each one.

"He did not touch it," I protested. "He merely hit it with his axe."

"It doesn't matter the method," she replied. "The only way the stone can be rendered useless is if someone crushes it. In doing so, they will surely succumb to the slumber of death. But how could he know such information? So few do . . ."

"I knew. And I told him." Chester straightened one of Kresten's arms. "This is my fault."

From where Jorg stood behind the queen, his expression was stricken. "No, it's my fault. When we parted ways, his farewell was too final. I should have stayed with him."

"I hold neither of you responsible." As much as I wanted to fall across Kresten and weep for all that had happened, I couldn't allow his sacrifice to be in vain. We had to finish this fight against the queen, and that meant lowering the drawbridge and allowing Pearl and the rest of the attackers inside.

I pressed Chester's hand. My heart was breaking inside, but outwardly I kept myself composed. I had to. If Kresten could sacrifice himself to put an end to the queen's alchemy not only for my sake but for all people, then I could surely find the strength to do the same. "As much as we shall grieve for Kresten, we must go now and bring swift victory to Mercia."

He bowed his head. "Your Majesty." When he rose, he looked at me with a new respect I'd never seen there before. And I understood then that respect was something one earned a little at a time with courageous feats in the face of fear.

I retrieved Kresten's sword. "We shall take the queen with us and have her order her men to stand down and open the gate. If she refuses to comply, we shall slay her."

At my order, Chester and Jorg ushered the queen between them out of the chapel. I followed on their heels, pausing in the doorway to gaze back at Kresten and fight down the tears that I wouldn't allow. Not yet. Not until I had privacy and could weep for the loss of the only man I would ever love.

As we made our way into the courtyard, Chester stopped in the center and held his torch high so it illuminated Queen Margery as well as me. "Your fight is over," he called.

Several of the guards standing at the arrow loops in the gatehouse wall turned. And at the sight of Queen Margery bound as our prisoner, they took aim at us with their arrows. In an instant, Chester had his knife out and against Queen Margery's throat while Jorg shoved me to the rear out of harm's way.

I stepped around him and raised Kresten's sword, unwilling to cower and needing these men to see me as the strong woman I wanted to be. Though I still had much to learn, I could start here and now. "Your queen is vanquished!"

My call drew the attention of more guards, and within seconds they were all facing us, their weapons still poised to fight but surprise registering on their faces nonetheless.

"If you lay down your weapons and cease fighting," I called, "I shall spare you and the queen your lives. If not, you will force me to a bloodbath, starting with your queen."

Silence descended over the crowd of soldiers. Behind them, a figure darted out from the shadows of a nearby building and slunk along the perimeter toward the gatehouse. Ruby. I needed to buy her another moment or two to climb into the tower and release the lever that would lower the bridge.

"I am Queen Aurora Leandra Floretta, the true queen of Mercia, the granddaughter of the greatest king the Great Isle has ever known, King Alfred the Peacemaker. I shall take my rightful throne, and it will not be denied me by anyone, especially not this woman." I pointed the sword at Queen Margery, who peered ahead, her chin held high and her eyes haughty.

The soldiers remained quiet, their gazes upon the queen, waiting for her orders.

"Tell them to cease fighting," Chester growled, shoving her.

"I will die first," she hissed.

"If that is what you wish." Chester tilted her head back farther and positioned the blade.

I hoped the soldiers would see reason, would realize Margery could no longer be their queen. They had no loyalty to so cruel a queen, did they? "Choose this day peace between Mercia and Warwick forevermore. If you do, I shall return to Mercia with no thought of taking Warwick for myself the way Queen Margery has always envied Mercia. I shall even allow you your own king. Prince Ethelbard will take over ruling the country in his mother's stead, and she will be locked away where she can do no more harm for the rest of her days."

Several of the guards lowered their weapons. I waited for more to do so, the silence stretching.

Suddenly, a clicking and creaking rent the night air. The soldiers glanced around trying to place the noise before realizing, as I did, that it was coming from the chains lowering the drawbridge.

Ruby had done it. I let some of the tension ease from my body, knowing we may still have a bloody battle ahead if the soldiers continued to resist surrendering.

The closest guards bounded toward the tower, likely intent upon keeping the bridge from falling in its entirety.

But it was too late. The momentum downward went much too quickly, and the bridge landed upon the opposite side of the ditch with a bang that reverberated and cracked the beams. Some pieces fell into the pit below, but regardless of its sturdiness, those on the opposite side charged across with the cries of battle.

As they spilled into the courtyard, Queen Margery's soldiers must have realized they were defeated. While several lifted swords to engage in fighting, the rest lowered themselves to their knees and placed their weapons in front of them in the symbol of surrender.

My heart swelled as I watched our troops stand back and cease their fighting, thankful that we'd come to a peaceful resolution.

I was surprised at how many soldiers continued to cross the drawbridge and pour into the courtyard. With numerous blazing torches lighting up the complex, I caught sight of Pearl hugging Ruby, swaying back and forth, both of them crying. And I was glad for their reunion, wishing Pearl could become Warwick's next ruler instead of Ethelbard. But I would only anger Warwick if I attempted to usurp their tradition of primogeniture going to the oldest son instead of the oldest child.

Behind Pearl, I caught a glimpse of two warrior-like men with the same broad shoulders and tall build as Kresten. I guessed they were his brothers, the other princes of Scania who'd come to the Great Isle for their Testing. They were all handsome men with a strong family resemblance.

What would they say when they learned their brother had sacrificed his life so everyone else could have freedom?

Ill and overcome at the thought of losing Kresten, I grabbed Jorg's arm. "Take me to Kresten. Please."

Jorg nodded, his expression grave. After whispered words with Chester, he led me back into the complex, but not without several of Chester's guards accompanying us. As we reached the chapel, we found Kresten lying where we'd left him, unmoving. I rushed inside, my heart thudding a misery I hadn't allowed myself to feel until this moment.

I dropped to my knees beside him and did what I'd longed to do since the instant he fell. I threw myself over him and let silent tears wet his cloak. Beneath my cheek, I could hear the soft thud of his heartbeat and feel the gentle rise and fall of his chest.

He was still alive.

But if Chester was correct about the slumber of death, then Kresten would remain asleep forever, until he died.

I held him at length, until I became conscious that others were in the room. I straightened from him, seeing first Pearl and Ruby kneeling on the opposite side of Kresten. Pearl's expression was somber as she reached for my hand and squeezed it. Ruby did likewise.

"I am truly sorry," Pearl said softly. "I know your loss is great. But Prince Kresten is a hero for his sacrifice."

I nodded and wiped the moisture from my cheeks. At the sight of Kresten's brothers nearby, I stood and walked toward them with as much dignity as I could. Upon reaching them, they both bowed, kissed my hand, and introduced themselves.

"He saved my life," I said, "and in destroying the white stone, I believe he saved many more people from experiencing heartache."

"I believe this as well." Prince Mikkel, the brother with the fairer hair had a leader's authority about him. He was Pearl's husband, and they made a handsome pair.

"If it pleases you," Prince Vilmar said with a sad smile, "we shall make him comfortable for the duration of our stay here while we make arrangements for his transport back to Scania."

I wanted to deny his request, but to do so would be foolish. I needed to return to Mercia and take my place at court as queen. Erelong, I would wed the man chosen for me. And I couldn't delay simply because I was brokenhearted.

Kresten had shown us all that we must oft do hard things—even impossible things. If I would be a queen worthy of Mercia's throne, then I must do this hard— impossible—thing and let him go so his family could care for him as they rightly should and so I could get on with my life as queen as I rightly should.

Chapter
28

Aurora

"We must go, Your Majesty," Chester said from the doorway of Kresten's chamber.

I'd hardly moved from the chair beside his bed over the past two days since he'd destroyed the stone and we'd captured Queen Margery.

Even now, I clasped his hand, unwilling to part ways. Vilmar and his bride, Gabriella, planned to travel with Kresten and attend to him. They would take Kresten south to the closest river, and from there they would go by boat to the East Sea before they sailed to Scania.

In the meantime, Mikkel and Pearl had already left for Kensington with a large contingent of knights to deliver Queen Margery to the capital city. From there they would take her to a remote mountain fortress where she would be locked in a tower for the rest of her days. Mikkel and Pearl intended to stay in Kensington until Ethelbard's coronation, then sail back to Scania with Ruby.

I'd learned Mikkel and Vilmar had both abdicated their claim to the throne because they'd given up their Testing before the six-month commitment ended. As a result, Kresten had been the first in line to become king. According to his brothers, Kresten had never aspired to be king the way they had, but he'd taken it upon himself to attempt to finish his Testing and do his duty for his country.

Now that Kresten was unconscious in a sleep of death, the Scanian Lagting would have to decide between Mikkel and Vilmar. But since neither had finished their Testing and both had married without permission, they feared the censure that awaited them upon their return.

I brushed a kiss against Kresten's listless hand and thought back to the days in the cottage when I'd sat beside his bed many an hour. And now, this would be the last time I'd ever be able to do so. Though I'd contemplated visiting him in Scania in the future, how could I? How would I explain a desire for another man to my husband? Even if I never loved my husband, I resolved to do my best to remain faithful and true. I couldn't do that if I clung to Kresten.

This had to be farewell.

I forced myself to stand.

Aunt Elspeth slipped her arm around my waist. "Oh my sweeting," she said with a gentle squeeze. "I always knew he was a special man. Right special, I said."

I nodded even as I leaned more heavily upon her.

"He should have told us he was a prince," Aunt Idony remarked dryly as she rolled up a scroll she'd been reading from among those she'd discovered in the monks' chambers of the lodge.

My two dear aunts had ridden in the morn after our victory, led by several dozen of Mercia's best knights who were now waiting to escort me to Delsworth.

"If we'd known he was a prince," Aunt Idony continued, "maybe we wouldn't have worried so much."

She was just trying to make me feel better, and I loved her for it. However, even if we'd known Kresten's identity from the start, our relationship had been doomed. We would have been in an impossible situation with my needing to return to Mercia and become queen and his departing for Scania to take up the kingship.

"The men are eager to be leaving," Chester said, his tone tight with impatience. Outfitted in his elite knight armor, he was an imposing figure. He'd proven himself to me time and again, even if he did still irritate me.

"I need a moment of privacy." I straightened my shoulders and faced him, lifting my chin and daring him to resist granting me a final farewell.

He scowled. "Fine. One more minute."

"Two."

He heaved a sigh of exasperation.

"Alone, please." I glanced to Aunt Elspeth and Aunt Idony.

Aunt Elspeth hurried across the room, fanning her flushed face. "Of course, dear heart, of course." As she exited, I held back a smile. Surely the dear woman didn't think I still needed a chaperone, not at a time like this.

Aunt Idony's steps were slower and more calculated, and when she reached the doorway, she paused. "Your Majesty, a legend has been passed down amongst the healers who have come and gone from St. Cuthbert's. The legend says that true love's kiss is the strongest weapon for fighting the battle with death."

"True love's kiss?"

"If you truly love someone more than you love yourself, then a kiss filled with that love may have the power to bring life where there is none." She bowed her head and then motioned to the few other remaining servants, who followed after her, leaving me alone.

Once the door closed, a sob slipped out before I could hold it back. I'd done well keeping my emotions in check, but now that I was alone and had no need of pretense, I could let my sorrow loose, couldn't I?

I looked down on Kresten's handsome face, his features so peaceful and relaxed, just as they'd been so oft when we'd spent time together. His lips even seemed to be slightly turned up into one of his winning smiles.

With a glance to the door to make sure I was alone, I lifted my hand to his cheek and traced the scratchy stubble there before I moved to his forehead and brushed a wisp of his hair back. Then I grazed his fine nose and tentatively skimmed his lips.

Did I dare kiss him?

I'd relived the kisses we'd shared in the woods dozens of times. They were embedded into my memory. A kiss now would be nothing like it. But I wanted to do it to say farewell.

I bent over him, leaning in toward his face until I was only a handbreadth away. His form under the covers was so still, so silent. And yet I could hear his laughter and teasing like a whisper taunting me with what could nevermore be.

After casting another glance toward the door to ensure privacy, I closed the distance and pressed my lips to Kresten's. I expected them to be cold and lifeless and was surprised to find them warm and pliable.

I pressed both of my hands against his cheeks and kissed him more deeply, loving him with every breath and heartbeat. I thought I felt him respond, lift up, and move in tune to my kiss, but when I pulled away a moment later, he was as still and silent as he'd been since we'd laid him in the chamber.

True love's kiss? The strongest weapon for fighting the battle with death?

I would try one more time. One more kiss. And in it I would pour out all the love for him I could. "Kresten," I whispered. "You are the only man I have loved and will ever love. You have my heart, soul, and body."

I touched my lips to his again, willing him to feel my love, to know how much I needed and wanted him. Again, as before, I could feel him stirring, his kiss melding with mine. At least, I didn't think I was imagining it. I lingered, kissing him longer than I knew I ought to but hoping the kiss would awaken him this time.

When I pulled back, I kept my eyes closed, praying that when I opened them, his blue eyes would be peering up at me and he'd give me one of his easy smiles.

Slowly, I pried one eye open and then the other. Disappointment coursed through me. His face, his expression, his coloring—they were all unchanged. His steady breathing and the slow beat of his heart remained the same.

I stood, frustration rippling through me. So much for true love's kiss. Aunt Idony's legend was just that— a legend, better off left unspoken rather than lending false hope.

"Farewell, Kresten." I smoothed my hand across his forehead again. Then I spun and stalked from the room. I had to leave before it became too hard to force myself to walk away.

Chapter 29

KRESTEN

THE SLEEP OF DEATH WAS PEACEFUL, EVEN BEAUTIFUL, AND I didn't want to wake up, didn't want it to end. It was unlike anything I'd known, almost as though I were residing in a little place of heaven and earth at the same time.

Until the kisses . . .

I wasn't sure how I'd known Aurora was there, only that I had. When she'd kissed me the first time, I'd seemed to come out of a trance and into the reality that I was in bed and she was standing above me, holding my cheeks and kissing me with every part of her heart.

When she'd finished, I'd tried to lift my hands and grab her back. I'd wanted to pull her down and kiss her again and again. But I hadn't been able to move and let her know I was aware she was kissing me. That I wasn't oblivious.

She'd pulled away, and I'd despaired she'd leave before I could try opening my eyes. And then before I'd known what was happening, she was over me again, kissing me and whispering words I'd never believed I would hear again: "*You are the only man I have loved and will ever love. You have my heart, soul, and body.*"

Why hadn't I been able to awaken and tell her she was the only woman I have loved and would ever love? That she had my heart, soul, and body?

Frustration had rolled through me and stayed to torment me since those kisses. I didn't know how much time had passed, but I sensed many days, perhaps even weeks, had come and gone.

Then one day I knew I was home in Scania. I felt it in my mother's touch, her hand upon mine, her soft weeping above me. And still, all I could think about was Aurora's kisses. They beckoned to me louder every passing day until I began to cry out and thrash in my bed.

I heard the whispers of the servants, heard the concern of the physicians, and realized they believed I was in pain and would soon die. Little did they know it was not my body but my heart that was broken.

My mother's kind voice and soothing touch had the power to calm me. And surprisingly, so did Vilmar's and Mikkel's voices. Through all of the trials we'd experienced during those last days in Warwick, I'd come to realize that somehow I'd earned my brothers' respect, and that by sacrificing my life, I'd done something they likely wouldn't have been able to do . . . at least that's what both of them had whispered to me when they'd sat beside my bed.

I suspected they didn't know I could hear every word they spoke, or they might have been more careful. But as it was, I'd learned the Lagting had read through all of the scribes' journals from our Testing. Even though Vilmar and Mikkel had abandoned the Testing and hadn't finished the prescribed amount of time, they'd earned great esteem for how they'd conducted themselves and the lessons they'd learned during the process.

They'd relayed to me all the Lagting had said about my time in Inglewood Forest. While the first part of my Testing had been uneventful, they believed I'd more than made up for my slow progress when I'd rescued Queen Aurora and brought about the end to the cursed white stone.

My father had come in once, shortly after I'd arrived home. He'd gripped my hand. I'd felt his tears fall upon my face. Then he'd whispered words I'd longed to hear my whole life: "You have made me proud."

He'd gone, and he hadn't come back. Vilmar had talked about how hard it was for Father to see me in this state. And I hadn't begrudged my father his absence, not after the love I'd felt in that moment.

"The Lagting will decide on the morrow whether Mikkel or I shall be the next king," Vilmar said quietly from my bedside. "I have been thinking long and hard about it, and I've always known Mikkel is the best choice."

Yes, I'd known that too. Mikkel would make a good king. He'd been born to lead, and with Pearl by his side, they would do great things for Scania.

"I told you that Pearl was able to negotiate the return of Gabriella's estate and fortune, didn't I?" Vilmar paused as though he expected me to answer.

I wanted to, tried to. But I couldn't get my tongue to work or my mouth to open.

"At one time, her father was the wealthiest nobleman in Warwick. Queen Margery's sister-in-law, the Duchess of Burgundy, was given the estate and squandered Gabi's father's wealth after his death. Fortunately, Pearl convinced Ethelbard to pay Gabriella back for what she lost. And now King Ethelbard has requested that I reside in Warwick as Scania's ambassador. We shall stay at the estate in Rockland for part of the year and travel home to Scania for the other half."

I wanted to tell Vilmar I was genuinely pleased for him, that he was made to be an ambassador. People always liked him because he smoothed over difficult situations when no one else could. In the end, he would be happier in his role as a peacemaker than as king.

"Curly has agreed to be the steward of Rockland and will live there year-round with his wife, Molly. And Gabriella has opened the estate to any of the former slaves who need a new home. She's so kind and generous to everyone."

His voice contained admiration. I wanted to remind him of his own generosity in building a safe place for Grendel to live here in Scania. After Lord Kennard had safely and securely delivered the berserker, Vilmar hadn't wanted the madman to languish in the dungeons for the rest of his days, so he had begun to build a prison that was more humane in nature.

Not to be outdone, Mikkel had offered his friends from the Isle of Outcasts a new home in Scania, places to live and labor where they wouldn't face censure. He'd already begun advocating for them as well, dispelling long-held superstitions and promoting the need for people to accept differences.

A moment of silence prevailed, and I found myself growing agitated, needing Aurora, needing another one of her kisses, needing to be with her forever. If only I could say it, if only I could tell one of my brothers or my mother to send a missive inviting her to come.

"You know what's hilarious?" Vilmar laid his hand upon my arm, and the touch brought my thrashing to an end. "I wish you were awake to hear this. Because you'd laugh, and I'd sure like to hear that sound again . . ." His voice trailed off with sadness.

He cleared his throat. "Father and the Lagting had arranged a marriage between you and Queen Aurora. Of course, they'd never expected you to finish first in the Testing. They'd always assumed they'd marry a charming man like you to a foreign queen in order to make a good alliance."

Vilmar was right. I would have laughed if I'd been able to. How was it possible Aurora and I had spent those weeks at the cottage together not knowing our advisors had already arranged our marriage? How might things have changed if we'd known?

The truth was, I wouldn't have wanted anything to detract from the simple pleasure of knowing each other for who we were rather than for our noble titles.

"Mercia's ambassador arrived earlier in the week to cancel the arrangement—"

"No."

Vilmar stood, knocking over his chair. He was silent for a long moment. "Mercia's ambassador arrived earlier in the week—"

"No." The word came out of my mouth again, a hoarse whisper. "Do not cancel the arrangement."

Vilmar dropped to the edge of the bed, pressed his face against my chest, and wept.

I opened my eyes to discover I was under the great canopy of my bed in my chamber in Bergenborg Castle. I found that I could lift my hand, and I placed it on Vilmar's head. And when he raised his face a moment later to look at me, I managed a smile even as tears coursed down my cheeks too.

Within hours, I was sitting up in bed. By the next morn, I'd managed to take some steps. And by afternoon, I was ravenously hungry, and the servants brought me a feast in bed.

I had visitors nonstop, and I was more than eager to hug my mother and kiss my father's hand. Both of my brothers and their wives visited me often, as did old friends. Jorg was a constant companion, and I learned he hadn't left my chamber since I'd been moved there after the voyage of many weeks.

But amidst the good-natured teasing and friendly camaraderie, I couldn't shake the unsettled feeling of needing Aurora. When my father, brothers, and the Lagting filed into my room late in the day, the feeling only deepened.

They circled my bed. The thirteen men from the Lagting wore their long, white robes trimmed with lynx and fox fur. Most had white hair and white beards—to reflect their age and wisdom. My father stood at the center, his rugged countenance, broad frame, and light-blue eyes so much like all of his sons. Even at his age, he was still an impressive and handsome man.

"You know why we have gathered here today, Prince Kresten?" my father asked solemnly.

"Yes, Your Majesty."

"You outlasted your brothers in the Testing and so have earned the right to become the next king of Scania—"

"With all due respect, Your Majesty." I pushed myself

up farther in bed. I had to speak up now, or I'd lose the opportunity forever. "The Lagting was willing to bestow upon Mikkel or Vilmar the crown just yesterday. Why not today?"

My father's brow rose. "You suffered from a sleeping illness."

"But if the Lagting was willing to give the crown to one of my brothers yesterday, then they should also consider them yet today. Though they did not finish their Testing in the prescribed manner, they finished it in their hearts in all the ways that truly matter. And that is what the Lagting should consider."

Mikkel's brows shot up, making him look identical to our father, and I almost smiled. I squelched my humor, knowing no one would listen to me if I made this moment into a jest. And now, more than ever, I needed them to take me seriously.

"If I may speak freely, Your Majesty?" I asked.

My father cocked his head, as though seeing me, truly seeing me for the first time. "Very well, Prince Kresten. Speak freely."

"Mikkel should be the next king of Scania. He is ready, willing, and able to take on the role. He was born a leader and will continue to make Scania into a great nation." At my declaration, murmuring broke out amongst the men. Mikkel's face registered surprise, and again I had to stifle my humor at his expression.

"Vilmar, on the other hand," I continued louder, "is ready and willing to become an ambassador to other nations."

Vilmar smiled slightly at my bold statement. I'd told him already that I'd heard everything he and Mikkel had spoken to me over the past weeks. His response had been to punch me in the arm.

"He will be a good ambassador, first to Warwick and then to other nations as needed. He is a born peacemaker and will make Scania proud."

My father's brows rose higher with each of my pronouncements. And the Lagting's murmuring grew louder.

"I, Prince Kresten, was made to form an alliance with a neighboring country. With my marriage to Mercia's Queen Aurora, I shall solidify the ongoing peace and prosperity between our two nations that Mother started when she married you." Joanna, as the youngest sister of King Alfred the Peacemaker, had begun the alliance. And now I would be honored to continue it.

By the time I'd finished, everyone was talking. I sat back against the cushions at the headboard, attempting to look relaxed, but inside, I was twisted into a dozen knots. I'd already spoken to Mercia's ambassador earlier in the day and urged him to wait to make a decision about cancelling the betrothal until I met with the Lagting. He'd been hesitant, since he'd been given strict orders to sail directly to Norland from Scania and make arrangements with one of the princes there.

After a few moments more of arguing, my father raised his hand. The Lagting's discussion tapered to silence. And when he had everyone's attention, the king nodded at me, a new look of respect in his eyes. "Prince Kresten has spoken wisely. We will do as he says."

Most of the men nodded in agreement, and I released a soft breath of relief. The discussion continued around me, but I couldn't focus, could only think of Aurora.

When the Lagting filed out of the chamber, my father stopped at the side of my bed and peered down at me with his serious eyes. "Let us be clear on one thing. I always believed you would make a worthy king for Scania. Your wise decision in this matter of kingship proves it. Now you must go and be a worthy king for Mercia."

"I will, Your Majesty."

As he strode out of the room, tears stung the backs of my eyes. I would do my best to be a worthy king and worthy husband. Now I just needed to make sure Mercia and her queen would still have me.

Chapter 30

Aurora

I stood rigidly at the front of the cathedral. **My father** and other members of the royal court had assembled to witness my betrothal ceremony. In the four months since All Saints' Day and my coronation, I'd been dreading this day.

I faced the nave and the doors at the back of the cathedral, my nerves tensing more with every passing moment. Though the early March sunshine was bright as it cascaded through the long stained-glass windows, I could take no pleasure in the beauty of the colorful glass or the arched ceilings and massive colonnades as I had the other times I'd come to worship.

I could also take no pleasure in the elegant gown I wore, one that spilled over in thick layers, the train filling the floor around me. I'd chosen the cornflower-blue color in memory of the flowers I'd picked so often in the woodland around the cottage. But now the color served to remind me of the crowns Kresten and I had woven, crowns I'd rather be wearing than the circlet of gold and pearls.

Only that morn, before allowing my maidservants to attend to my needs, I'd finally folded up and set aside the scarf Kresten had given me. I'd worn it underneath my garments every day since then. And though I'd loathed to part from it, I'd known I couldn't meet my future husband wearing another man's token.

Mercia's ambassador had been gone for weeks working out the details of my betrothal. The first prince my father had chosen was now unavailable, and so the ambassador had been traveling to make new arrangements, which had taken more time due to the constraints of winter.

I'd wanted to tell my father and his advisors I would rather remain single than wed a man I didn't love. But I had to do my duty as queen. I must put my country and people first, just as I'd been doing over the past months.

Even if I'd wanted to delay this moment of meeting my intended, the joy I was experiencing in my new role as queen would surely carry me through the days ahead. Though I hadn't been able to travel far during the winter months, I'd made a point of visiting smaller villages and hamlets close to Delsworth, always with my ladies-in-waiting and always with an escort of knights, including Chester. I'd relished the opportunity to see the countryside and meet people, stopping often, entering their humble cottages, and listening to their concerns.

I had no trouble interacting with them on their level nor they with me. I realized, then, that one more blessing had come of living all those years as a peasant. I could relate to the people as no other could. I understood their problems intimately. And I truly cared about helping them through the difficulties.

One of the first issues I'd addressed was their desire to put an end to the threat of basilisks. I'd given Chester the task of eradicating them from Inglewood Forest and the surrounding areas. I had every confidence Chester would be able to accomplish the feat.

I'd recently heard that they'd started calling me the People's Queen, because I was one of them. And when I'd heard the name, I'd realized God was using my inadequacies and insecurities in a way I'd never anticipated. I was becoming the queen God had planned, one unlike anyone else, one based on my unique strengths.

I was eager for the spring thaw, when I'd be able to sail up the Cress River and visit the industrial towns and mines in the Iron Hills. I loved my country and loved being able to fulfill my destiny as queen.

Even so, through all the visiting and meeting people, an emptiness remained, a spot that would always be reserved for Kresten.

As the double doors in the nave swung open, I tensed so much that Father, who was standing at my side, touched my arm gently. "Aurora, my dear, if you do not like him, you are not bound to wed him. Have I not assured you of this many times?"

Being with my father again was another joy of becoming queen. The past months had been filled with love, laughter, and many conversations. Even now, as he regarded me with his kind eyes, I smiled at him in return.

Tall and regal and with a dignified countenance, my

father had served as my regent these many years without once considering taking the throne for himself. As a result, I respected him even more for his loyalty and wisdom. "And I have told you, Father dear, it does not matter who I marry as long as he is good and kind like you."

As the ambassador entered, I couldn't keep from stiffening again. Who would he bring? And even after everything I'd just told my father, could I truly make myself go through with the betrothal?

I twisted my hands together, staring at them and wishing for a bouquet of wildflowers from my garden behind the cottage. What I wouldn't give at this moment to hold something in my hands.

"Oh dear heart, oh dear heart." At Aunt Elspeth's gasp from where she stood in the front row, I cringed. What was wrong with my future husband that my aunt would react this way?

I finally peeked up, chancing a small glance. The man stood in the doorway, leaning casually against the frame as though waiting for my attention. Arms and feet crossed nonchalantly. A lazy smile on his face. And silvery-blue eyes that could light the darkest night.

I squealed and cupped my hands over my mouth. Then without thought to being a queen of one of the greatest nations on earth, I ran. I ran as fast as I could toward the man I loved.

With a growing grin, he pushed away from the door and waited for me.

When I reached him, I flung myself into his arms. I didn't care that I was laughing and crying or that my courtiers were staring at me and likely murmuring about my unruly behavior. All I cared about was being in Kresten's arms.

He squeezed me tightly as though he might never let go.

Finally, I tugged back. "How? When? What happened?" I couldn't get my voice to work properly, especially as he gazed down at me with eyes full of love.

"I'm here to marry you, if you'll have me."

"You're the one arranged for me?"

"Yes. And I couldn't have picked a better match myself."

I smiled through my tears of joy. "But I thought you were dying in the sleep of death."

Over my head, he looked at Aunt Idony standing speechless next to Aunt Elspeth and winked at her. "There's something called true love's kiss. I've heard it's the strongest weapon for fighting the battle with death. That if you truly love someone more than you love yourself, then a kiss filled with that love may have the power to bring life where there is none."

Wonder blossomed inside me. "You heard Aunt Idony?"

"And I heard you. I think you said I'm the only man you have loved and will ever love. Is that still true?"

"It is." It was more than true. "You still have my heart, soul, and body."

"Then I pledge to you this day to give you the same."

I wrapped my arms around him again, and he drew me into another embrace. "Why don't we just skip the betrothal and get married today?"

Heat rose in my cheeks. "I am agreeable." Heartily

so, but I couldn't say that.

"And before we do anything else, could I have another one of true love's kisses? Just to make certain it worked?"

His roguish grin made my heart patter hard, and before he could say anything more, I rose to my toes and kissed him with all the love that I had, love that had the power to bring life where there had been none.

As he kissed me in return, my heart thrilled that somehow, someway, God had brought us through the testing fires to this place where we could finally be together. I hadn't believed it even possible. And though the future would still be full of challenges, I would rule alongside the man I loved. We would serve the people well. Together.

Jody Hedlund is the best-selling author of over forty books and is the winner of numerous awards. She writes sweet historical romances with plenty of sizzle. Find out more at jodyhedlund.com.

More Sweet Medieval Romance from Jody Hedlund

The Fairest Maidens

Beholden

Upon the death of her wealthy father, Lady Gabriella is condemned to work in Warwick's gem mine. As she struggles to survive the dangerous conditions, her kindness and beauty shine as brightly as the jewels the slaves excavate. While laboring, Gabriella plots how to avenge her father's death and stop Queen Margery's cruelty.

Beguiled

Princess Pearl flees for her life after her mother, Queen Margery, tries to have her killed during a hunting expedition. Pearl finds refuge on the Isle of Outcasts among criminals and misfits, disguising her face with a veil so no one recognizes her. She lives for the day when she can return to Warwick and rescue her sister, Ruby, from the queen's clutches.

Besotted

Queen Aurora of Mercia has spent her entire life deep in Inglewood Forest, hiding from Warwick's Queen Margery, who seeks her demise. As the time draws near for Aurora to take the throne, she happens upon a handsome woodcutter. Although friendship with outsiders is forbidden and dangerous, she cannot stay away from the charming stranger.

The Lost Princesses

Always: Prequel Novella

On the verge of dying after giving birth to twins, the queen of Mercia pleads with Lady Felicia to save her infant daughters. With the castle overrun by King Ethelwulf's invading army, Lady Felicia vows to do whatever she can to take the newborn princesses and their three-year-old sister to safety, even though it means sacrificing everything she holds dear, possibly her own life.

Evermore

Raised by a noble family, Lady Adelaide has always known she's an orphan. Little does she realize she's one of the lost princesses and the true heir to Mercia's throne . . . until a visitor arrives at her family estate, reveals her birthright as queen, and thrusts her into a quest for the throne whether she's ready or not.

Foremost

Raised in an isolated abbey, Lady Maribel desires nothing more than to become a nun and continue practicing her healing arts. She's carefree and happy with her life . . . until a visitor comes to the abbey and reveals her true identity as one of the lost princesses.

Hereafter

Forced into marriage, Emmeline has one goal—to escape. But Ethelrex takes his marriage vows seriously, including his promise to love and cherish his wife, and he has no intention of letting Emmeline get away. As the battle for the throne rages, will the prince be able to win the battle for Emmeline's heart?

Knights of Brethren

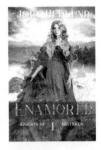

Enamored

Having been raised by her childless aunt and uncle, the king and queen, Princess Elinor finds herself the only heir to the throne of Norvegia. As she comes of age, she must choose a husband to rule beside her, but she struggles to make her selection from among a dozen noblemen during a weeklong courtship.

Entwined

After growing up on a remote farm, Lis learns she is the rightful heir to the throne of Norvegia. Even as she does her part to thwart a dangerous plot against the king, she resists pursuing her new identity and resigns herself to a simple life helping her elderly father with their farm.

Ensnared

Nursemaid to the Earl of Likness's two young daughters, Mikaela despises the earl for his cruelty to his subjects, and she longs for the day when she can make a difference in the lives of her suffering friends and family.

Enriched

Lady Karina lives in a convent and expects to become a nun someday. When her wealthy father asks her to help his textile business become more successful by marrying one of the popular Knights of Brethren, Karina complies, ever the dutiful daughter.

Enflamed

When Sylvi Prestegard discovers that her father has arranged for her to marry a wealthy nobleman known for his thieving ways, she's desperate to avoid the union. She turns to her childhood friend Espen, a Knight of Brethren, counting on his loyalty and kindness to help her escape.

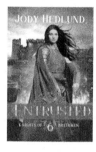

Entrusted

Hoping to minimize the death and destruction of the coming war, Princess Birgitta of Swaine leads the Dark Warriors as part of her brother King Canute's efforts to take the throne of Norvegia. As she engages in a skirmish with a band of elite Knights of Brethren, she's kidnapped by Kristoffer Prestegard, a cunning warrior.

The Noble Knights

The Vow

Young Rosemarie finds herself drawn to Thomas, the son of the nearby baron. But just as her feelings begin to grow, a man carrying the Plague interrupts their hunting party. While in forced isolation, Rosemarie begins to contemplate her future—could it include Thomas? Could he be the perfect man to one day rule beside her and oversee her parents' lands?

An Uncertain Choice

Due to her parents' promise at her birth, Lady Rosemarie has been prepared to become a nun on the day she turns eighteen. Then, shortly before her birthday, a friend of her father's enters the kingdom and proclaims her parents' will left a second choice—if Rosemarie can marry before the eve of her eighteenth year, she will be exempt from the ancient vow.

A Daring Sacrifice

In a reverse twist on the Robin Hood story, a young medieval maiden stands up for the rights of the mistreated, stealing from the rich to give to the poor. All the while, she fights against her cruel uncle who has taken over the land that is rightfully hers.

For Love & Honor

Lady Sabine is harboring a skin blemish, one that if revealed could cause her to be branded as a witch, put her life in danger, and damage her chances of making a good marriage. After all, what nobleman would want to marry a woman so flawed?

A Loyal Heart

When Lady Olivia's castle is besieged, she and her sister are taken captive and held for ransom by her father's enemy, Lord Pitt. Loyalty to family means everything to Olivia. She'll save her sister at any cost and do whatever her father asks—even if that means obeying his order to steal a sacred relic from her captor.

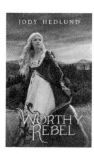

A Worthy Rebel

While fleeing an arranged betrothal to a heartless lord, Lady Isabelle becomes injured and lost. Rescued by a young peasant man, she hides her identity as a noblewoman for fear of reprisal from the peasants who are bitter and angry toward the nobility.

A complete list of my novels can be found at jodyhedlund.com.

Would you like to know when my next book is available? You can sign up for my newsletter, become my friend on Goodreads, like me on Facebook, or follow me on Twitter.

Newsletter: jodyhedlund.com
Goodreads:
goodreads.com/author/show/3358829.Jody_Hedlund
Facebook: facebook.com/AuthorJodyHedlund
Twitter: @JodyHedlund

The more reviews a book has, the more likely other readers are to find it. If you have a minute, please leave a rating or review. I appreciate all reviews, whether positive or negative.

Printed in Great Britain
by Amazon